IF MY
WORDS
HAD WINGS

PRAISE FOR DANIELLE JAWANDO

'Powerful'
Cosmopolitan

'A searing debut novel'
Evening Standard

'Sensitive, moving and engrossing'
i News

'A gripping, Manchester-set tale of troubled young masculinity'
FT

'Thought-provoking and timely, yet filled with hope'
The Bookseller

'Jawando's writing is incredibly raw and real;
I felt completely immersed'
Alice Oseman, author of the Heartstopper series

'Sears with truth, and soars with hope.
Fiercely moving and devastatingly real'
Josh Silver, author of *HappyHead*

'An outstanding and compassionate debut'
Patrice Lawrence, author of *Orangeboy*

'One of the brightest up and coming stars of the YA world'
Alex Wheatle, author of *Crongton Knights*

'A raw, unflinching and powerful story that
will stay with me for a long time'
Manjeet Mann, author of *The Crossing*

'An utter page turner from a storming new talent. Passionate,
committed and shines a ray of light into the darkest places'
Melvin Burgess, author of *Junk*

'A beautiful ode to found family, and a compassionate
look at the power of connection borne from
the ashes of tragedy and apathy'
Christina Hammonds Reed, author of *The Black Kids*

DANIELLE JAWANDO

IF MY WORDS HAD WORDS HAD WINGS

SIMON & SCHUSTER

First published in Great Britain in 2024 by Simon & Schuster UK Ltd

1 3 5 7 9 10 8 6 4 2

Simon & Schuster UK Ltd
1st Floor, 222 Gray's Inn Road
London WC1X 8HB

Simon & Schuster: Celebrating 100 Years of Publishing in 2024

www.simonandschuster.co.uk
www.simonandschuster.com.au
www.simonandschuster.co.in

Simon & Schuster Australia, Sydney
Simon & Schuster India, New Delhi

A CIP catalogue record for this book is available from the British Library.

PB ISBN 978-1-3985-1403-4
eBook ISBN 978-1-3985-1404-1
eAudio ISBN 978-1-3985-1405-8

Printed and Bound in the UK using
100% Renewable Electricity at CPI Group (UK) Ltd

MIX
Paper | Supporting
responsible forestry
FSC® C171272

For all of the incredible young people I've had the honour of meeting and working with, this book is for each and every one of you. Never forget how much your voice matters. Never forget how much of a difference you make to this world.

1

They say you can get used to anything, if it's part of your life for long enough; even somewhere like here. It's mad, cos never in a million years did I think I'd ever get used to prison. The noise, the smell, the way you've always gotta be on constant alert, looking over your shoulder for the next fight that's about to kick off, or the next load of screws that are gonna start beating the shit outta someone. Being in here feels like you're constantly stuck inside a ticking time bomb that's about to explode and take you down with it. And if you don't keep your guard up, if you don't watch to see who's looking at you funny, or if you get too cocky, or if you come across like too much of a pushover … then you won't last a minute in here. Not one.

All I've tried to do, in the eighteen months since I've been here, is survive. Make it back from the servery to my cell with a tray full of food. Make it to the end of my sentence alive. I guess I've learned how to block out bits of my life. How to keep this place ... separate ... from who I am. Which is hard, *fucking hard*, when you're banged up for hours, with nothing but your thoughts going around in your head.

If you start to let it seep in, tho, into your skin and your veins. If you start to properly think about the constant alarms and the slamming of the metal hatch or the banging against the cell doors. If you let in the shouts of: *'Oi, you listening? You listening, yeah? When I catch you on wing, you're dead! Fucking dead – y'hear me, bruv?'* Or all the shit that the screws say about you. That you're a lowlife, an animal, scum, a worthless piece of crap that's ruined his life for ever. If you let in the fact that you ain't even seen as a person any more. You're just a thing. A criminal. An *it*. Prison number 88582LD.

Or you stop to think about how much of your life you've already wasted, and how you threw it all away in one dumb moment. How every day feels like you're slowly starting to disappear, cos the outside world forgot about you. When you let all those thoughts take over, that's when it can feel like there's no point even trying to make it to your release date. Cos you just feel so hopeless and empty.

That's when things get really bad. Or you end up on Ibis

Wing, cos cutting yourself seems like the only way you can cope. I was on Ibis for a bit when I first got here too. All the wings are named after birds, which is mad, cos why would you name a place where people are locked up after something that shouldn't even be kept in a cage? That pulls its own feathers out when it's kept behind bars. When doing a sentence is called 'a bird' as well. I dunno if it's a coincidence or what, but it's like at every moment, you're reminded that you won't ever be free. Not really.

Everyone on suicide watch gets put on Ibis. And the thing is, once you end up there, you're marked too, cos everyone else sees you as weak. You might as well walk around with a fucking target slapped to your forehead ... so then you've gotta work five times as hard not to be seen that way.

All my mates back home tried to give me advice when they found out I was getting locked up, but unless you've actually been inside, you can't say shit. No one tells you that where your cell is on the wing properly makes a difference to how easy or hard your life is gonna be. Or that there ain't no such thing as 'keeping your head down'. Or that you need to make sure you have a loaf of bread in your cell at all times, cos prison food is nasty, and even then, they don't give you enough of it.

When I first got sent down, I was on a secure unit cos I was only fifteen. That was hard enough, but as soon as I turned sixteen, they shipped me off to Ryecroft Young Offenders. My

3

first week here, this guy called Spider, who has a scar down the right side of his face, started giving me a hard time. His real name's Wesley, but everyone calls him Spider cos of the eight plaits he has, tied up in a bobble, that look like tarantula legs. Even tho Spider was the same age as me, he already seemed to have so much respect from everyone in prison. Spider decided that he didn't like me from the get-go. That's another thing about being inside: people don't need an excuse to hate you. You don't always have to of done something. It ain't always about rival wings or being from different ends on the outside. Someone can decide that they just don't like your face, and then it becomes your problem. I started off having to 'pay rent' – that's what they call it – giving Spider or some of the other guys a shower gel a week or the food off my tray, or anything else they wanted out my cell, all to stop me from getting my head kicked in.

Eventually, when I started running out of stuff to give him, he started pulling me off the pool table, even tho I'd been queuing for ages. And that gave the go-ahead for everyone else to start taking my food off me, and pushing me about too. Spider took my CD player, my Maryland cookies, my Pot Noodles – he even took my Adidas sliders. All the things that mean nothing to you when you're on the outside, but everything when you're in prison.

And the thing is, I never said anything cos I was too scared. I'd seen Spider slam some guy's head onto the tiled floor of the showers, and once throw boiling water mixed with sugar in someone else's face. I'd heard that he'd kept another inmate hostage and threatened to burn the entire prison down. So when he'd shout, *'Forrester, I'll kill you, y'know!'* through the bars of his window at night, I fucking believed him; and I didn't know how I'd even get through a week, never mind 548 days – that's what it said on this shitty slip of paper that got pushed underneath my cell door on the first night. They call it a sentence calculation and everything's broken down into all these different sections. The amount of time I got in total is on there – 1,095 days. Then, my CRD – conditional release date – which is the date I'm supposed to be getting out, and my LED – license expiry date, which is when I won't have to go to probation anymore, is on there too.

At first, I couldn't work out why they write your sentence in days instead of years, but now I do. Cos getting through each day is like passing another milestone.

So that's when I first started cutting myself. I used this sharpened bit of my lighter. You ain't even allowed lighters inside, tho there's a lot of stuff you ain't allowed that you can easily get hold of. It fucking hurt, but at the same time, it was the only thing that made me feel ... I dunno. *Normal.* Like I had some tiny bit of control over my life. Cos nothing made sense and everything had been taken away from me, and I just wanted to be back home with my mum and my brothers, Kias and Isiah.

I figured that even if Spider didn't kill me, my life would be ruined anyway, cos once you go prison, that's it. You'll only ever be seen as a criminal and nothing more. When I was on the outside, I'd sometimes wake up in the middle of the night and my heart would be beating proper fast and my whole body would be shaking. I'd have moments where I'd find it hard to breathe as well, or I'd end up crying for no fucking reason. I never bothered to try and talk to my mum or Isiah about it. I dunno why. Maybe cos I didn't really get what was going on myself. Or maybe cos that's when things were really bad at home. Me and my older brother, Isiah, were fighting all the time and I could tell that my mum was fed up with all the dumb shit I was doing and I didn't wanna give her *another* thing to be pissed about. Besides, all that stuff was easier to handle when I was on the outside. I'd just go to town or play a game on my Xbox or hang out with Clinton, Abass and Shaun, and it was like I could push everything else to the back of my mind. You can't do that in here tho.

Those first few weeks in Ryecroft were the hardest. What with Spider hassling me, and me trying to figure out all the unspoken rules in jail, and seeing people being jumped almost every day. Then there was all the hours in my cell. Thinking about my dad and everything I'd ever done wrong. Or how my mum and Isiah, and maybe even Kias, must hate me. Or how Elisha, who used to be one of my closest friends, must think that I'm a lowlife too. I never started cutting before prison. I never even thought about it. But loads of people do it here. Even before I realized that that's what was going on, I'd clock the scars on people's arms or other parts of their body.

At first, I'd do it to try and block out all the thoughts I was having. It made me feel like there was one tiny thing in my life that I had some sorta control over too. Not just that, tho, but a part of me felt like I deserved it. It would always make me feel better while I was doing it, and for a split second, I'd almost forget. Forget everything that had happened and the fact that I was locked up. But then the pain would hit, and I'd be in agony. Every time I did it, I'd hate myself for ages afterwards, but I still couldn't stop. Soon, cutting myself just weren't enough, cos I didn't wanna be here any more and I thought that everyone else would be better off if I wasn't. At least then I wouldn't be such a burden.

One night, I got so desperate that I couldn't see a way out. I don't think I wanted to die; I just didn't wanna be alive any more. It all just felt too much. Too painful, and I didn't know how else I was supposed to handle it. How else was I supposed to cope? It wasn't just prison I had to deal with; it was all these low feelings I kept getting too. Ryecroft was like being stuck inside this black hole, and no matter how hard I tried, no matter how many days I struck off my calendar or how many visits I had coming up, it was like there was no end in sight. And I just wanted it to be over. *I just wanted to be free ...*

I don't even remember much about that night, really. I used my bed sheets tho. I just remember that there was all this noise from the wing around me one minute; then the next, I passed out. I woke up after one of the screws resuscitated me, and that made me feel a million times worse cos I didn't get why they'd saved me. Part of me wished that they hadn't bothered. Then I got checked out, and that's when they moved me onto Ibis Wing.

I was there for a couple days, and I had to have some psych assessment with the nurse. When I'd convinced her that I weren't having suicidal thoughts and I wouldn't try and do it again, they moved me back to my cell on Jay Wing. I don't even know if I meant what I said. At least, I don't think I did at first. But then the prison phoned my mum and told her what had happened, and when she came to visit me, she stretched her hand out across the plastic visiting table and held on to mine. She cried for pretty much the whole hour, and when it was time for her to go, she said: *'Please, Ty. Don't do anything like that again. I know it's hard, but promise me you won't. You've just got to hold on. You'll be out soon, okay? I love you. I love you more than anything . . .'*

I nodded, even tho I wanted to cry, cos I hadn't heard her say she loved me in such a long time. Even tho I wanted to hug her and tell her not to go, cos I missed her and Kias and Isiah like mad. I didn't. I held all that inside me, cos I could feel some of the other guys from Jay watching me and I knew that if I started getting emotional in a visit, then that would be another target on my head. It would be *another* reason to see me as weak, on top of the fact I'd tried to kill myself. I dunno if it was seeing my mum like that and knowing that I'd caused her even more pain, or the fact she'd reminded me that I was loved, but I decided that day that I wasn't gonna die inside. That I had to make it to the end of my sentence. *No matter what.* I waited until association, which is where they unlock all the cells on the wing and you're allowed out to socialize with the other inmates for an hour and a half a day. Then I went and got all my shit back out of Spider's cell.

As soon as I'd done that, I went downstairs to the main bit of the wing, where I knew Spider would be playing pool with all his mates, and I jumped on his back. I didn't stop punching and I managed to bust up his lip and his eye. Spider never in a million years expected me to fight back, so he was caught off guard. Before he could even get a proper punch in, the alarm went off, and all these screws came running over. About ten of them grabbed me off Spider, then twisted up my arm so much that I yelled out in pain. Then there were knees in my back and my face was pressed to the floor. They did the same to Spider too. I couldn't see them, but I could hear Spider yelling at them to get off him. It didn't matter which one of us started it.

They yanked me up, and one of the screws had his hand on my neck, pushing my head towards the floor, so I couldn't see where I was going, but they dragged me away. They took me round the back of the block, tho, and they put me on basic for two weeks. Which is where they take all your privileges off you and you're pretty much left in an empty cell. With no TV or radio or kettle, like you're usually allowed. Being on basic made me realize that I *never* wanted to be put on it again tho. There's just too much time to think. It was shit, but it was worth it, cos at least I'd stood up to Spider.

After our fight, everyone on the wing started saying I was mad, cos no one in their right mind would mess with Spider. But I'd had no other choice. I had to fight Spider, and everyone had to see it, if I wanted to survive. They had to see that I could hold my own. Spider left me alone after that. Even tho I kept waiting for him to get his revenge. Part of me was scared that he'd do it when I was least expecting it.

That was time ago now, but I know that Spider ain't forgotten. I can tell by the way I see him glaring at me in association. I also know that people don't let go of grudges too easily in here. No matter how long ago it was, or how minor it may seem, it ain't that sorta place.

Now, I get up off my bed and make my way to the tiny window in the corner of my cell. I'm getting out in three weeks. It's the only thing that's keeping me going right now, even tho it still feels like forever. Time has a way of moving mad when you're locked up. A couple of days can feel like a lifetime, and you don't believe anything till you see it. You can be due to be released one minute; then the next, you end up doing something dumb. Breaking the rules, or being found with some shit in your cell. Or people set you up. Then suddenly you've got more days added onto the end of your sentence. Most of the lifers don't give a fuck about what happens to them, cos as far as they're concerned, they're being locked up for ages anyway. So, they'll move proper mad. Someone on Quail even got stabbed the day before he was about to be released. He died as well. That's why no one ever has any hope in here. Cos the moment you start to dream, or believe, or think that some sorta future is possible, it gets ripped to shreds right in front of you.

I press my face against the window and try and breathe in the little bit of fresh air from the outside. Through the bars, I can see the other wings of the prison and a bit of the path that leads up to the main gates. Sometimes I see other inmates getting released as well. I used to feel mad jealous whenever I saw that, cos they were getting out and not me. But I know that my time's coming soon. That I'll be walking down that path with a whole load of people watching me, wishing that they were the ones who were leaving instead.

I turn my head so that I'm facing as much towards the cell on my right as possible.

'Yo, Dadir!' I shout. 'Dadir!'

'Yo!' I hear a voice shout back. I can't see him cos of the way that the windows are positioned, but I can hear him, which is all that matters. Dadir was one of the first friends I made in here, he was at Ryecroft six months before me. He feels more like a brother than a friend tho. Even tho he noticed all the scars up my arms, he never once treated me any different, either. Although there's bare people who self-harm in Ryecroft. The longer you're here, the more you realize that too. I'm gonna properly miss Dadir when I go. The thought of leaving him behind almost breaks me, cos never in a million years did I think I'd come to prison and find someone who I'd be mates with for the rest of my life. Who I care about and would back just as much as my brothers, Kias and Isiah. Probably more than Isiah, if I'm honest, cos even tho he's my actual brother, he still pisses me off most of the time.

The faint smell of weed catches in my throat and I hear Dadir cough. Sometimes people crumble the inside bits of a teabag into their spliff to stop it stinking so much. Or they put a wet towel over their heads and blow the smoke down the toilet while they flush. Most of the time, tho, the screws just turn a blind eye to drugs. Especially if it's something like weed that's just gonna mellow people out. It's easier for them, I guess. Cos then they don't have to break up fights twenty-four-seven or deal with people who are giving them aggro.

'I'd offer you some,' Dadir says. 'But there's *no way* I'm

gonna let you fuck up your last few weeks. Not when you're so close to getting out . . .' He pauses. 'It ain't worth it.'

I shake my head, even tho he can't see me. 'Nah,' I say. 'I know! I'm good anyway.'

I can almost picture Dadir nodding, the way he always does. He don't say shit just to fill the silence, either. Even when we ain't talking, it never feels awkward. That's how you know when you're tight with someone. When you can just sit there, comfortable, and you feel like you can truly be yourself. The only other time I had that was with Elisha, before we stopped talking. Elisha and me had been best mates for as long as I could remember. We'd lived in the same street since we were born and went to the same primary and secondary school for a bit. We just clicked. Not just that, tho, but Leesh felt like the only person in the world who truly got me. Maybe cos she lived so close, so she'd see or hear all the shit that would kick off with my dad. Then I just started talking to her about stuff. One time, I was too scared to go home, so I stayed at Elisha's for what felt like ages. I didn't tell anyone apart from her that my dad would hit my mum. Or how frightened I really was of him whenever he got mad. Imagine that, being frightened of your own dad.

Then, when I got kicked outta my third school and got sent to some pupil referral unit, people call it PRU for short, which is where you go when no other schools want you, I met Clinton and his mates, Abass and Shaun, who were a bit older than me and Clinton. When I was with them, tho, I felt ... safe. I'd never felt that before, and it was like having a second family, almost. Not only that – I could pretend to be someone else when I was with them, even if deep down I knew that that someone else wasn't really me. It was like I could forget about all the other crap that was going on. But at the same time, it wasn't like the way it is with Dadir or even Leesh. Shaun and that lot were always starting shit with people or going on a mad one, and most of the time, I felt like I had something to prove. I know that if they saw the scars up my arms, they'd probably rip into me as well. Or make me feel dumb or pathetic for doing something like that. Dadir doesn't tho.

I hear Dadir cough again and I know he must be trying to finish his spliff quick-time. Drugs, phones, shit like that ain't as hard to get hold of as you might think. There's always a way to get something inside. People usually dig a hole through the wall around the pipes and pass stuff through that way. Or it gets brought in during visits. One guy on Nightingale even got one of his mates on the outside to try and fly stuff in using a drone. They got caught tho. It's mainly this drug called spice that people smuggle in, cos it's harder to detect. But I don't touch none of that stuff. There are people in here who are addicts as well. Which is mad, cos before I got sent to Ryecroft, I thought addicts were all older people, not kids around my age, who were sixteen and seventeen. And sometimes they start using even more, maybe to try and block out all the stuff that happens inside.

They've got a special wing in the prison for people like that. Cos as soon as they get locked up, they start having a comedown and screaming down the whole jail, and that can be rough to hear.

I rest my head against the brick wall. 'How'd it go with your barrister?' I ask. 'It was today, innit?' I pause after I say it. Part of me doesn't wanna ask, cos I already know the answer. And even tho it might be dumb – cos everything about this place and the world and my life has taught me that it's wrong to hope; that you should never, ever have even a glimmer of it – I so badly want Dadir to prove me wrong. You don't realize how fucked this whole system is until you get caught up in it. I did some dumb shit – that's how I ended up in Ryecroft – but Dadir shouldn't even be in here in the first place.

He kisses his teeth. 'Same bullshit, man,' he says. 'It's fucked up, *I swear*! My solicitor is such a wasteman. I'd prefer anyone else but him. He just keeps using all these big words and telling me he's "trying" to appeal it. Well, try harder, then ... And the worst thing is when he goes, "I understand." Can you imagine? Nah, you fucking don't, bruv. You roll up here in your Merc, come inside for fifteen minutes, then go back to your nice house in Cheshire, and you wanna tell me that *you understand*?

Get outta here!' Dadir pauses. 'I told him that he ain't the one serving a life sentence for murder, when I didn't even do nothing! And d'you know what he said as well?'

'What?' I ask.

'How there's a risk I could end up being deported back to Somalia as soon as I turn eighteen. They'd ship me out to a prison there, cos now that I'm a "convicted murderer", I ain't classed as a British citizen any more. How are my family gonna come and visit me when this place is far enough as it is? I've been in England since I was two … This place is my home. Manchester's all I've known, my whole life, and they're gonna take that from me too? *It's just fucked!*'

Dadir sucks in a breath, and it's like I can feel the heaviness of it all. For as long as I've known Dadir, he's been trying to appeal his sentence. To be honest, I dunno how he does it. I've just about managed eighteen months, but if I was serving life for something I didn't do … I ain't sure I'd cope.

'It's like I can't win,' Dadir adds. 'If this appeal keeps getting dismissed, by the time I get out, I'm gonna be an old man. I'll be thirty-six, and even then, I'll still be a murderer. And that's if they don't try and send me back to Somalia.' Dadir pauses. 'Who makes these fucking laws?' he continues. 'Cos they weren't made for people like me and you.'

I go silent. Dadir's been here for two years and he's got nineteen more years to go. *Nineteen!* He's right, tho, cos the more I try and wrap my head around it, all these laws, the way that everything goes when you're in court and then in prison, the more I really don't understand. I'd never even heard of joint enterprise till I went to prison. Which is mad, cos there's *so* many guys in here locked up for it. That's what Dadir's in here for. The first time he told me about this whole joint enterprise thing, I thought he was taking the piss or something, cos it just didn't make sense. You can be sent down for something like murder, even if you didn't do anything. Even if you didn't kill or hurt anyone. You don't even have to know the people who did it, either. You just have to have been there, and that's enough.

I soon realized that Dadir wasn't lying tho. Cos I kept seeing more and more guys coming here cos of joint enterprise. All of them Black or brown, and from council estates too. It's always big groups as well. Like, ten, fifteen guys, around the same age as me or a bit older, all being sent down at once. Dadir had told me that he was coming out of this takeaway place, not too far from his house, when something kicked off between these two guys, Lance and Marlon, and some other guy called Yusuf. Dadir didn't even really know Lance and Marlon; he'd just seen them around the estate. But he'd never seen this Yusuf before. This argument started between these two boys and Yusuf, and they chased Yusuf onto the main road, then stabbed and killed him. It was this Marlon who'd done it. There were loads of witnesses as well, cos it was early evening when people were coming back from work.

And even tho this Marlon murdered Yusuf, the police arrested ten other boys who were in the area or near the takeaway shop at the same time as Dadir as well.

They said it was a 'planned gang killing'.

All Dadir did was nod at Marlon cos he'd seen him around. *That's it.* Then the next minute, he was up for a murder charge. He wasn't even allowed bail while he was waiting to go on trial, either. They just picked Dadir up and sent him straight to Ryecroft. They tried him at this new super court they built in Manchester that cost almost three mil. I got tried there too. It's this proper massive courtroom that they built especially for 'gang cases'. Even tho me, Dadir, or the rest of the guys who got sent to Ryecroft for joint enterprise ain't even in a gang. But, I suppose, if they're gonna build a special court for gang cases, then they need 'gang members' to actually put on trial there.

When Dadir was on trial, the prosecution started saying all this stuff about Dadir being the 'lookout' who had let Marlon know exactly where Yusuf was, and how he'd been keeping an 'eye out' to make sure that the police weren't about. Then they started saying all this stuff about an eye witness seeing Dadir nod, which was a signal for Marlon to kill Yusuf. And how Dadir was 'dangerous' and 'calculated' and 'cold' when it comes to stuff like this, cos he was 'from Somalia' and was clearly used to being around war and violence from a young age, so would have no problem setting someone up to be murdered like that.

They even used the lyrics from some of Dadir's drill music videos as well, and decided that that was enough 'evidence' to prove that he was in a gang and guilty of Yusuf's murder. When you're in court, it's like they create this whole new story about who you are and what your life is like, and why you did what you did to end up on trial in the first place. They did it with me and Abass and Shaun too. I didn't even recognize the version of me they told everyone about in that courtroom.

'I know,' I reply finally, and I dunno what else to say. Cos I know that whatever comes out of my mouth just ain't gonna be enough. How can it? I don't just want to say nothing, tho, so I add: 'I'm so sorry, bro.'

But my words feel flat, empty. What could I even say to make any of this feel bearable? To give him some sorta comfort? I could tell him to keep fighting, but he's already doing that. Besides, there's people in here that tried to fight in the beginning, but it didn't make any difference. Cos once you get sent down for joint, there's no way they'll overturn the sentence. Not from what I've seen anyway.

Dadir goes quiet for a moment. 'It is what it is,' he says. But I can hear the pain in his voice. 'Y'know some guy's just come onto Wren,' he continues. 'Same thing. Only – check this, yeah. Him and nine other guys have been given life sentences

19

for conspiracy to murder, over some messages in a WhatsApp group chat . . .'

'What the fuck?!' I say.

'Swear down!' Dadir continues. 'Cem was telling me about it. They're from somewhere in south Manchester. They got sent down for some messages, cos they were saying how they wanted to get some guy, yeah, who murdered their friend. Nothing even happened to the guy they were talking about, tho. He weren't hurt. None of them were planning anything. They were just grieving in a private chat, that's it. I swear, if that had happened to one of my mates, I'd be running my mouth in the group chat, as well. They were hurting – that ain't no conspiracy . . .'

I shake my head. 'Yeah, if my friend had been killed, I'd be saying all sorts Anyone would!'

'*I know!* And the thing is,' Dadir continues, 'the victim don't even wanna press charges, y'know? It's the CPS and them lot that still decided to take it court.' Dadir pauses. 'It's a different case, but it's the *same* story again and again. They're all "part of a gang". They're "too dangerous to be on the streets" . . . When's this all gonna stop tho? It's like they're locking us all up for the joke of it. Just cos they can.'

Dadir sighs loudly and I rest my head against the brick wall by my window. It kinda makes me scared for Kias. Cos it ain't even about 'staying out of trouble' any more, like my mum used to say to me. You can end up inside so easily, for sending

WhatsApp messages, or nodding to someone outside a fast-food place, or having a saved drill music video on your phone. People don't realize just how easy it is. Especially when you look like me and Dadir. Or when you're from an estate too. I glance around my cell at the cramped space that's been my home for nearly eighteen months, and I wish more than anything that I could tell Dadir that everything will be all right. That he'll get some sorta justice, cos how is shit like this even allowed to happen? And it ain't just a one-off, either. It's happening all the time. I know that it ain't just in Manchester too, cos people have been sent to Ryecroft from London and Nottingham and Birmingham, even Bristol.

'It's so fucked!' I reply. 'I just wish there was something we could do.'

Dadir doesn't say anything and I'm not sure if it's cos he's thinking the same thing as me – *What can we actually do?* We're just two boys, two prisoners ... caught up in something that's so much bigger than us. That's out of our control. How are we supposed to do anything?

I dunno if Dadir's still standing by the window or if he's gone over to his bed at the other side of his cell, but he doesn't say another word. I stare out the window at the metal fencing that runs all the way around the prison, and the narrower parts of the massive building that stick out. I stare down at Quail and Ibis and Wren Wing, and all around me, there's the usual sounds.

The yelling and shouting and banging against cell doors. I try to look beyond the building, to the sky above me. But even tho I know it's there, I can't see anything. All I can see is bricks and bars, and I can't help but think that even when I do get out, even when it's time for me to be released, what chance do I have?

What chance does someone like me have out there?

2

I lay back on my bed. Dadir didn't come back to the window
after that, which I know meant that he was done talking about
it. He tries to make out like it doesn't bother him that much,
but I know he gets proper upset whenever he has one of those
meetings with his barrister. I dunno what I'd do if I was him.
Knowing that I've got nineteen more years to serve, that I'll
have to go to an adult prison when I turn twenty-one as well.
Being in Ryecroft is bad enough, but the shit I've heard about
adult prison ... That's one place I definitely don't wanna end up.
That's where Shaun and Abass will be going in about a year or
so. I feel bad for Dadir, cos it's not like he even did anything.
It's not like he got caught up in some dumb shit, like me. I got

sentenced when I was fifteen. It was mainly robberies and stuff like that with Shaun, Abass and Clinton. It started off small at first, like robbing bikes or stuff from the off-licence. Then, before I knew it, everything just seemed to snowball, and get bigger and bigger. One minute, we were walking into shops and nicking booze and cigs – the next, we were breaking into places.

The last robbery we did, where we got caught, was pretty bad. We had weapons. We broke into this jewellery shop, and Abass and Shaun had knives. I had a metal bar. I still remember the feel of it as I held it ... and how my hand wouldn't stop trembling. I never would've used it or nothing. It was just supposed to scare the bloke behind the counter into handing the cash and other stuff over. But he refused, which we never expected, so Shaun whacked him hard in the face, and pulled out his knife. The man gave us the code for the safe then, and I just sorta froze. Cos for a split second, I saw a Shaun that I'd never seen before, and I honestly thought that he might use the knife. My mates all fell about laughing, grabbing as much as they could and frightening the man even more, and I just ... stood there. I didn't even wanna take any of the stuff in the end – I just wanted to go.

It was horrible, *fucking horrible*, seeing how scared that man was. How he cried with his face pressed to the trodden-down carpet, begging for us not to hurt him, begging for us just to leave. Shaun and Clinton and Abass thought it was hilarious. I could see

24

how much Shaun seemed to be enjoying it as well, telling the old man what would happen to him if he phoned the police. And I just wished right then and there that I could disappear. Or that I'd never even gone with them in the first place. Then Shaun started smashing up the shop, even tho we already had everything, spraying glass and wood everywhere. He only stopped when I told him to 'leave it', but even then, it's like he wanted to keep going. Maybe he would've if I'd never told him to stop.

I replay that night over and over in my head. The fear in the jewellery shop man's eyes. The way my mum looked at me when armed police busted down our door, then dragged me off. I'd never seen my mum look at me that way before. I can't explain it, but for a moment, it was like she didn't even know who I was any more. Like I'd suddenly transformed into some next person and I wasn't Tyrell, I wasn't her son. My older brother, Isiah, was on the floor with his hands on his head, cos the police had told him to get down as well. My little brother, Kias, started screaming and crying cos the police had twisted my arm up behind my back, and our door was off its hinges. And all I remember is my mum saying: *'But Ty wouldn't do something like that!'* Over and over, like she was trying to convince herself more than anything else. Like, if she said it enough, it would somehow make it true. Then they put me in the back of the van and took me to the station. They didn't even put me on bail, either. I got sent straight to some holding cells.

I've never gotten over that look on Mum's face. It never left. Not really. Even tho she tried to hide it. Even tho she tried to push it down, somewhere, I could still see it, caught flashes of it when she came to visit me. Disappointment and shame. And sometimes I'd catch her searching my face, like she was trying to figure out how it had all got to this point? How I'd ended up in Ryecroft? If it was something she'd done? I know she blames herself, and I hate that I've put her through so much. That I've made her feel this way, cos I love my mum more than anything, and I guess the only person to blame for me being here is me. She asked me '*Why?*' once, which I suppose is a normal thing to ask. But I couldn't even answer, cos even tho I know why I'm here, it's like I don't even know how it ended up happening.

Not really.

One minute I was in school, being kicked out my lessons – then the next, I'm in prison. My mum stopped visiting me as much as she used to. Now that Isiah's at uni, she's been travelling down to London to see him instead. Which is probably for the best anyway, cos by the time I'd get through all the security checks and be let into the visiting hall, I'd just be sat there, on my own. Waiting for my mum. I'd always be the last one to get a visit, which would be proper embarrassing too, cos everyone else's friends and family would walk in, and I'd have nothing to do except stare at the door, and hope and pray that she hadn't changed her mind. That she was still gonna show up. And I'd feel unloved and forgotten about all over again.

When she'd eventually turn up, she'd say something about being held up at work or getting Kias ready for school, but it always felt like some sorta excuse. It's mad, cos even tho she's still my mum, every time I'd see her, she just felt ... I dunno, more and more like a stranger to me. Like she was slowly fading away and I didn't know how to fix it. How to make things go back to the way they used to be. Before prison and getting kicked outta school and all of that stuff. But I guess there's only so much you can fix, when all you have is an hour ... less than that, in a crowded visitors room.

My mate Clinton should be getting out soon as well, he'd only just turned sixteen when we got sent down. Not Shaun and Abass tho. They got the maximum sentence for armed robbery. Life. Clinton, Abass and Shaun got sent to Fanmoore, which is another young offenders prison near Birmingham. Abass and Shaun were both eighteen when they got sent down, so they'll be going to adult prison as soon as they turn twenty-one. Maybe it was dumb of me, but I never expected Shaun to get life, cos he'd only ever been in trouble for minor stuff before. He said he was on some police 'watch list' or something tho. That they've got one for kids who've been in care, or kids who they think are in 'gangs.' Shaun said they'd been raiding the houses of his foster carers ever since he was twelve. It would happen in every placement he ever got sent to. The night of the robbery, they found all the watches and cash stashed underneath the floorboards in his bedroom. He tried to get away, and that was another thing they got him for, resisting arrest.

When we were on trial, the judge said that we were given the sentences we got cos an 'example needed to be set'. That we were 'dangerous and had already done enough damage, inflicting terror on an innocent victim' and that we were 'a risk to civilians', so we went straight to prison. I wasn't even allowed to go home, say goodbye, nothing.

It's mad, cos even tho what we'd done was wrong, I just kept thinking about this kid, Ibrahim Saleh, who was this dead clever straight-A student. I'd heard about him on the news. He moved over here from Iraq and got a scholarship to go this private school outside of Manchester. He was murdered by one of his friends: a posh white boy, whose dad had some proper good job. This boy and his friend, who was also there the night that Ibrahim was killed, had both been carrying knives. They'd even posted pictures on IG of them holding shanks, and there were all these Snapchat videos of them rapping about being about 'that life' and 'taking people out'. Even tho their life couldn't be further from what they were talking about. The court and all the papers said that these kids were just playing at being gangsters and that it was all part of some ridiculous fantasy, and that was it. The boy who killed Ibrahim got acquitted of murder and manslaughter, even tho he admitted to stabbing Ibrahim and lying to the police. He was only given a sixteen-month detention order for carrying a knife and perverting the course of justice. Even then, tho, he was released after eight months.

Then there was this student, from one of those top universities, who stabbed her boyfriend and was given a suspended sentence cos they said she was 'too smart for jail' and that sending her to prison would ruin her dreams of becoming a surgeon, or some crap. No one thought about Dadir's dreams when they sent him down for life. I guess some people's dreams matter more than other people's tho.

I hear the sound of the key in the lock, and one of the screws, Longman, opens my cell door. He barely even looks at me. I'm just glad that it ain't Davidson tho. He's my personal officer. They're supposed to look after you when you get sent here, kinda like a form tutor, but in prison. I can't stand the guy and I know he can't stand me, either. I can tell by the way he looks at me. By the way he looks at most of the other inmates in here too. Some of the screws can actually be kinda safe and some of them can be nobs. Then there's the ones who make your life a living hell. There's bare people in here who've been bullied by screws or beaten up proper badly by them. Nothing ever happens about it, either. Even the screws who are all right, I'd never trust fully, cos they can still switch on you in an instant.

'Forrester,' Longman says, 'association!'

Then he goes to open the next cell. God was clearly taking

the piss when he gave Longman his surname, cos he's gotta be one of the shortest guys I've ever seen. Maybe that's why he's always doing the most, getting in people's faces and acting all aggressive all the time. I get up off my bed and make my way onto the wing. There's already a few people out of their cells and others hanging about on the landing, and I hear someone behind me spitting some drill lyrics. I shove my hands into the pockets of my tracksuit bottoms and I look around me, just to get a sense of who's about and who exactly is out of their cell.

Anything can kick off at any time, but association is where you've gotta be extra careful. It's not just cos of the other inmates, either; it's when you find out if there's someone new in as well. Sometimes people end up in Ryecroft and they've already got grudges with other inmates from being on the outside. I head down the stairs to the ground floor of Jay Wing, where the pool tables are. The T-shirt I'm wearing feels way too tight and there's loads of small holes in it too.

That's one thing I can't wait to do when I get outta here: get some new clothes and a decent pair of trainers, and a trim as well. You can still get your hair cut inside tho. The screws normally let a trusted prisoner on the wing take a pair of clippers out so they can cut hair. Morgan's the one who does it on Jay. The one time he did it, tho, Morgan gave me a wonky trim and proper messed up my hairline, so I'd rather wait! I look around. There's a few screws watching to see if there's gonna be any trouble as usual, and I scan the groups of people. I see Dadir making his way down the stairs, but he clocks me before I'm about to shout him.

'Saying?' he says, and he holds his hand out for me to fist-bump him. He seems in a slightly better mood than earlier, which I'm relieved about as well. 'You heard about this poet or something that they've got coming in?' Dadir adds. 'I said I'd do it, yeah, cos it gets me outta my pad and that, but now ... I dunno, y'know.'

'Yeah, me too,' I say.

He shrugs. 'I wish I hadn't, cos is it gonna be like English lessons at school? I tell you now, that was my worst subject. *Fucking hated it!* Give me Maths any day. Didn't know what half the people in them books were even going on about, bruv. It was *so* boring! I just used to sleep, innit. And I tell you what, the sleep you would get in Mr Fisher's class ... better than any sleep you got at home!'

I laugh. 'There's no way any of my teachers would've let me get away with that,' I say. 'I'd just breathe and I'd end up getting kicked out. I weren't even in proper lessons after Year Eight. I'd just be sat at this table outside the headteacher's office, facing the wall. I'd get escorted *everywhere*. Couldn't even have dinner the same time as everyone else. And there was this one police officer who was always in our school doing the most—'

'Them ones!' Dadir interrupts. 'Yeah, we had some police officer at our school as well, only they gave him some next name … "engagement support officer" or some shit like that. Like calling them something else is gonna make a difference. He was always manhandling me, asking me why I was late, looking through my bag …'

'Yeah, the one at my school took my Afro comb off me!' I say. 'Never gave it me back, either.'

'You serious?' Dadir replies.

'Yeah,' I add. 'Said it was a "bladed article".'

Dadir shakes his head. 'Taking the piss! It was bad enough having to deal with that on the road, never mind inside the school gates as well. And they said it was for our "own safety" – it just made everything worse.'

'I know,' I say.

Talking about school makes me think about this upcoming poetry session again, tho, and I dunno why I said I'd do it. Even if it does get me outta my cell. I fucking hated every minute of school. And I ain't just talking about one subject like Dadir is, either. I hated it *all*. I didn't like any of my teachers, but my English teacher, Mr Howe, was the worst. Before I got taken out of my main lessons, he'd always say something to try and humiliate me in front of everyone else in the class. He'd always say that if I 'carried on' the way I was going, I'd 'end up prison'. One time, in Year Seven, I overhead him say to this other teacher that me and my mates all looked 'like a gang' that day. Just cos we were a big group of Black boys. When I kicked off about him saying that, tho, I was the one who ended up in trouble. And the joke is, school weren't all that different to prison for me. I was pretty much used to being escorted everywhere and kept in isolation. It's almost like it prepared me in a way, which probably made Ryecroft that bit easier to handle.

Maybe I was always meant to end up here tho. Maybe it was always my fate. Cos it's like my teachers said it would be, long before it even happened. Still, I bet Mr Howe would love to know that he was right about me all along.

'I'm proper dreading it now tho,' I say.

'Can't be any worse than being banged up, tho, can it?' Dadir goes.

I shrug. 'I hope not!' I reply.

Dadir gestures towards one of the pool tables. We only get an hour and a half for association, so you've gotta make the most of it. No matter how quickly you try to get to the pool tables as well, there's always someone there before you.

'We having a game, or what?' Dadir asks.

'Yeah,' I say. 'Don't expect me to go easy on you tho. Cos I know you're a sore loser!'

'Bruv,' Dadir continues, and he screws up his face. 'I've been letting you win the past few times, y'know. You ain't even competition any more!'

'Yeah, yeah,' I go. 'The past eighteen months, you mean?'

'All right, all right,' Dadir says, and he shoves me playfully.

'Fighting talk, yeah? Let me wipe that smile off your face!'

He laughs and I see the chipped tooth in the right side of his mouth. We make our way over to the pool tables. Michael and Oxy are finishing up a game, so we wait by the wall at the back. I spot a new face on the wing, and I'm about to say something to Dadir when I feel someone's eyes on me.

Out the corner of my eye, I clock Spider staring at me. He doesn't look away, either. He's with his two mates Kofi and Jason. I feel myself tense. Spider says something to them. Then they all make their way over to me and Dadir. I don't wanna look like I'm scared or nothing, cos I know that Spider gets a kick outta that. People can smell fear in this place. I've pretty much been left alone since that fight with Spider, which was ages ago now. I catch a few people looking to see if anything's about to kick off. My heart starts beating fast. I know there's a couple of screws not too far from me, but that never stops anyone from going for you. Not during association.

I feel Dadir tense next to me. 'What the fuck does he want?' he mumbles.

Even tho me and Dadir spoke when I first got to Ryecroft, we weren't anywhere near as tight as we are now. Back then, I knew that I *had* to fight Spider on my own, without any back-up, to show people that I could handle myself and that I wasn't an easy target. But now, I know that if anything happened, Dadir would back me. He doesn't start trouble, either, but he's had to have a few fights to be left alone in here too. Cos even losing a fight is better than doing nothing.

Spider nods when he reaches us. He's even more hench than he was eighteen months ago when I arrived at Ryecroft. Probably cos he spends most of his time working out in the gym or in his cell. I don't just feel a few people looking at us now; it's pretty much everyone. There's barely anything to do in here, so whenever there's some sorta fight, people get all caught up in it and take sides, cheering either you or the other person on. It doesn't matter how badly you're getting your head kicked in, cos it's entertainment. Like it's the best new series that's just dropped on Netflix or something. It's contagious as well, and sometimes one fight can spark another one. I force myself to look Spider right in the eye, even tho my legs are trembling and I feel a tightness in my chest. I try to calm my breathing down, but I'm getting ready to fight cos I don't know what Spider's about to do. I clench my fist by my side and I feel the adrenaline coursing through my veins.

'You good?' Spider says. 'Heard you're getting out soon?'

I dunno if this is some sorta trick question, cos Spider's never said a word to me since our fight, but I nod.

'Yeah,' I reply, and I try to stop my voice from trembling. 'Three weeks.'

Spider nods. 'Three weeks, yeah?' he says, and I watch to see what Kofi and Jason are doing. They don't look like they're gonna start something, but I see Spider glance at them for a split second; it's like they're all part of some inside joke that I know nothing about. Spider shakes his head.

'You not excited?' he continues. 'Cos you don't sound too happy for someone who's got their freedom right around the corner.'

I see Kofi and Jason smirk again, but I can't read what's going on. I don't even know why they've all come over here. I'm still shaking, cos this ain't just Spider having a random convo. It feels like a loaded question and I've gotta be careful how I answer it. Yeah, I'm proper buzzing to be getting out – it's the best I've felt in ages. But if I act too happy, then people will think I'm being cocky and that's when you get set up. Or put in situations where you end up with more days added onto your sentence.

I shrug. 'Yeah,' I say. 'Suppose!'

Spider laughs. '*Suppose?!*' he repeats, and he turns to Jason and Kofi. 'You heard this guy? He's getting out in a couple weeks and he *supposes* that he's excited?' He shakes his head. 'It's all right, you're allowed to be happy, y'know. I would be bouncing off the walls if it was me ... but it's gonna be a while before I even get so much as whiff of the outside.'

He takes a step closer and I move back, quick. I don't even care that I look scared now, either. Spider stares down at my hand and he notices that it's balled up into a fist. He laughs hard and loud, like it's the funniest thing he's ever seen. Kofi and Jason clock it too, and I see Kofi mumble something under his breath.

'Eh, relax, man,' Spider says, and he reaches a hand out and puts it on my shoulder. I flinch and move to the side, but this only makes Kofi and Jason crack up more. 'This guy,' Spider says; then he shakes my shoulder. 'Anyway, we're cool. All that stuff that happened . . . it's forgotten. Water under the bridge, y'hear me? If I had a problem, d'you not think I'd have done something by now? It's calm, *trust me*!'

I stare at Spider. I don't believe a word that's coming outta his mouth, but I nod anyway. Even the people I chat to in here I don't trust. The only person I trust, one hundred per cent, is Dadir. Spider shakes my shoulder again, and I swear I just want him to get the fuck off me, and move.

'All right,' I say. 'Cool!'

Spider smiles wide. 'See,' he says, and he lets go of me. 'We don't have to be all hostile and shit. We can get along! I ain't about all that madness any more. I'm just trying to keep my head down. Live a quiet life. Y'know what I mean?'

'Yeah,' I say.

Spider nods; then he straightens himself up. 'Make sure you have a game of pool with me before you go tho. Cos, y'know, I'm the real pool champ over here. I'll come find you if you don't, y'know . . .'

I stare at him. Is this guy having a laugh? All he's done is glare at me for the past year and a half. And not just that, I mashed up his face in front of the whole wing, and now he's talking about having 'a game of pool'? I don't know what Spider's playing at, but I just nod.

'All right, yeah!' I reply. 'We'll have a game before I'm out.'

Spider smiles. 'Good,' he says. 'I'll catch you in a bit, Forrester.' Then he heads off, Kofi and Jason behind him.

I turn to Dadir and he looks even more confused than I feel. Even tho I'm shaken up by Spider coming over, the look on Dadir's face almost sets me off laughing.

'What the fuck just happened?' Dadir asks. 'Man said, "Are we having a game of pool?" Pool?! Why's he just chatting to you like it's nothing?'

I shake my head. 'I don't know,' I reply, and I genuinely don't. All that stuff about him wanting to stay outta trouble is bullshit tho. He got into a fight with some guy in the yard a couple of weeks ago. Spider's never been one to keep his head down – everyone knows that.

'You don't believe him, do you?' Dadir asks.

'Nah,' I reply. 'D'you think I'm stupid?'

Dadir looks at me as if to say, *Well* ... and I shove him.

'Yeah, funny!' I reply, and Dadir laughs.

I glance over to the other side of the wing, where Spider's talking to a group of people. I catch his eye again, and even tho Spider nods at me, there's a glint in his eye that makes me feel uneasy. Even more uneasy than that first week back on the wing after our fight.

'I dunno what he's playing at,' I add. 'But whatever it is, I know we ain't cool.'

Dadir nods. 'You've just gotta try and stay outta his way. Even if you've gotta stay in your cell during association. Like, it ain't ideal, but at least it'll only be for a few weeks. Then you'll never have to worry about that fool ever again.'

'Yeah!' I say.

The thought of never having to think about Spider or bump into him when I'm out my cell makes me feel so happy. But me and Dadir both know that staying 'out of someone's way' when you're locked up with them is easier said than done. Just cos you're safely behind bars, it doesn't mean that you're safe. You can be on a completely different wing to someone and they can still end up getting to you. They'll just find someone else who's on the same wing as you to do it. When it comes down to it, no one can protect you – not really. And even tho I don't tell Dadir just how scared I am, deep down, I'm terrified. It feels just like those first few nights in Ryecroft, all over again. Cos that day I beat up Spider, I ruined his rep. And in here, reputation is everything, cos what else do you have? How else are you supposed to get by? And if you let people disrespect you, then you can slide right to the bottom of the food chain, and that's one place you defo don't wanna be. *Trust me!* Spider didn't quite go

39

there, cos he'd already done way worse and people still feared him. He found a new target after me as well, but that didn't change the fact I'd still got one over him.

'Here!' Dadir says, and he points to the pool table that's now empty. 'The guy's a bully anyway – never does anything without his two sidekicks. He thinks he runs Ryecroft now, but we'll see what happens when he gets moved to the older wing. Never mind adult prison ...'

I know that Dadir ain't wrong, cos things can change so quickly in here. Plus, each wing and who runs it is so different. I'm glad I won't be at Ryecroft long enough to be put on the older wing, cos then, I'd have to prove myself, all over again. I feel guilty for even thinking that tho, cos I know that's where Dadir will be going as soon as he turns eighteen. That's if they don't end up sending him to Somalia.

Dadir grabs both the cues and he hands one to me. I take it and try not to think about Spider as I make my way to the other side of the pool table. Maybe that was the thing as well. Most of my life, I've been pushed around – by my dad, or other people at school who used to say stuff. When I started hanging around with Shaun, Clinton and Abass, all that stopped. I felt protected. Like I finally had people who were looking out for me. I guess I was wrong about that tho. Dadir starts arranging the balls inside that triangular thing. He doesn't look at me; he just keeps his head down and reaches for an orange ball at the far end of the table.

'I'm happy for you tho,' he says suddenly. It kinda catches me off guard cos it seems to come from nowhere. 'Don't think that I ain't,' Dadir continues. 'It's just . . . I'm gonna proper miss you when you go.' He looks at me, finally, and I shake my head.

I wish more than anything that Dadir was getting out too. Every time I think about it, my heart breaks and I feel this pain, deep inside me. But it isn't just about Dadir. It's this whole fucking system. To people on the outside, it's black and white. If you get sentenced for murder, if you go down for joint, then that means you did it. You had a part to play. But Dadir and all the other guys in here who are serving time for joint enterprise will tell you different. It ain't just joint, either. There's so many other ways you see this happening. There's so many other ways you can get caught up in it. I look at Dadir – by the time he gets out, he's gonna be a grown man. He will have spent most of his life inside. It's mad, cos I can't even imagine that. I can't even think about how much of his life is gonna be wasted behind bars. Dadir moves a hand to rub underneath his eye and I suddenly clock how upset he is. I see a glimmer of it flash across his face, but it soon disappears.

He told me once that he tries to keep everything inside, cos that's the only way he can make it through another day. I shake my head and I just wanna let Dadir know that I'll *always* be here for him. Even if I might not be able to actually see him for a while.

'Nah,' I say, and I look him firmly in the eye. 'Don't even start

41

with that, cos whatever happens, yeah, this ain't it! *We're family.* You're my family, and me leaving here ain't gonna change that. Besides, you ain't getting rid of me that easily. I know I ain't allowed to visit, but I'll write to you and shit ... and I'll speak to you on the phone ... Curtis Coombs, remember?'

'Ha!' Dadir goes. 'Yeah. Even tho you don't look like no Curtis.'

It's part of my licence conditions that I ain't allowed to visit another serving prisoner. Even tho people still find ways to get around it. I don't wanna risk it tho. Me and Dadir came up with the fake name so I can still write to him, and he's already added me to his phone pin list, which is a list of numbers that you have to get approved, so he'll be able to call me too. I pause. 'I wouldn't have been able to get through Ryecroft if it weren't for you,' I say, and it breaks me to think I'm leaving him behind. 'I'm always gonna be here for you. No matter what.'

Dadir smiles. People say a lot of crap about keeping in touch once they get out, and they never do, but I actually mean it. I can tell that Dadir knows it too, cos his face suddenly lights up, and I see some of the pain disappear.

He nods. 'Safe,' he says, but his voice cracks. 'Don't be starting all this now tho. Having me get emotional at the pool table and shit. With bare man around.'

I laugh. 'All right, all right,' I say, and I pick up my cue stick. 'I won't say no more.'

'I appreciate you tho,' Dadir adds.

I nod. Never in a million years did I think that something good could come out of prison, but in a messed-up way, something has. In the darkest moment of my life, it's like there was some sorta light. I just know that me and Dadir will be friends for ever. Dadir straightens himself up and he glances quickly around. You've always gotta be careful about what you think, or feel, or say. If you show any kind of weakness or emotion, then people just use it against you. It ain't just other inmates who do that, either. When you're in court, it's the same thing. If you feel guilt about what you've done and get upset, or try and say you're sorry, then no one believes you. The barristers and that say you're 'playing up to it'.

Why are you never allowed to show any emotion as a Black boy? Why are you never allowed to be seen as human? Cos if you try and keep everything in and just do what you can to get through, then you're told that you're 'heartless' and that you don't have any 'remorse' for what you've done. It's like you can't win. I just wanna be able to think and feel what I want and express it, without it putting me in danger. Without someone twisting it and using it against me. Even when Dadir's dad died last year and some officers escorted him to the funeral, he wasn't allowed to be there for the *Janazah*, which is the goodbye prayers, but they let him go to the grave. Dadir didn't say a word about how upset he was. He got into bare fights that week, tho,

43

cos he said that when he got back to his pad, all he could do was sit there and think about how upset and angry he was. How he never even got to say bye to his dad properly. How he could've at least had more time with him if he wasn't locked up.

I ain't been through what Dadir has, but I've felt like that too. I never got to say goodbye to Elisha, even tho we weren't really talking then. When you're stuck staring at the same dry walls, with all these thoughts and feelings that you don't even know what to do with going around and around in your head, it feels like you're drowning. Only, there's no point in shouting for help, cos no one listens to you anyway.

Dadir lifts the triangle bit off the pool balls. 'Don't forget, you need to swap your TV with me before you go tho,' he says. 'My one's stuck on that *same*, one, channel. Been like that for months. I swear, if I have to watch the Yorkshire vet one more time, I'm gonna go mad. Can't even get *EastEnders*! I ain't having some new guy that's been here two minutes get a TV that actually works.'

I laugh. 'Yeah, yeah,' I reply. 'I ain't forgotten, don't worry. Anything else I got left is yours as well.'

Dadir grins. 'Cool, cool,' he says, and he leans forward to take the first shot with the cue ball. 'Release day can't come soon enough,' he says, and even tho he's smiling, I can still hear the sadness in his voice.

3

The whole of last night, I couldn't stop thinking about Dadir, or the way that Spider had acted towards me. I couldn't even sleep properly. I just kept tossing and turning, trying to figure out why he'd made out like everything between us was all good. Unless he was doing it just to mess with my head. I know that I ain't just being para, either. Some people take it a step too far. They can pretend to be your mate, even when they ain't. Even Dadir told me that there was a kid on the same induction wing as him – which is where they put you the first week of prison to help you get 'used' to it – who went out of his way to chat to this guy called Lucas and make friends with him, when the whole time he was planning to get him cos they were both from different ends. I swear, you've gotta have eyes everywhere in this place.

I try to push my worries about Spider to the back of my mind. I've got twenty days left. That's it. That's all I need to get through. I thought I'd be proper buzzing this close to release, but it feels ... weird. In the eighteen months I've been inside, I've seen people leave prison, then come straight back, cos they've breached their licence, or committed a crime again, and they've ended up right back here. There's some people as well who don't have nowhere to go. They come out and they don't have no family or nothing, or all their family's disowned them, so they end up in a hostel with a load of other people who've just come out of prison, or sleeping on the streets – then the next minute, they're back inside. One kid on my wing, Morgan, told me and Dadir that he'd been in care all his life and didn't have any family. When he got released, the hostel they put him in was only temporary and he couldn't find anywhere to live, cos no one wants to give you a job or help you out with somewhere to stay once you've been inside. Morgan didn't have a fixed address, which was part of his licence agreement, so they recalled him straight back to Ryecroft.

Then Cem, who's in the cell next to mine, said that being in pen was way better than being on the outside. He didn't really say why or nothing, but it made me wonder how bad things must be back home for him, cos being in Ryecroft is awful. And there's no way I'd choose this place over my freedom.

Never in a million years. I guess I'd never really thought about what happens afterwards before. What happens after you get released . . .

When I get out, I'm gonna be on tag and licence for the rest of my sentence, which is another eighteen months. My probation worker, Becky, has already told me my licence conditions. I can't go near Shaun or Clinton or Abass; I can't go to north Manchester; I can't go anywhere near the jewellery shop, or the guy that we robbed; I can't visit anyone in prison; I've gotta be in by my ten p.m. curfew – and a whole load of other stuff. If I break any of my conditions, then they'll lock me back up again, without so much as a second thought.

I sit up in my bed, if you can even call it that. The mattress is proper thin and it's so uncomfortable that I'm surprised I've even managed to get any sleep since I've been here. That's another thing I can't wait for: a bed, without a plastic mattress that sticks to you when it's hot. I'm waiting for one of the officers to come and take me to this poetry thing. Only, I ain't in the mood at all now and I'm properly regretting that I even agreed to it in the first place. I never liked all the poetry stuff we did at school. Most of it was proper old and I felt like it didn't relate to my life in any way. Not the way that music or lyrics do. Most of the time, I was never really paying attention in school anyway, cos there was always something else I was thinking about.

Like how my dad had smashed up the living room. Or how

Isiah would wet the bed cos he was that scared of our dad. Or how I was the one who would try and stop him from hitting our mum, even if it meant that I'd end up covered in bruises too. I dunno if my teachers noticed the bruises, but no one ever said anything. They were quick to get on my case about anything minor tho. It was like each school I went to couldn't wait to get rid of me.

I stare at the drawings stuck to the wall by my bed. Mum won't let Kias come to visit me. I ain't even seen him once since I got locked up. Not that I can blame her. It ain't just that tho. It's almost like she thinks that if she keeps Kias away from prison, then it'll stop him from ending up here too. She still sends me the drawings he does tho. Sometimes I talk to him on the phone when I ring home too. Kias has always done pictures for me, ever since I got locked up. Most of them don't even make sense, or I can't really tell what some of them are supposed to be. Cos there's, like, drawings of me and him, walking on this giant sun. Or the two of us, like, flying over this massive ocean and stuff. Kias is only seven, so he still draws people with those big round heads and tiny stick arms and no neck. Some of the drawings are just scribbles as well, and on one of them, he's written: *I miss you, Ty, Kias xxx*. At the beginning of my sentence, Kias's drawings were at least something to look forward to. Every time I'd get one, it was almost like he was giving me a bit of light. Some brightness in a place like this, which is so hard to find.

They don't give you the original tho. Mum said that Kias had spent ages colouring the drawings in too. The prison destroys them, in case they're laced with spice or other drugs, and gives you a black-and-white photocopy instead. I had to lie to Kias and tell him that I loved all the colours he'd used, cos I couldn't face telling him what they'd really done with his drawing. Still, it made me feel like I at least had my baby brother with me. Even if it was only for a little while.

Thinking about what I'm supposed to do in this poetry workshop is stressing me out, tho, cos when I had English at school and I had to do creative writing, or answer questions or whatever, I never knew what to say. Or how to say it. So, most of the time, I just wouldn't write anything.

Leesh wrote me a letter when I first got sent to Ryecroft, even tho we hadn't spoken in ages. She was the only one of my friends to even bother keeping in touch. I tried to write a reply back so many times, but I could never do it. Probably cos I felt so ashamed. Not just about being locked up, but cos of the way I treated her as well. We were best mates and I messed it all up. I sacked her off as soon as I started hanging around with Abass and Clinton and Shaun. And when Leesh tried to tell me that I'd changed and I wasn't acting like myself when I was around them, we got into a massive fight. I guess I didn't wanna hear it back then. One time, Shaun even took the piss out of Elisha to her face while I was standing there and I didn't say anything.

49

I just laughed, even tho I could see how upset she was. I've never forgiven myself for that.

Anyway, another reason I don't really like words that much is cos of the way they've been used against me all my life. At school, I was a 'problem'. Then in court, I was 'callous' and 'heartless'. Even in court, they used my own words against me too. I hate the way that all the barristers and the judges and the things that they say are so difficult to understand too. Like, they might as well be speaking some next language, cos when you're sitting there in the dock, you don't even know what it is they're going on about half of the time. It's mad, cos all these strangers are talking about you and your future, and you can't even follow what they're saying. Even when me and Shaun and Abass and Clinton were in court, our solicitor was telling us how to speak. How we couldn't use slang or any of that. How we had to talk 'properly', cos otherwise they'd think that we really were in a gang or they'd judge us for it, cos we weren't using standard English or whatever. I did try, but I couldn't do it. Cos it's, like, how am I supposed to change who I am? The way I talk, is the way I talk, innit.

My cell door opens. This time, it ain't Longman or one of the other screws tho; it's Officer Davidson. He's one of those screws who does things just cos he can. Cos he likes the power or whatever. One time, after Spider kicked off on the wing, Davidson left him banged-up for twenty-four hours a day, for a whole week. He wouldn't even let him out his cell to shower. He just left Spider in his pad, sitting in his own stink.

Davidson gestures with his head. 'Forrester,' he says, and he almost scoffs when he adds the next bit: 'Poetry workshop. You ready?'

'Yeah, sir,' I say, and I follow him out.

Even having to call the screws 'boss' or 'sir' just reminds me of being back at school. You've gotta be escorted everywhere in this place as well. Even when you're going to education. That used to happen when I was in main school too. Then, when I got sent to the PRU, they'd lock you inside the classroom when you had lessons. I suppose they don't lock you in the classroom here tho; they just keep the door closed. So that's something. They lock you in the education block tho, so if you do leave the classroom, you ain't gonna get very far.

We walk along the landing and the usual commotion is already going on. I can hear an emergency alarm going off in the distance. I still ain't in the mood for this poetry workshop, but I guess that it's better than being padded up. You can either spend time in education, or you get a job doing maintenance work, or laundry, or cleaning the wing, or helping out in the kitchen and that while you're here. And if you don't wanna do any of those, then you're just stuck in your pad for most of the day. I did sit some exams while I've been in here. Not GCSEs or nothing like that. They don't do those – probably cos most of the guys in here are like me. They either hated school, or can't read properly, or got kicked out. There's quite a few people who can't read at all as well. But there's also some kids in here who are proper clever. Dadir was at college and there's a couple of guys in here who planned to go to uni as well. Not any more tho.

I don't even know if it was a waste of time, me doing these entry-level English and Maths qualifications. I mainly did it for the money at first, cos you get £2.50 a week if you go to your lessons. And I know that it doesn't sound like much, but you can spend it on sweets or phone credit and stuff. When I passed, tho, I felt proud, cos I'd never passed anything in my life. To other people outside of prison, they might just be crappy qualifications, cos it ain't like I passed my GCSEs or my A-levels, like Isiah has, but they mean something to me. I'll never be as smart as Isiah, but I wanna try and carry on with studying when I leave. I wanna try and go to college or something, even tho it's embarrassing to say, cos Abass and Shaun and Clinton would take the piss outta me if they knew that.

We head along the walkway, past the rows of cells and down the stairs. I hear someone screaming and kicking off, shouting through one of the doors about being let out for a cig. Another couple of screws walk past, but they don't go to the door of whoever's shouting. That's the thing you realize about being here – you can make as much noise as you want. You can scream and yell and shout till your throat's dry and you've got no more air left inside you, and it feels like you're all out of words, and scream, and noise, but it still don't make no difference. This whole place makes you feel like you have no voice. Cos you don't matter, not in here, and not out there, either …

We walk along the ground floor, past the pool tables, and Davidson unlocks one of the heavy metal doors. The door slams behind us and he locks it straight back up.

'Not long now, is it, Forrester?' he says. 'What is it, four weeks? Five?'

'Three,' I say.

'What's the first thing you're gonna do when you get out?'

I shrug. People keep asking me this, and the thing is, I don't really know. There's so much I wanna do and I've probably thought about it a million times. I used to think I'd go straight to town or something, but I'd have to make sure that I'm back by ten. Or maybe I'll just play Xbox with Kias. Or go to my favourite takeaway … I swear, the way I'm looking forward to never having to eat prison food again. Never mind my Afro comb being taken off me cos it was a 'bladed article', the chips in here are so tough, they should be classed as a bladed weapon as well. You could do some serious damage with them, let me tell you. Davidson unlocks another door, then closes it behind us. I ain't even sure why he's asking me this, or trying to make small talk in the first place.

'Dunno,' I say. 'Probably get a trim, to be honest … and some decent food.'

I ain't joking about the trim, either. I swear, I can't wait to get rid of the prison 'fro.

Davidson looks at me and I can't really explain what the look is, but I've seen it before. It's the same cold stare that the judge gave me and Clinton and that lot the day we got sentenced. We head up the next set of stairs that leads to the education block.

'Well,' Davidson says as he closes the metal gate behind us. 'Don't be getting too comfortable on the outside, will you? It won't be long till you're back here again. I give you five months.'

I feel the anger rising inside me and I wanna ask Davidson who the fuck he thinks he's talking to! But if you even try and go up against one of the screws, they'll all come down on you, and I don't wanna kick off and risk having more days added onto my sentence when I'm so close to getting out. I don't say anything, even tho I wanna tell Davidson that he's wrong. *Fuck that!* Once I leave, I ain't ever coming back to this place, despite what Davidson and anyone else thinks. He pushes open the classroom door, but I'm so mad, I'm even less in the mood than I already was. Maybe cos, deep down, a tiny part of me is worried that Davidson might be right.

Or maybe it's cos he can just say shit like that to me and there's nothing I can do.

4

I spot Dadir in the far corner of the room and I go over and sit at one of the desks closest to him.

'What you saying?' Dadir goes, and he reaches a hand out for me to fist-bump him.

Another screw, Johnson, is already in the room. It's the classroom where we'd normally have our Maths and English lessons. I'm still pissed about what Davidson said, but I try to ignore his words echoing in my head: '*It won't be long till you're back here again. I give you five months.*' Davidson don't know what he's talking about. I stare around at the other people in the room. There's a few guys off Jay Wing here – Lewis, Morgan, Oxy – and I clock one or two people from

Quail and Nightingale, who I don't really know too tough. You normally only get to do stuff like this if you've been well behaved, so I dunno why Oxy's in here. He's usually in trouble for all kinds of shit. Fighting, or doing something dumb, like jumping on the metal safety netting that they have underneath the balcony of each of the floors. Me and Dadir have always got on all right with him tho. Oxy says he does all that cos he's bored, cos there's nothing else to do in Ryecroft. Which, to be fair, is true. Maybe the screws have only put him in this workshop to take the piss? Sometimes, tho, they put the inmates who don't have privileges in stuff like this to try and get them interested or whatever. I know that whoever this poet is that's about to step through that door, tho, Oxy won't be having any of it.

The screws have made sure not to pick anyone who has any beef, tho, cos as soon as you put two guys who hate each other in the same room, it doesn't matter if there's ten screws there or one – it's gonna kick off and they won't stop till someone ends up hurt.

I notice a box of pens at the table near the front. It's always the same ones. These tiny blue plastic ones with a long tip and no proper grip. They give them out to you with paper and colouring books to help with your mental health or something like that. One guy on the wing broke this sharp bit of plastic off his and used it on another inmate. That's another thing I've learned about being in here. How anything can be used as a weapon. *Even a pen.*

Oxy starts kicking off about the fact he got taken out of his pad when he'd much rather be sleeping and how he got chosen to come to this workshop cos one of the screws said it would be a 'good opportunity' for him. I'm pretty sure that most of the people here hate writing and words just as much as me, but you'll do anything if it gets you out of your cell. Then I turn and notice this guy sitting to my right. He looks about sixteen. Even tho he's quite a bit older than Kias, he reminds me so much of my little brother. He doesn't look like him, but it's something about the way he's sitting, like he's trying to make himself as small as possible. And the way he seems to be taking in everything that's happening around him. I've seen him a couple of times when I've had dentist or healthcare appointments, but he ain't a familiar face or nothing. I can tell he ain't been in Ryecroft for that long, tho, cos his clothes still look kinda fresh. His sweatshirt doesn't have any holes in it yet, and the cuffs don't have those frayed bits of thread hanging off them, either. It ain't just that that makes me realize he's new tho: it's the bags under his eyes, which you only get when you ain't used to all the noise yet. It's this look he has as well, almost like he's drowning . . . and how frightened he seems too. He must feel me staring cos he turns around, and I nod.

'You all right?' I say. 'I'm Tyrell. Most people call me Ty, tho.'

'Emmanuel,' he replies, and his voice is barely above a whisper.

'Emmanuel?' Dadir cuts in. 'Ain't you that kid that's in for joint? Over those WhatsApp messages?'

Emmanuel gives us both a nod and he shifts over in his chair. It doesn't take long for certain names to get around in here, and for people to put those names to faces, either. I remember Dadir telling me that the kid who was in for joint had been put on Wren. No wonder Emmanuel looks like he ain't slept in ages. You get to know how many years people are doing and how serious their crime is by the wing they're put on. Jay's pretty serious, cos I'm on there for armed robbery and Dadir's on there too. Wren's the same. People doing long sentences are put on there – only it's way worse than Jay. There's always stuff kicking off on Wren. I bet Emmanuel ain't got anyone to look out for him, either.

'Yeah,' Emmanuel goes, and he looks like he's still trying to get his head around it all. The fact that he's even here. I see this look flash across Dadir's face and I can't quite figure out what it is at first, but it's almost like a mixture between knowing *exactly* what Emmanuel's going through and feeling broken, at the same time. Cos if even more kids are being sent down for joint enterprise like it's nothing, what chance of appeal do Emmanuel and Dadir even have?

Dadir opens his mouth like he's about to say something, but

before he can, the door opens. Longman's there this time, and with him there's another guy, who must be this poet or whatever. I glance over at Dadir and he pulls a face and I can tell that he's wishing he never even signed up to do this dumb poetry session, for two hours as well! I look at this guy and, to be honest, I'm bare shocked. He ain't what I expected *at all*, and I can tell that everyone else is just as baffled as me. I mean, it ain't like I've seen any poets in real life or nothing, or even any writers to be honest, but there's no way I expected him to look like this.

I just thought he'd be some posh old white guy with grey hair who looks like he's about to keel over at any minute. Or that he'd at least look like most of the pictures that my teacher would put up on the whiteboard whenever we did poetry. I mean, I remember my English teacher in one of the schools I went to showing us this poem by this Black poet. I don't even remember his name, to be honest. I just know that we did one of his poems and it was actually all right. I liked it more than any of the other stuff we did anyway. I guess I thought that he was the only one.

Apparently, this poet guy's called Malik, and he looks pretty young, which I never expected, either. He's probably in his twenties or something like that. He's Black, with these long dreadlocks that reach down to his waist. He ain't even dressed like a poet, either. I expected him to be in some sorta stiff suit, but he's just wearing normal clothes. Shit that me or my mates would wear. Trainers, a hoodie with the sleeves rolled up so you can see all these tattoos up his arms, and some jeans. It's mad, cos from the day I was first arrested till now, I ain't ever really seen anyone who looks like me on the other side of this whole system.

And I ain't talking about the Black and brown faces that you see in the visits hall, either. I'm talking about the people who make all the decisions. Who decide your future. I mean, I know you can get Black barristers and that, but I ain't ever seen one. Not in my case anyway. Everyone was white. The police, the barristers, the judge, even the jury. Apart from Clinton, Abass and Shaun and our families and that in the public gallery, I didn't see one other Black person till I got put on the induction wing. Don't get me wrong, there's white guys inside too, but there's nowhere near as many. And, even then, they're mainly the ones from poorer areas and from council estates, like me. I know this sounds weird, but when the only other Black and brown faces you see throughout this whole process are behind bars, a small part of you starts to wonder if that's all you'll ever be good for.

Longman clears his throat. 'Right,' he says. 'I want you to all listen up! We're very lucky today to have Malik with us, who is a renowned poet and will be running some poetry workshops with you all over the next few weeks. I want you to remember that each and every one of you have earned the right to be here. It's a privilege, okay? And I want you to remember that you're representing Ryecroft.'

'I ain't representing this fucking place,' I hear Dadir mumble under his breath.

'So, if we could all make sure that we behave accordingly and give Malik the respect and attention he deserves. Any misbehaving and you can go straight back to your cell,' Longman finishes. Then he turns and heads out the room.

It's just this Malik guy and Johnson then, which I'm glad about, cos I wouldn't have been able to relax properly if Longman was still around. It's kinda awkward for a minute as everyone waits for Malik to get going. I ain't never done anything like this, so I dunno what to think, or how to act, and I can tell that everyone else feels the same. I turn to the front and give Malik a nod tho. He doesn't even seem fazed that he's in a prison, to be honest. Even some of the teachers who've been here for time still get a bit twitchy whenever something kicks off. Or they look at you funny sometimes as well.

I sink down in my chair. Malik seems all right so far, but I still don't know what to make of the whole thing. What if he shows us some poem, then asks us to tell him what it means? Cos I won't be able to do that . . . That's what they used to make us do in school anyway. I suddenly wanna get out of here, cos I can never work out what half these poets are even going on about, and I don't wanna look stupid. I've already had years of that at school.

'Hi,' Malik says, and he makes sure to look each of us in

the eye. 'It's good to meet you all! I'm a spoken-word poet and performer. I've been writing for pretty much my whole life. Poetry is my way of trying to understand the world and everything that happens in it. Of putting the things that I think, and feel, and have lived through onto the page.'

Dadir pulls a face. 'This guy,' he mutters. 'It ain't that deep. I swear, it's just writing a few random words down.'

I try not to laugh and Dadir shakes his head. I dunno if Malik is expecting us all to start making a load of noise cos of what he's just said, but we mostly just stare at him, sizing him up. Oxy and Morgan and pretty much everyone else in the room look unimpressed, but I notice Emmanuel nodding. It's weird, cos there's something about Emmanuel that's changed in the last few minutes. Like something in him has shifted, just through Malik being here. It makes me wonder where Emmanuel was before Ryecroft and if he actually enjoyed school. Maybe he likes all this poetry stuff?

'Anyway,' Malik says, 'I've told you a little bit about who I am. I wanna know who you all are. Especially as we'll be working together over the next few weeks.'

Malik gives us a small nod, and then he goes round and asks us each to say our names. Even tho it's just my name and I've been saying it for most of my life, I feel my throat tighten, and I start to feel proper nervous, cos there's people in here I don't really know, and I don't like being the centre of attention and saying stuff in front of everyone else.

Malik looks at each of us properly, which is another thing that the screws, or even some of the teachers, don't really do. But this Malik guy, even tho he's just come in ... I dunno. It's like he sees us as more than just a bunch of criminals. As more than just a prison number.

My hands won't stop trembling underneath the desk and I feel everyone's eyes on me. *It's my turn.* I stare down into my lap. Even tho it ain't the same, it just reminds me of being asked to answer questions I never knew the answer to at school. Malik clears his throat.

'What about you?' he asks.

'Ty,' I say, but it comes out much quieter than I wanted it to. 'I'm Tyrell.' I glance up and I see Malik nod. I'm relieved when he moves on to the next and last person. Dadir straightens himself up.

'Not like I need an introduction,' he says. 'But I'm Dadir ... and I ain't being funny, bruv, but you don't look like no poet to me!'

Malik laughs. 'All right,' he says. 'Dadir, who doesn't need an introduction ... I'm intrigued! What do you think a poet looks like?'

Dadir shrugs. 'I dunno,' he says, and then he glances around the room and points to Johnson standing in the corner, who's proper old and has this bald patch on the top of his head.

'I expected suttin like him, innit,' he says. 'No offence and that. I just ain't ever seen a poet that looks like you before! Like, I ain't tryna be rude or nothing, but you just seem like a normal guy. Nothing special. If that makes sense.'

Malik laughs harder and a few other people in the room start sniggering too.

'None taken,' Malik says. 'I am a "normal guy". There's loads of poets who look like me, though,' he continues. 'Benjamin Zephaniah, Lemn Sissay, Caleb Femi, Linton Kwesi Johnson, Kayo Chingonyi, George the Poet . . . You heard of any of those?'

Dadir narrows his eyes. I must've been to about three different schools and I ain't heard of any of those names before, altho Benjamin Zephaniah is kinda ringing a bell. We only ever really looked at poems by dead white men. Dadir looks just as confused as I feel.

'Nah,' he says. 'I ain't really heard of any of those. Apart from maybe Benjamin Zephaniah. None of them were in the GCSE anthology.' Dadir pauses. 'But just so you know,' he continues, 'I can't be writing no poem about hills and nature and shit. How am I supposed to tell you that I'm going through it by describing a leaf?' He shakes his head. 'That ain't for me . . .'

'I see. So, is that what you think poetry is?' Malik asks.

'Ain't it?' Dadir replies. 'All the ones we had to learn at school were like . . . daffodils, clouds, then some next one about postcodes that weren't even about a turf war or nothing. It was, like, "*I want to write to my window in Devon.*" Who the fuck wants to write to a window, bruv? What's a window gonna tell ya? Maybe I'm dumb, but I just don't get it.'

'Yeah, I did that one too, y'know,' Morgan says. 'It was *dead*. Oh my days. Like, I didn't know what it was going on about, either. When I tell you that poetry ain't for me ...'

I nod. I remember doing that one as well. I couldn't even tell you if it was good or bad; I just knew that I couldn't relate to it. Or connect to it. I felt like that about pretty much everything we did in English tho. The books as well as the poems.

'Yeah, same!' I add. 'I did that one too!'

'See what I mean,' Dadir continues. 'How have we all gone to different schools all over the place and we all end up doing the same, dry poetry?' Now Dadir's on one, I can tell that he ain't about to shut up. 'It's never anything I care about,' he continues. 'That's the problem with all of this stuff. I don't see myself in none of these poems. I don't see my experience, or my upbringing. It's like I don't exist ...'

'Where do you see yourself? Malik asks.

Dadir shrugs. 'Music,' he says.

I agree with Dadir. I ain't never been into reading or anything like that, but I know that whenever I hear anyone talking about a life like mine, living on an estate, my mum not being able to pay the bills sometimes, being kicked outta school, or being stopped and searched by the police, it's always in music. Maybe the countryside and seeing hills and all that stuff is normal for some people, but it ain't for me. Before I got sent to Ryecroft, I'd never even left Manchester.

'Okay,' Malik says. 'Now, I'm not saying you're wrong, at all. For a long time, I only ever saw my experience through music too. I never really connected to poetry or books in the way I connected to music. I didn't think that poetry – or writing – was for someone like me, from my background. But when I started reading more, that's when I started to see myself more. That's when I really fell in love with words and the power that they have.' Malik shakes his head. 'They can move you, they can help you to escape, they can fill you with rage, they can make you feel things you've never even felt before . . . and sometimes they can make you feel that little bit less alone. Poetry's saved my life many times,' Malik adds. 'And, let me tell you, there's so many poets and *so* much poetry out there that I guarantee you'll find something that speaks to you.'

I've never seen anyone as passionate about anything as the way Malik seems to be about poetry and I'm kinda intrigued. Especially cos he said that it's saved his life. Surely if it was that dry, he wouldn't be going on about it so much?

'What type of music do you listen to?' Malik asks Dadir.

Dadir shrugs. 'Drill, grime, hip-hop – normal stuff like that.' He pauses. 'I used to spit bars, innit. I was in this music group. We made a few drill music videos and that . . . and one of them

66

had over a hundred thousand likes. It just kept getting shared, again and again. Even my mum said it was good and she don't even listen to music like that . . .' He pauses. 'But I don't do none of that stuff any more.'

I watch Dadir sink back in his chair. In all the time I've been at Ryecroft, I've never seen him as alive as he was then, in those few seconds, talking about making music and his life before.

'Yeah,' Oxy adds. 'Dadir's actually proper good, y'know. I ain't even from round 'ere, but I heard his music before I came to Ryecroft. He had this one track and I just used to have it on repeat. Like, his flow is actually sick. Y'know how you get some people who spit and they think they're cold, and you're just, like, *Bro, shut the fuck up. No one wants to hear you chatting rubbish.* Well, Dadir ain't like that! *At all!*'

Dadir gives him a nod, and a look of pride spreads across his face. Oxy never has a good thing to say about anyone, so you know it must be true. It made me wish that I'd listened to Dadir's music too. I knew about it; I just had no idea just how good he was.

'Appreciate it,' Dadir says.

'So you've been writing poetry already, then?' Malik says.

'Nah,' Dadir says, and he practically jumps out of his chair. 'Drill's drill, and poetry is some next thing. I'm just expressing myself through music, talking about my struggles and that.'

'Well, that's what poetry is,' Malik continues. 'What all

67

art is ... a form of self-expression. And let me tell you now some of the things those artists do ... that *you* would've done.' Malik whistles. 'The clever wordplay, the imagery, building to a hook ... I'm telling you now – you put down some of the best drill, hip-hop and rap lyrics next to some poetry, you wouldn't even be able to tell the difference.'

Dadir looks at him and he seems surprised. I won't lie, I'm a bit surprised too, cos never in a million years would any of my teachers have compared drill to poetry.

'You know what?' Dadir says. 'I ain't never even thought about it that way before. It makes sense, tho, cos there's just some lyrics, yeah, that are mad clever ... and you think you must be some kinda genius to have thought of that! And I guess with poetry you've gotta, like, think of each line and stuff too.'

Malik nods. 'Exactly,' he replies. Then after a minute, he goes, 'Why did you stop? You said you don't do that any more?'

Dadir looks down at his hands. Loads of people do music in here – I'm probably one of the few people who don't. Quite a few guys had drill channels, or made videos and stuff before Ryecroft. More people get into it inside tho. They've got a music studio and stuff too, which you can use as one of your privileges if you've been well behaved. They even have producers who come in especially from this charity that makes music with kids inside. Or people will still make music and upload it onto YouTube on a phone they've smuggled in. Dadir shakes his head. Pretty much everyone in Ryecroft knows why he's here. You don't get to find out about everything that happens on the outside, but there's some cases that you hear about cos they're just so big. Dadir's was one of them.

'I used to love writing music, yeah,' he says. 'I mean, I still listen to it and that, but I used to love writing the bars, making them fit with the beat, all of that stuff. Like, I went to college and I did well in all my lessons, but music was all I could think about. Even wanted to do it at uni. Then, when I got arrested, they ruined it for me. They didn't just take away my freedom and my family – they took away the way that music used to make me feel. They ruined that for me. They just started saying how all my videos "proved" that I was a gang member, and cos I mentioned some lyric from this famous drill artist who's inside for murder in one of my tracks, the prosecution and that started saying how I obviously knew him and how I'm a murderer too.' Dadir kisses his teeth. 'It's a well-known bar – it's in bare people's songs . . .'

He goes quiet for a minute, and then he shakes his head, and I know it's cos Dadir don't really talk about his feelings like that. Maybe cos no one cares about how you feel. Or cos of the way that everything about this whole process – from the moment you're arrested, right up until the minute you're in the dock and then locked in your cell – is so silencing. What if music is Dadir's way of being heard tho? Of trying to speak out?

'They used every single fucking lyric I'd ever written,' Dadir continues. 'Then they twisted them to fit this whole gang-warfare thing they're tryna say is going on. Making music and rapping about certain experiences, and all that stuff. It ain't gang behaviour. It's just ... what kids my age do. What people who look like us do. It's normal for us. But they don't see it that way. Imagine someone taking something that you're proud of and using it to help put you behind bars? That's why I don't do music no more,' he finishes quietly.

The room is silent and even Malik looks shocked. He shakes his head, and for a minute it's like he doesn't know what to say, cos he can see how much Dadir's already had taken away from him.

'I'm so sorry,' Malik says, finally, and I can tell that he really means it. He looks hurt and angry, almost as hurt as Dadir.

'Yo, that happened to me as well, y'know,' Morgan says, and he leans forward over the desk.

I don't really know Morgan too well, but I heard that he got taken into care when his mum died cos he didn't have no other family and his dad was inside. Then he began hanging around with these guys who were twice his age. When he was about thirteen, they started driving him to country, which is what they call it when they take you to these *far*-out places in the middle of nowhere to deliver drugs, and that was the first time he ended up inside.

'Before I came here,' Morgan says, 'I was in some next prison in Coventry, when I was, like, fourteen. I was well behaved and that, so they let me use the music studio. I made this track, yeah? And they've got this rule in prison, where if you rap about anything that shows you're a risk or whatever, then they have to let the governor know. They didn't say anything about my track being a problem or nothing like that. Then, when I got released and re-arrested again over some stupidness, they used that same track as "evidence" in court. And even tho one of the screws came on the stand and said that the song weren't a risk or nothing, they still wouldn't listen. They did the same thing that they did to you –' he points to Dadir – 'using my bars and that, even the way that I said some of the lyrics, to try and show how "dangerous" I am.'

Dadir shakes his head. 'Nah, that's fucked up,' he says. 'How they gonna keep using music like that, against us?'

Malik leans back against the edge of the table. 'Language is so loaded,' he says, and I can hear the emotion in his voice. 'Sometimes it can be the most freeing thing there is. Being able to make a difference in the world with your words, or get things off your chest. But, other times, when it comes to people who look like you and me, anything we say can be criminalized.'

I glance around the room and I notice people nodding. I've never even thought about that before really, but it's true. When I was in school, it was the same thing. If I called a teacher a 'wasteman', then he'd say I was threatening violence and talking about how I was gonna 'do something to him'. Even had teachers calling me and the other Black kids I'd hang around with a 'gang'. From the age of eleven. Even when we were in court, they read out the messages that me and Abass and Clinton and Shaun sent each other leading up to the robbery. The prosecution twisted all the slang we used to try and say we were violent and that if we weren't locked up, then we would go on to do some serious damage. They did the same to Dadir as well, but they went next level, cos the only 'evidence' they had were his drill music videos and some random messages he'd sent to his mates about something completely different. They got some police officer in to go through all the slang he'd ever used.

Stuff like 'kmt', and 'pattern it up'. Dadir told me how this police officer just said he had 'no idea what it meant', whenever anything was read out. So, of course, a jury full of posh white people are gonna think that it's probably some gang abbreviation, or means he was planning to stab someone. They ain't gonna get to understand that that's just how we talk.

'Like I said before, words carry so much good power,' Malik adds. 'I want you to always remember that. They've given me a voice when I've felt silenced. Even if whatever I'm writing is just for me.' He pauses. 'Right,' he adds, and he clasps his hands together. 'We're going to look at structure and different types of poetry and all of that in due course. But for now, I want you to just get used to putting yourself on the page. I want you to think about what it is you've got to say . . . or what it is you want to say. I want you start off with a word. Just one, about how you feel. Then I want you to describe it in more detail. We're going to use that as a starting point. A way in. Then we're going to build from that. The only thing I ask,' he continues, 'is that it's truthful and that it comes from here.' He puts a hand to his chest. 'You've got to mean it.'

'Nah, that's bare cheesy,' Dadir mutters, but he shakes his head and picks up his pen anyway.

It's strange, but I suddenly feel excited to write something down. I'm nowhere near as bored as I thought I'd be, and I dunno what it is that Malik's said exactly to make me feel this way. If it's all the stuff he said about words being powerful. Or if it's cos he's actually made poetry or whatever feel like something we can all do. Or maybe it's cos he actually wants to know what we think. What it is we've got to say. No one ever wanted to know what I thought or cared about in school, and now it feels . . . *good*.

Malik hands out some paper and gives us each a pen, but it feels different in my hand, somehow. It feels heavier than it ever has before. I run my thumb along the smooth plastic.

'Yo,' Oxy says. 'What is it we're actually supposed to be writing?'

'How you feel, bruv,' Dadir cuts in. 'Were you not listening to the man?'

'That's it?' Oxy says.

'That's it,' Malik replies.

'What if I feel bored?' Oxy says. 'Like this is all a waste of time. Like, I could be in my pad right now. Or in the gym ...'

'This guy!' Dadir says, and he shakes his head.

A few people start laughing, but Malik doesn't go into teacher mode and start having a go at Oxy. He just shrugs.

'Boredom's a genuine emotion,' he says. 'If that's how you're feeling, then write it down. You've got your first line there too. "*I could be in my pad right now, or in the gym.*"'

Oxy looks like he doesn't believe Malik at first, but when he realizes that he ain't taking the piss, he shrugs and picks up his pen.

'I'll give you ten minutes,' Malik says.

Everyone around me starts writing, even Dadir. The excitement that I felt at first quickly vanishes now that I'm staring down at the blank page. I know that there's probably loads of things that I wanna say, but it's just hard to get them out. The sound of everyone writing is proper stressing me out and I just carry on staring at the sheet of paper on my desk. Malik must notice that I ain't writing anything cos he comes over.

'You all right, Tyrell?' he says.

I shrug. 'I dunno what to put,' I say.

'Maybe just a word,' Malik says. 'Just one … about how you feel.'

I look down at my hands. 'Stuck, I guess,' I say.

He nods. 'Write it down.'

My hands start to shake. I've never been too good with spelling and that, either, and I suddenly feel para with Malik standing next to me, even tho I know how to spell *stuck*. I stare at the letters.

'Anything else?' he asks.

'Nah,' I say. 'I've got it.' And I shift over in my chair.

Malik nods and walks off, and I dunno what it is about writing that first word down, but more and more are coming. Not just *stuck*, but *powerless, voiceless, scared. Frightened,* cos as soon as I walk through those gates, I've gotta face everything that's on the outside. And even tho I hate prison, even tho it's shit, at least you know everything is kinda the same. You might always be watching your back, but there's rules and routine – and out there, there ain't none of that.

Malik tells us to stop writing and I stare down at the words on the page. It's shit that I didn't even realize what I was feeling, to be honest, and at the bottom of the list, there's another word. *Dad.* I didn't even clock that I'd written it, but I stare at the word. That's who I don't wanna end up like. That's who I'm frightened of becoming. My dad's been in and out of pen for most of my life too.

'All right,' Malik says, after time's up. 'I'm gonna get everyone to share a word. Who wants to go first?'

The room goes proper quiet and no one looks at him. We don't do shit like that here. You don't really talk to no one about what you're thinking or feeling. Even your closest mates, the people you trust the most. I've never spoken to Dadir about cutting myself, or anything like that. You just keep it all in, until it builds, and it builds, and you can't contain it any more. That's when it spills out. You don't talk; you fight. You don't feel; you survive.

The silence feels like it's lasting for ever, but Malik ain't letting it go. He just sits there, waiting for someone to speak. I've never known a group of us to be this quiet in all the time I've been here. The noise from the wing drifts in, and still no one says anything. It feels unbearable, sitting here like this, and I want someone to speak just to make it feel less awkward, but it ain't gonna be me.

Finally, Lewis goes: 'All right! I'll say mine, then, shall I? Seeing as no one's talking!'

I clock Lewis's leg shaking and he looks proper nervous. He stares down at his piece of paper and he mumbles something under his breath. It's so quiet that I don't even catch what he's said at first and I don't think Malik does, either, cos he takes a step forward towards Lewis.

'Sorry,' Malik says. 'Can you repeat that? Just a bit louder.

Be proud of what you've written.'

No one's ever told me to be proud of what I've done in my entire life. This is all so new and unfamiliar and I don't know how I'm supposed to feel. Lewis's whole body is shaking now, and even my heart is pounding, knowing that Malik's gonna ask me to share as well.

Lewis clears his throat. 'Stuck,' he says. Then he looks away quickly. 'It don't matter.'

I'm kinda surprised that Lewis said 'stuck', cos that's the exact same word that I'd put down. I'd never even thought that someone would feel the *exact* same way that I do, and I never thought it would be Lewis, either. He's always seemed like one of those guys who's never really been fazed about being inside. He's always pissing about, and I've never seen him so serious, to be honest. I see a couple of people shift in their seats and I dunno if it's cos they feel the same too.

'Nothing you say in here is stupid,' Malik says. 'Nothing you say about who you are, or how you feel, is stupid. Can you tell us what you mean by "stuck"?' Malik adds.

'I just . . .' Lewis shrugs. 'Dunno. I just feel stuck in here. And I don't just mean cos I can't actually go nowhere. It's like, I get stuck in my head sometimes . . . stuck in my thoughts and that. Like, I struggle a lot with my mental health and I'm on medication and stuff, yeah, but it's like, I just feel trapped . . .' He pauses. 'I used to find it hard and that on the outside, but in

77

here, things are ten times worse. You just feel all those things even more.'

I see a look flicker across Dadir's and Morgan's faces. Lewis only came to Ryecroft a few months ago. He got transferred over from some other prison in Norwich. It's mad, hearing someone talk so openly like this, and even tho it feels strange, at the same time, it's kinda refreshing. Prison has this way of, like, magnifying whatever the fuck you came in here with.

The room is still bare quiet and I can tell that Lewis wishes he never said anything, but then I hear Morgan say: 'Yeah, same, y'know. I get like that when I'm in my cell too, bro. Cos you're just going over the same shit again and again, and it's like you proper question everything you've ever done and that. At first, yeah, I was just mad, cos of how they dealt with me when I was in court and that. Before I even started dealing, my house was getting searched, like, raided every day. Even banned me from going carnival every year ... Can you imagine? I was in care, innit, so y'know how they have certain people on that watch list ...'

'Yeah, yeah, yeah!' Oxy goes. 'It's that gang watch list, innit? My house was always getting raided too.'

I don't say anything, but I nod, cos that happened to me a couple times as well, even before I started doing robberies and that with Shaun and the other guys, and I remember Clinton telling me about the watch list. He said it was called like a gang matrix or suttin like that, and certain people were more likely to be on it. Like, if you're in care, or live in a certain area. Which is probably why they were doing it to me. Cos of where I live. They ain't even supposed to use the matrix thing any more, but that doesn't mean they won't.

'Yeah, that one!' Morgan continues. 'So it was, like, I went to live with some random aunt I didn't know for a bit and then she didn't want me. Then I got put in foster care. The house would get raided, and the carer wouldn't believe that I never did anything, so I'd get kicked out, yeah. Then I'd get moved to another one. Then that one would get raided too. I ended up being told I had no other placement I could go to. Imagine, it's like the only family you have don't want you and you've got *nowhere* to stay.' He pauses. 'I started hanging round with these older boys, yeah, and they became my family. And I just thought, *fuck it*! I didn't even have nowhere to live. I needed to make money.' He looks at Malik. 'I felt like I didn't have no choice. Like, I dunno … that's the way it was always gonna be for me, from the beginning.' He shrugs. 'No choices,' he continues. 'Those are my words.'

Everyone carries on saying their words: *regret, guilty, ashamed, worthless, forgotten, powerless, angry, mad, hurt, broken*. Hearing everyone say this stuff makes me feel less alone, cos I've felt every single one of those things too. The way this place is built, it's like we're always so busy fighting

79

each other, acting like big men, or trying to work out the things that make us different – postcodes, what areas we're from, weaknesses – that I've never even thought that someone might actually feel the same.

Oxy says that he's hungry, then starts going on about how shit prison food is. Malik doesn't shut him up tho; he just listens to him rant. Then it's my turn. I still don't say nothing. Even tho everyone has said something, I'm still too scared to speak up.

'Tyrell, what about you?' Malik asks.

I shrug, then Dadir goes: 'Go on, Ty, man. Everyone's said suttin. Just say whatever.'

I feel everyone's eyes on me and my heart starts beating fast again. I hate being the centre of attention, even tho if you spoke to my teachers, they would probably tell you something completely different cos of the way I carried on. But I guess it was all a front. My whole life, I've just been made to feel stupid, or like I'm a problem. So, I'd just prefer to say nothing. I'd just prefer to stay silent. I look down at my hands, trembling underneath the desk, and I already know that Malik ain't gonna let this one slide, cos he does that thing where he just waits again.

I swallow hard and I can't stop my hands from trembling, but I don't wanna piss people off. Especially if I'm the one holding everything up. If I'm the only one who doesn't say anything, how will I look then? The thing is, tho, when I'm alone, when it's just me, I can't stop thinking about stuff. Replaying all the shit that happened, or getting flashbacks, or just going over and over stuff in my head. And it's, like, I wanna get it all out, I really do. But this ... *this is different.*

'Just one word,' Malik says. 'You can say anything. It can be *hungry* too, if you like.'

A few people laugh and I feel a bit less pressure. I could just say that, like Oxy did, and be done with it. Then Malik will move on. But even tho I'm scared, I dunno ... it feels like a waste of a word. Especially when you never get asked to do anything like this in here. I stare down at my list and I try to pick a word that ain't already been said. I breathe out.

'I dunno,' I say, finally. 'Like, *voiceless*. Like you could be screaming at the top of your lungs in here, but no one listens, no one cares. Cos anything you've got to say ain't worth shit.'

I blurt out more than I mean to. I was only meant to say the word, and I feel a bit embarrassed. I expect everyone to start cracking up and taking the piss, the way people would do in school. Or the way they would in here, if you ever came out with something like this on the wing. But no one does. I glance up and I see a few people are nodding. Dadir is one of them. Now that I've actually said it, it doesn't feel too bad, either.

'Yeah.' Dadir nods. 'I get you. You feel like that, every step of the way. Like when the papers write all this crap about you, like they did with me ... saying how I was part of some big

81

"gang" warfare. You can't do nothing. You can't even get your side of the story out there.' Dadir pauses. 'Look at all the shit you've got us saying, bruv,' he says to Malik. 'Thought we were supposed to be writing poetry, not doing some therapy session.'

Malik laughs. 'Sorry,' he says. 'My bad. But writing is like a form of release, like therapy. This is a safe space, all right, so I want you to take each one of the words you've already written and start to develop them. Use them as a springboard to write a few lines. You might want to flesh out the emotions, or write using images, if that's how it comes to you. If any memories come up, you might want to write those down too.'

'Ain't we supposed to do some *A*, *A*, *B*, *B* rhyming shit?' Dadir asks.

'No,' Malik replies. 'Not today. We'll look at form in the next session. For now, just get it down on the page. How you feel, what your hopes are, what you're scared of, even.'

There's no pause this time. People pick up their pens straight away and start writing. Even Oxy, who looked like he couldn't be bothered at first, is proper concentrating. It feels different staring at the paper this time. It doesn't feel as scary or intimidating as it did before. I ain't never done anything like this in all the time I was at school.

'I can't really spell too good,' I blurt out. 'I just get everything wrong, y'know.'

'It doesn't matter,' Malik says. 'Just get the words down first.

We'll look at the spelling later. I'll help you if you get stuck.'

'Right,' I say.

It feels strange hearing someone say that, cos I've never once been taught that in school. I've always been told how important spelling is, which sometimes made it harder for me to even start.

Everyone in the room is writing bare fast, but I don't know how to start. How am I meant to begin? I pick up my pen and I think about the night of the robbery and how I broke my mum's heart. I think about my little brother and how much I miss him and how I really wish I could've seen him, at least once, these past eighteen months. Or how I wish things were the way they used to be between me and Isiah. I think about being in the back of the prison van, and how I didn't even know where I was gonna end up. I think about cutting and *that night* in my cell. I think about all the times my dad had hit my mum, and how I even called the police once, cos I thought he was gonna kill her and kill us, but they never came. I think about how scared I am ... How scared I *was*. And all the names of the wings in here ... How something so terrifying could be named after something so beautiful and full of hope and supposed to be free. Then, for the first time ever, it's like the words just come rushing out ...

Scars

I carry the pain in my scars
Beneath raw skin the colour of dirt
Each line a brush stroke that never made it
onto the page
My body is a canvas, that I rip and tear apart
Carving lines from forearm to wrist
To try to forget
To try and block out the noise
Cos maybe it's easier that way?

I carry survival in my scars
Of trying to exist in a place that doesn't really want
me to live
Screams and sirens pulsating through my veins
Coursing through blood and flesh and arteries
Close to bone
And nothingness
If you opened these scars back up again, would
poetry pour out?

I carry the silence in my scars
The thick heaviness of it
That feels like a stone in my throat

*A clenched fist shattering my jaw into a thousand
tiny pieces
My mum's screams, echoing over the sound of the TV
And if you opened these scars back up again, would
words come out?*

*I carry his voice in my scars
He'll kill her
He'll kill us
He'll burn the house down with us all in it, if
she leaves
Only maybe he'd already done it
Cos inside, I'm empty
And inside, I'm empty*

*I carry the heaviness in my scars
But when I open my mouth
Only feathers fly.*

5

I'm by one of the phones that's in between Jay and Quail Wing.
I wanted to call Kias cos it's his birthday today and I didn't
want him to think I'd forgotten it. I even made him a birthday
card and posted it back home the week before last, just in case
there were any delays, cos everything you post out has to be
read. You don't get long on the phone, either. You only get ten
minutes max before it cuts out, and if you wanna carry on with
your conversation, you have to rejoin the back of the queue
again. And even tho you barely get any time on the phone in
the first place, there's always someone behind you, telling you
to hurry the fuck up.

Not that I mind so much about that when I'm talking to

my mum. Sometimes I even use it as an excuse, cos our conversations just seem to fizzle out these days. It's like neither of us knows what to say any more. She makes small talk and asks: '*How are you?*' But there's always *so* many pauses. *There's always so much silence.* And I swear, even tho I'm however many miles away, in the middle of nowhere, I can feel it. The weight of it all. And when that happens, I just catch myself wishing that I knew what she was thinking. Or that there was a way I could piece together all those spaces between her words and figure out what it is she's really saying. If it's that she loves me, or she hates me, or she's ashamed of me, or that she just ... misses me. But I can't tell which one it is and I never say owt, or ask her about it, cos I'm too scared to find out.

The phone rings a couple times and I pray that someone picks up. I'm calling a bit later than I said I would cos Malik's session this morning ran over. The phone clicks, and then I hear a voice say:

'Hello?'

I was hoping that it would've been Kias who'd picked up, but I guess I ain't that lucky.

'Hi, Mum,' I say quickly. 'You all right?'

There's a pause that feels like it lasts for a lifetime and then she says: 'I'm fine ... I'm good. Are you okay?'

It's funny, cos whenever she'd ask if I was okay in the past, I'd almost wanna laugh. Cos how can you ever really be okay

87

when you're inside? I swallow hard. Ever since I came here, eighteen months ago, I feel like all I've been doing is holding my breath. Holding my breath and hoping that one day it'll all be over. I'll be out, and it'll all be ... *okay*. And now that that day is almost here, it just doesn't feel the way I thought it would do. I still feel like I'm holding my breath, cos even tho I'm excited to see my mum, and Kias and Isiah again – even tho I can't wait to *finally* get my freedom back – I still don't know how things will be back home.

I move my hand to my face and I try to push down all the hurt. It ain't just the ordinary hurt that's usually there, either. Since Malik's session, it's like every feeling is right on the surface. I try to make sure that there's none of that hurt in my voice. But it's hard, cos whenever I think about Mum, or talk to her, I just think about how much I let her down. How much pain I caused her, and it makes me feel even worse. I never told her how hard it was when I was first sentenced. Or how hard it still is, now. Maybe cos deep down, I felt like I deserved it. And I don't wanna worry her any more. I've already put her through enough.

'Yeah, I'm good,' I lie. 'I'm good, y'know.' I dunno why I say it twice. Maybe to try and convince her, or myself. I almost tell her about the poetry session with Malik and how much I enjoyed it, but for some reason, I suddenly feel embarrassed. No matter what I do, I'll never be the talented one, like Isiah. I'll never make my mum proud the way that he does. She tells everyone she's got a son at uni, but I bet she doesn't go around bragging about me. Mum goes silent again and I strain through the phone. Just in case I miss something. A joke, or Mum going on about Dianne next door, who she's always beefing with. Or just the way she'd laugh and laugh whenever she was around me. But it ain't like that any more. It hasn't been for ages now. I dunno if you can stop loving your kids, but I think that's what's happened with me.

I know I ain't got long, and I'm just about to ask her to put Kias on when she goes: 'I'm sorry, I've got to go ... Kias is having some friends over and I need to get some bits sorted. Do you want to speak to him?'

'Yeah,' I say. 'Please.'

She pauses and I wonder what she's gonna say for a minute. 'I'll see you soon, though,' she says. 'Just ... stay out of trouble, Ty, please? You don't want to be getting extra days added on over something stupid. Not when you're so close ...'

'I won't!' I say. It pisses me off that she *always* thinks the worst of me. But then again, what do I expect? She doesn't say bye, but I hear her shout for Kias, and then a voice down the phone.

'Hello?' Kias says, and it almost catches me off guard. All the awkwardness I felt with Mum suddenly disappears. It's weird, cos you'd think that talking on the phone would make it easier. That it would make being in here more bearable, somehow.

And I guess, in some ways, it does. It hasn't with Kias tho. I've missed him so much, more than I've missed my freedom. But knowing that I'll be coming home in a few weeks, and that I'll actually get to hug him, and hold him, and chat to him, in his room, in *my* city makes me so happy that I swear I could fly.

'Happy birthday, mate,' I say.

And even tho I can't see him, I can tell that Kias is proper grinning through the phone. I can hear it, and I know that the one, random dimple on the left side of his face will have made an appearance too.

'Ty!' Kias yells, and I swear he almost bursts my eardrum. 'I got your card! I love it!'

'You do?' I say, and my heart swells just hearing my little brother sound this happy.

'Yeah,' he continues. 'I've put it up on top of the TV so everyone can see it! And guess what I got? Guess what Mum got me for my birthday ... ?'

I laugh. 'I dunno,' I say. 'Trainers?'

'*No!*' he shouts, and I shake my head. 'She got me one of them ... how'd you say it, now? Skai ... skay ... skaya—'

'Scalextric?' I say.

'Yeah! That's it! You should see it, Ty. I've got it all up in my room and it's *proper* massive. It's, like, twenty feet ... *No! Bigger!* It's, like, fifty feet, and it goes all the way from my bed, right down to my wardrobe and back again. And you can race 'em. I've been racing the cars, yeah, and they make this proper loud noise. But you've gotta be careful, cos there's this upside-down loop bit, and if you don't go round it proper slowly, then your car just flies off and you've gotta start *all ov*er again.'

Kias pauses to take a breath and I can't stop smiling. I've never been able to get a word in edgeways once Kias gets going. I don't mind that tho. It's nice to hear him getting excited about stuff. I suddenly notice that I've got the phone pressed proper hard to my ear. Like doing that will somehow transport me out of here and back home. I can almost picture it all in front of me. The bits of plastic track slotted together in a *U* shape around his room. I can almost see Kias kneeling on the floor beside me, putting the two cars carefully on the starting line. But then a loud shout makes me jump, and I'm quickly reminded that I ain't at home, or with Kias. I'm still very much in Ryecroft.

'Maybe we can play it when you're back?' Kias continues quietly.

My heart feels like it could burst, knowing that soon I'll get to do normal stuff like this with my little brother again. I honestly can't wait.

'Yeah,' I say. 'I'd really like that. In fact, that's the first thing I'm gonna do when I'm out. After I've given you the biggest hug.'

'You can't use the blue car tho,' Kias says. 'That's my favourite! And we need to have three ... no, four goes!'

'We'll have as many goes as you want!' I say. 'What you doing today?' I ask. 'It ain't every day you turn eight, is it?'

'I'm having a party!' Kias says. 'Mum's bought loads of pizza and she got me some sweets to take to school. Which doesn't make sense, cos I dunno why everyone gets sweets on *my* birthday. Shouldn't they be giving 'em to me?'

I laugh.

'Oh, and d'you know wot my teacher said ... ?'

'What?'

But I don't even get a chance to find out, cos someone reaches from behind me and presses their hand down on the receiver to end the call. The phone goes dead. I turn around, mad.

'Yo, what the fuck?!' I shout, and I see Spider standing there.

Everything Kias says is precious to me. No matter how small. And not to get to say bye, either – on his birthday as well – makes my blood boil. Even tho I'm scared of Spider, I'm still pissed. Messing with me is one thing, but not my family ... the people that I love. I'm shaking, but I still don't back down.

'What the fuck you doing?' I snap. 'I was on the phone to my brother! What's wrong with you?'

Part of me is surprised that I'm even able to stand up to him like this, but I guess my love for Kias is stronger than any fear I have of what Spider might do. Spider smirks; then he rubs under his eye and shoves me out the way.

'Yeah, yeah,' he says. 'You're boring me, Forrester!'

There's a few people on the other phones watching us. It's association, so the wing's packed as well. Spider picks up the receiver and turns to face me. He almost looks bored, which pisses me off even more. He knows that I'll have to wait at least half an hour before my phonecard will work again, and I'll have to rejoin the back of the queue as well.

'I need to phone my girl, innit,' Spider says. 'Anyway,' he continues as he dials a number, 'you're getting out soon, so what difference does it make? You can talk to your brother all the time when you're out. Some of us ain't so lucky . . .' He laughs and I stare at him, but I still don't move. I know I should, but I can't stop thinking about Kias standing there, with the phone in his hand, wondering what happened and why it went dead.

'That ain't the point,' I say before I can stop the words coming out of my mouth.

'Listen, Forrester,' Spider spits. 'I think you're forgetting who you're talking to. I told ya, we're cool. And this is what mates do for each other . . . I scratch your back – you scratch mine. But if you wanna make a problem out of this whole thing, we can do.' Spider leans in closer. 'Cos, y'know, I can make every second of every minute you've got left in this place a living hell.'

He laughs as if I've just said something proper funny, and I clock people looking in our direction to see if anything's about to kick off. I'm still shaking.

Spider's girlfriend must pick up on the other end of the line, cos I hear him say, 'Babes,' before turning to speak quietly into the phone.

Everyone's looking to see what I'm about to do, but as mad as I am, I don't wanna start stirring shit up between me and Spider when I'm so close to getting out. He starts laughing into the phone, but I don't bother to say anything else. I just turn and walk off, even tho my legs won't stop trembling.

'Good choice, Forrester!' Spider shouts after me. 'I'll catch you in a bit, yeah?'

His voice echoes around me, and I can tell that he's enjoying every moment of this. I head down along the wing. It's as noisy as it always is. I'm still so mad that I can't think of anything else. Plus, if I phone Kias back, then I'll only have one more call left to last me the rest of the week. I'm about to head up the stairs and go back to my cell, but I know that if I do that, then I'll just sit there going over and over everything in my head. Not just with Kias, but with my mum too.

I'm heading along the corridor that leads to the library. I never bothered going to the library in school, cos I hated being there, and I've never really been into books or anything like that. That was more Isiah's thing. Besides, when I got taken out of my lessons before I got sent to the PRU, I was only ever allowed at that one table outside the headteacher's office. Or in the playground for ten minutes, when everyone else was inside.

Even if I'd wanted to go to the library or whatever, they probably wouldn't have let me. I never would've thought that the first time I'd step foot in a library would be in prison.

I push open the double doors, and even tho it sounds stupid, I'm scared to go in at first. Cos I've always been made to feel like I'm thick, or stupid, or dumb or whatever, and that I don't belong in a place like this. What if the person working here thinks that too? But I suck in a deep breath, cos I'm curious about what Malik said. About there being different types of poetry. I look around. I don't have anything to compare the poem to, so I dunno if it's good or bad, but I see the rows of books and a librarian sitting behind the desk.

He must be in his forties. He's thin, with greyish hair and glasses, and he smiles at me as I head over to the desk. There's a couple of inmates in here too, sitting down at this little table, reading. I clock Cem, who's on the same landing on Jay Wing as me, stacking some shelves, and this other guy from Kingfisher, sorting through a trolley of books. You can get a job working in the library, but it's only the most trusted inmates who are allowed to do it. Just like working in the kitchens. I must look like I don't know what I'm doing here, cos the librarian stands up.

'Hello,' he says, and he gives me a kind smile. 'I'm Gareth. Welcome to the library! I don't think I've seen you in here before.'

'Nah,' I say, and I glance quickly around. I can see signs for FICTION and NON-FICTION, and CHILDREN'S BOOKS, but I can't see any for poetry. I don't even know how they sort all the books, either. I suddenly feel embarrassed and I look down at the floor.

'How does this all work, then?' I ask Gareth, and he gets up from behind the desk.

'Here, I'll show you,' he says. 'I didn't catch your name,' he adds, as we head over to the shelves at the back.

'It's Ty,' I reply. 'Tyrell.'

'Nice to meet you, Ty,' Gareth says, and I suddenly feel much more at ease than I did when I first came in. 'It's quite straightforward once you know where everything is,' he continues. 'All the books are arranged by genre, and then alphabetically by the author's last name.'

'Right,' I reply, even tho I don't really know what 'genre' means.

'All the genres are listed at the top here,' he says, and he points to one of the signs that says REAL-LIFE STORIES.

I nod, cos it seems easy enough now.

'You looking for anything in particular?' he asks.

I glance around to see if anyone's listening, but no one's paying any attention to me, or what I'm doing. Which makes a change.

'Nah, not really,' I say, and then I add, 'You got any poetry and that tho?'

Gareth's entire face lights up, and I swear the only other time I've ever seen anyone look that happy is on release day.

'Sure have,' Gareth says, and we head over to one of the bookshelves right at the back. 'It's just in this section over here,' he says. 'It's tucked away, and we really don't have much, but there's a few collections here. Do you know what you're looking for?'

I stare at him. 'No,' I say. 'Dunno. Just … we had some poetry session today and the guy, Malik, said there's all different types of poetry.'

'There definitely is,' Gareth replies, and he begins to scan the shelf. 'I heard there was a poet coming in. Did you enjoy it?'

'I did, y'know. I didn't think I would, but it was actually all right.'

Gareth pauses and pulls out a book. 'This is an incredible collection,' he says. 'And this one … Oh, and hang on.' He pulls out three more books and I catch a glimpse of one of the names.

'Lemn Sissay?' I say, and I recognize the name from earlier.

'Yes,' Gareth replies. 'Have you heard of him?'

'Not till this morning,' I reply. 'He's one of the ones that poet mentioned. Is he any good?'

Gareth smiles. 'One of the greatest, in my opinion, but I'll let you be the judge of that. Come on, let's get you checked out!'

We head back to the desk and I give Gareth my prison number. Taking books out the library is the only thing you don't need privileges for. The only time they'll ever stop you is if you're on basic, cos you can't actually leave your cell. Gareth hands the books to me. I don't even think I've ever held this many books in my life before.

'Will you let me know how you get on?' he asks me. 'What you think once you've read them?'

It catches me off guard, cos no one's ever asked me what I think before. At school, I was always just ignored, or told to shut up.

'Yeah,' I reply. 'I might not understand 'em tho,' I add quickly. 'Like, what they're even going on about. Or if they're even good.'

'Don't worry about that,' Gareth says. 'Whatever you think when you read them, it'll be right.' He smiles, and even tho I've never spoken to him before, he looks like he means it.

I nod. 'All right,' I reply. 'And thanks, yeah?' I add. Then I head out of the library and make my way back to my cell.

As I'm going up the stairs, I feel someone's eyes on me. I glance upwards, past the rusty balconies and the metal safety netting, and I see Spider on the top landing, staring down at me. He leans forward and I can't quite make out his expression cos of how far up he is, but I swear I see the corners of his mouth twist into a smirk. I look away, cos I suddenly feel uneasy, and somewhere in the distance, I hear an alarm go off. I'm on edge as I take the stairs, adrenaline coursing through my veins as I try to gauge who's about. I spot a few new faces as I reach the second landing, where my cell is. There's three guys, who must've just come off induction wing, hanging about outside one of the cells. I can tell by the way that they're laughing and cracking jokes that they all must know each other from outside Ryecroft. One of them, this white guy with a shaved head in a grey tracksuit, stares in my direction.

'Yeah,' he shouts. 'What the fuck you looking at?'

My hands clench around the books, cos there's a few of them and only me, and new people nearly always start shit. They dunno the lay of the land, or who runs the prison yet, so they do the most to try and prove themselves. And it won't be just a few punches, either. They wanna do damage. They wanna draw blood. My heart starts to quicken, but I don't want to fight them, cos it'll mean extra days on my sentence, but you only ever have a few options in this place, and none of them are ever good. Even tho my whole body's trembling, I try to keep my voice steady. I try to look like I'd fight them back.

'You what?!' I reply, and I stand my ground. The last thing I need is these guys *and* Spider on my case. No matter how close I am to getting out. 'You got something to say?' I add, and I stare him down. He looks at me for a minute and I can tell that he's sizing me up.

'Nah, nah, nah,' he says. 'It's cool. I'm just playing with ya.' That's the other thing about this place – sometimes people just test you to see what they can get away with. Relief floods through me, but I try my best not to show it; I just nod instead. Then I head into my cell.

I can relax a bit now that I'm off the landing, and I sit down on my bed and go through the books that Gareth gave me. Quite a few of them are names that Malik mentioned too: Benjamin Zephaniah, Linton Kwesi Johnson, George the Poet. There's a couple I don't recognize, like Casey Bailey and Isaiah Hull too. I dunno why, but I reach for the Lemn Sissay one first. Maybe it's the cover that catches my eye, or maybe it's cos Gareth said he thought he was really good. Malik did too. I'm still mad about Spider cutting off my call to Kias like that, but I try to distract myself by flicking to the contents page.

There's loads of titles of the different poems, and I dunno if you're supposed to read poems in the order that they're written in, but one of them catches my eye – 'Spell Me Freedom'. It almost leaps off the page. Another alarm goes off in the distance, probably cos there's been another fight. I stare down at the title again, and in a weird way, it kinda feels like fate, cos freedom's all I've thought about for so long. Then I turn to the poem and start to read.

6

We're in our second poetry workshop with Malik. It's been a week since he was last here, and I've only got two weeks till I'm released. Malik was right – and Gareth was right too – there's more than one type of poetry. I didn't expect to like Lemn Sissay, or even relate to any of the stuff that he spoke about, but I do. It's weird, but it's almost like the sadness and anger that he writes about in some of his poetry belongs to me, cos that's exactly how I've felt too. There was this one poem about his mum and how he doesn't know what to say to her. How he's scared to tell her the truth, cos she might be disappointed or ashamed of him. And another about the bruises he's had for most of his life, which reminded me of my dad.

But it weren't just those ones, either, tho. He mentioned places that I recognize, where I'd go all the time before I got locked up. There's a whole poem about Manchester Piccadilly, and ones that mention Moss Side and Hulme too. I've never read a poem that talks about my ends before. And even tho some of the poems are about hard times and death, and surviving each day, and what it means to just live in the world when you're Black ... they're hopeful too. It's like some of them are full of so much pride. Not just for the city and where Lemn's from, but for the people who live in it too.

There's one poem where he talks about a gym in Moss Side turning princes into kings, and I know which gym he's talking about. I've walked past it most of my life. I guess I've never heard of anyone like me, from an area like mine, being described that way before. I even read the book a couple of times, which I ain't ever done, either. I've never finished a full book in my life, never mind read one twice. I'm kinda excited to go back to the library and tell Gareth what I think, once I've read the other ones too.

We're in that same classroom as last week, and pretty much everyone's here again, apart from Oxy, who got into a fight yesterday and is still banged up in his cell. Dadir don't seem annoyed to be here, and I'm actually looking forward to it too.

This time, tho, Malik gives us two poems: 'Gentle Youth' and 'Boys in Hoodies' by Caleb Femi. They're only short, and he gets each of us to read a bit out loud. Even those of us who can't read that well. I recognize Caleb's name from one of the collections that Gareth gave me too. In the poems, it's like I can see myself and Clinton and Abass and Shaun, and every other kid I know my age who'd be hanging about on the estate. It's the first time I've really seen myself in words like that.

One of the poems talks about cracking jokes outside of a chicken shop. And how inside each hoodie, there's almost something magical that the outside world doesn't see. Or maybe doesn't want us to see, either. In the next poem, he talks about the streets being fragile, and boys like me being scared. How the news will say that we'll dead you in the night, but all we want to do is make music and live and laugh. It's like there's a beauty in the poems that none of us ever get to see, and a truth as well that we never even talk about.

'What do you think?' Malik asks us. 'Do you like them? Hate them? What?'

'I really liked them both!' Dadir goes. 'Even, like, the bits of speech on there or whatever – that's how me and my friends really talk. And all that stuff about being misunderstood and judged by the outside world as well ... It's almost like where we're from isn't just seen as being this harsh, tough place, either. There's, like, a softness to it. If that makes sense?'

Malik nods. 'Yeah, it definitely does make sense!' he says.

Everyone agrees and says something about the poem.

I really liked it too, and thoughts are going round in my head about what I think. But I stay quiet. I know it sounds mad, but I found standing up to those new guys on the wing way easier than the thought of talking about what I think in a room full of people.

Malik must clock that I ain't said anything, cos he goes: 'Tyrell? What do you think?'

My palms begin to sweat, but I know I need to say something, cos everyone else has and I'll just look like even more of an idiot if I don't.

I pause. 'I feel like he really gets it,' I say. I sneak a glance at Malik, but he ain't looking at me like I've said something wrong, or stupid. Instead, he nods.

'Go on,' Malik says.

I shrug. 'I dunno,' I continue. 'But it's like this Caleb guy just understands the things you *really* feel when you're hanging out with a group of boys. That we *all* feel, but no one talks about, cos no one ever says anything about being scared. No one ever talks about being frightened, or how hanging out with a group of boys that you know, on the streets that you know, is more than just "hanging out". It's like a lifeline ...' I finish quietly, and I can't look at Malik, cos I suddenly feel embarrassed. It's true tho. Even tho I ended up doing some bad stuff, I don't know what I would've done without Clinton and Abass and Shaun. And even tho Clinton never said anything, I could tell he was scared about going to prison too.

Malik nods again. 'That's great, Ty!' he says. 'Really. I felt like that the first time I read it too. It really spoke to me, because of the reasons you've said . . . you've *all* said,' Malik continues, and he glances around the room.

It feels strange, hearing that I've done something right for a change. Having an adult say they've thought the same thing as me ain't something that I'm used to, either, but it feels good. I shift over in my chair and I just wanna take in everything that Malik says. I just wanna take in all the poetry and all the words that I've been introduced to as well.

'Can anyone see what Caleb's maybe done with the imagery?' Malik asks. 'When he's describing the streets or young people?'

'Yeah,' I blurt out before I can stop myself, and I'm surprised that I've actually spoken again. 'It's like he's taken the things that are normal to us, or that other people would see as dangerous or whatever, and described them in, like, a beautiful way. Kinda magical, almost, cos he talks about hoodies being like trees, and boys pouring themselves into raindrops . . . and groups of guys who unwrinkle nightlight from their skin.'

'That's right!' Malik says, and he gives me a wide smile. 'There's so much beauty in everyday life. So much poetry in everyday life – sometimes it's easy to forget.'

Malik starts telling us about the way that poems are organized. How there's stanzas and verses and line breaks.

105

How everything the writer does – even when a word is on its own, surrounded by all this white space – is deliberate. I feel my whole body tense, cos I'm almost too scared to breathe, just in case I miss something that Malik says. Then he gets us to start writing our own poems, thinking about those moments of beauty in our lives. In places where we might not have seen or noticed it before. He gets us to describe our ends and people we hang around with and the things we don't let ourselves say. And he gets us to arrange it in lines and stanzas.

I pick up my pen, and this time I can't stop the words from coming. It feels good to try and put the lines in some sorta order, to try and structure them in a way I can understand, cos nothing else in my life feels like that.

I don't know how long I'm writing for, but time goes really fast, and I'm disappointed when Malik tells us to stop. My fingers are throbbing, cos I can't remember the last time I've ever written so much, and I'm still trying to work out the order of the last few lines when Malik goes: 'Does anyone want to read out what they've written? I do have one rule, though – I'll never force you to if you don't want to.'

There are a few nods, and I'm a bit surprised that Dadir says he'll read his too. One by one, people start to read out their poems. They're all so different. Some people have only written a few lines and that, but they still read them out anyway. My heart starts to quicken, cos it feels like I'm sharing another piece of myself, and I ain't sure I want everyone to hear it. I fold my poem in half and move it towards me.

'Tyrell?' Malik asks.

'Nah, nah,' I say, and he doesn't try and persuade me to read or anything. He just nods and moves on to the next person.

When the session finishes, we have to wait to be escorted back to our different wings. There's only me and Dadir and a few others from Jay left in the room. Before some of the screws take us back, tho, I go up to Malik. The poem clutched in my hands.

'You all right, Ty?' Malik asks.

'Yeah,' I say, and I feel my hands trembling. 'I just wanted to say thanks and that for today. I really enjoyed it.'

Malik smiles. 'I'm glad!' he says.

I can see Dadir and the other guys looking at me and I know I have to be quick, cos we're gonna have to go soon, so I hold my poem out towards Malik. I feel embarrassed, cos a couple of people are looking, but I don't want Malik to think that I weren't interested in the session or anything like that. Besides, I just want to know if I'm at least on the right track.

I clear my throat. 'I, err, I wrote something and I didn't wanna read it out in front of everyone, or nothing like that,' I say quickly. 'But d'you think you could, like, read it and see what you think . . . ?'

Malik pauses for a split second, and I swear it feels like a lifetime. I regret asking him right away.

'It don't matter if you're too busy tho,' I add. 'It's probably a load of rubbish anyway—'

But before I can finish, Malik shakes his head. 'I'd be honoured to read it, Ty,' he says. 'I'll let you know what I think in the next session, yeah?'

'Yeah,' I say. 'Thanks.'

Malik reaches his hand out to take the piece of paper from me, and even tho it's just a few words, it's harder to let go of than I thought. Cos it ain't just a poem. It's more than that. It almost feels like I'm trusting Malik with something precious and fragile and important. Longman and two more screws come to the door.

'Forrester, Hassan, Mullard, Biddy, let's go.'

'Yeah, boss,' I hear a few people say.

'I'll see you all next week,' Malik says.

'Bye,' I reply, and I find myself wishing that it was next week already as we head out the door.

I'm waiting in line at the servery so I can get my dinner and take it back to my cell. Dinner's been the same since I first arrived at Ryecroft. A dry sandwich, an apple and a packet of crisps. You only ever get two choices as well: rubbery cheese, or chicken that don't taste like any meat I've ever had. I scan my surroundings, cos the servery and by the showers are where the worst fights can kick off. Even tho I'm trying to see who's about, I can't stop thinking about the fact I gave my poem to Malik and if it was the right thing to do. What if it really is rubbish? What if he didn't wanna read it in the first place, but felt like he couldn't say no?

Dadir's in front of me in the queue and he says, 'Y'know what? I never thought I'd like all that poetry shit, but ... it's all right, y'know. It's actually made me miss writing music as well. Like, I swear, I just wanna get behind a mic again. I forgot how much music helps me to escape.'

'You still can,' I say. 'Just tell Davidson you changed your mind and you wanna do the music sessions.'

Dadir nods. 'Yeah, I think I might still, y'know. Could do with something else to help me pass the time in 'ere.' Dadir reaches one of the people handing out the sandwiches and he goes: 'Yeah, cheese, please,' and they put the sandwich on his tray.

I ask for the same. Out of the corner of my eye, I clock the new guy in the grey tracksuit who was on the landing last week. I see him arguing with some other guy who's a lot smaller. Then the next minute, he headbutts him in the face. They start fighting, tho it ain't really a fight, cos the guy in the grey is about twice the size as the kid on the floor. The noise starts too, the shouting and the banging, and my heart starts to race quicker. Even when you're prepared for it, when you're constantly waiting for it to happen, it can still come out of nowhere, the violence, and that's the scariest thing. Cos it's like one explosion after the next. An alarm goes off; then some screws run over and break them apart, and twist them both up. Then another fight breaks out. Me and Dadir walk off with our trays, and even tho I'm shaking, I don't look back. Some people are jeering and shouting, cos they just see it all as entertainment. I hate it tho.

'Another day in the madhouse,' Dadir goes. 'Eh,' he continues, as we make our way along the wing. 'Did I tell you what my mum said when she came to visit yesterday?'

Dadir's words sting, cos over the past couple of years, I'd have given anything for Mum to have visited me more. It's like she'd always find some reason not to come and it was usually to do with Isiah. I swallow hard and try to push down some of the pain.

'Nah,' I reply. 'What did she say?'

'She said how the trial was in the paper,' Dadir continues. 'But not how it was the first time, when they were calling it a "gang conspiracy". They actually said it was a miscarriage of justice, and my mum reckons it'll help my appeal ... I mean, it has to? Innit?'

I hear a bit of hope in Dadir's voice, and the thing is, I don't know. It's hard to believe in any kind of justice when people like Dadir and Emmanuel are even in Ryecroft in the first place.

'Yeah,' I say, and I think I say it out loud, cos I desperately want it to be true. Dadir smiles, and I'm about to say something else, when Spider, Jason and Kofi come down the stairs. Dadir shoots me a look, probably to check that I'm all right. Even tho Spider and them stare Dadir down, they let him pass. I go to follow Dadir, but Spider steps in front of me and blocks my path.

'You all right, Forrester?' he says, and the corners of his mouth twist into a smile. I feel my body tense, and Spider glances down at the tray in my hands. 'Don't think you need that, do you?' he says. Then he reaches down and grabs my sandwich before I can try and do anything to stop him. 'Just like old times, eh?' he says, and there's a glint in his eye.

Jason and Kofi laugh, and I know what Spider's doing. I know that he's trying to get some sorta reaction out of me. First, my phone call with Kias, and now this. My heart starts to pound in my chest, but I turn to Spider. You barely get enough to eat as it is in prison, and now I'm gonna have to wait another five hours till my next meal. It's like he's taking away anything that gives me even the tiniest bit of happiness.

'E-yar, yo—' I start, but Spider gets right in my face.

'What?!' he spits, and he's so close to me that I can feel his breath on my skin. I dunno why I even said anything back in the first place. Maybe cos I'm still so upset and mad that I never got to finish talking to Kias yesterday. I can feel people circling us, waiting for whatever's about to happen to kick off. My legs start to tremble and suddenly I wish I'd never said anything. That I'd just kept my big mouth shut.

'You going to do anything about it, Forrester?' Spider asks me. 'Go on,' he continues, and he moves his head so that he's staring right at me. 'I dare you.' His mouth curls up and I catch a glimpse of one of his chipped teeth. I'm proper frightened and I just wanna get out of here quick-time, but I know I can't. I try not to show Spider and everyone else just how scared I am, but I move away. Spider and his mates all laugh.

'Better make sure nothing don't show up in your cell, Forrester,' Spider says. 'Especially when you're so close to getting out. The last thing you need is one of them screws finding a phone, a chiv, some spice … I'd watch my back if I were you,' Spider finishes, and then him and his mates head off.

I let out a breath, now that Spider's cleared off, and even tho I was scared, a part of me just wishes I could stand up to him again. I guess there's more riding on it this time tho. I turn to Dadir and he looks really worried.

'I knew all that stuff he was spouting the other day about you two being cool was a load of bullshit,' Dadir says.

'Yeah, I know,' I reply. 'Never trusted him for a minute.'

'You need to be careful, tho, Ty,' Dadir adds, and he lowers his voice. 'I swear, you didn't make it this far just for him to set you up.'

'I know,' I say, and I mean it. Cos if my cell got searched and they did find something, there ain't no way they'd believe that it wasn't mine. And it ain't like I could grass and say that Spider planted it, either, cos then my life really wouldn't be worth living.

7

I'm in my cell. The first thing I did when I got back here was check to make sure that Spider hadn't planted anything. The last thing I need is one of the screws doing a random cell spin and finding something. Everything looked exactly the same as it had done when I'd left, but I still checked in all the places people usually stash stuff to make sure that there was nothing hidden. Between the layers of tissue paper in a loo roll, down the hole in the drain, inside the back of the telly and behind the metal panel that's part of the sink. I had to undo the tiny screws that keep the panel in place with some nail clippers, but I was relieved to see that there was nothing in there.

Spider was just trying to make me even more para. As if being in prison didn't do that already. Even if Spider was just messing with my head, tho, I still wouldn't put anything past him.

After we looked at those poems in Malik's session, I just want to read more. So I'm reading through Caleb's collection that Gareth gave me. It ain't just cos I connected to his poetry tho. I'm trying to distract myself from how hungry I am too. That packet of crisps and dusty apple barely did anything, and all I can think about is food. In a weird way, reading these poems seems to help tho. It's almost as if I get lost in them, and for a split second, I can forget about my stomach rumbling, or that I'm even banged up in Ryecroft, cos I'm thinking about all the images and the sadness and anger and joy that I feel. And even tho I was brought up in Moss Side and not in Peckham, I recognize it. It feels like home to me, but at the same time, it helps me to escape too. Just like Lemn Sissay's poetry did. I've never had that before. I've never really been able to get lost in something and escape.

I read through 'Thirteen' and 'Coping' and 'Things I Have Stolen', then 'Schrödinger's Black', 'On Magic / Violence', 'Poor', 'Concrete (IV)', then 'East Dulwich Road' and 'Yard'. Then 'Here Too Spring Comes to Us with Open Arms' and 'On the Other Side of the Street'. I even re-read the poems that Malik showed us in our session too. Only, it's kinda like I'm reading them for the first time, now that I've read what goes before and after them.

My mind is buzzing. Caleb talks about brotherhood and pain

and music and loss. And how sometimes you behave a certain way or do certain things cos that's just how you've learned to cope. He talks about being hassled by the police, and rich people moving into your area, and the people who've lived there for years being kicked out. He talks about fear and frustration and anger, and how kids from areas like that are judged. How we constantly feel like we're walking on a narrow ledge, with no one to catch us. Cos maybe the world wants us to fall. But it's also about imagination and love, and the beauty of being from a place that's made up entirely of concrete and walkways and tower blocks.

I kinda want next week to hurry up even more now so I can talk to Malik about the rest of Caleb's poems. I turn over the page and I try to think about some of the stuff we learned today – about the verses and the line breaks and why some of the words are on their own – when I hear a scream. It echoes all around me, piercing and thin. Then the next minute, I hear someone shout: '*Get off me!* Get the fuck off me! My hands ... You're hurting my hands ...'

An alarm goes off on the landing, screeching loudly, and I get up off my bed. The screaming only seems to get worse and I rush out my cell. Maybe it's cos of the noise and the fact that the alarm is barely even drowning out the cries, but my chest starts to feel tight, and my whole body is trembling. A few other people come out their cells to see what's going on, and a couple more screws come running.

Oxy's across the landing from me. He's on the floor and they've got him folded up, with his thumbs pushed right back. I already know that they're gonna take him to segregation, which is a wing in another part of the prison, where they keep you separate from everyone else. They do it as a form of punishment and it's even worse than being on basic, cos you ain't allowed no letters, or visits, or to go to education, or nothing. They put you in an empty cell and you're only allowed out for fifteen minutes of 'exercise' a day. So you can walk around the yard, by yourself, while a screw watches. That's if they even let you do that. They can keep you there for days or even weeks and it proper messes with people's heads, cos you're just there, on your own, for all that time.

There's about six screws holding Oxy down, and the other ones who came running over try to hold him down too. Someone's kneeing him in the back, but Oxy's still trying to fight them, and I hear one of the screws say: 'Oxy, we're taking you to the seg, all right? If you resist, it's only going to hurt you more, cos we're allowed to use reasonable force. Do you understand me? Do you understand?'

Oxy just yells again. Then he says: 'My hands – you're hurting my hands. Get off me!'

Then Davidson shouts: 'All prisoners back in their cells. I want all prisoners back in their cells, *now*!'

But I can't stop staring at Oxy. Even tho he's mouthing off, there's tears streaming down his face, and I can see how much pain he's in. I ain't never seen Oxy cry before. Someone's holding his head down, and two of the screws make their way down along the landing and shout: 'In your cells – get in your cells, now!'

But I can't move. Someone else protests, and Longman goes: 'If you don't get in your cell, I'll nick ya.'

Then the doors slam. One by one. But I still can't look away from Oxy.

One of the screws gets to me.

'Forrester,' he says. 'Did you not hear me? In your cell, now. Get back in your cell!' he shouts.

I take a few steps backwards, and I'm only just inside when the door slams shut in my face. I hear the sound of the key, and he pulls the metal hatch down too. They'll probably have us banged up for a while now. At least till they get Oxy out of here anyway. I dunno why, but I suddenly feel like my cell is too small, even tho I've been in the same one for almost eighteen months. Oxy's screaming and the sound of the alarm seems so loud – louder than usual.

I start to feel proper hot. I'm sweating and then I feel this rush of emotions, like it's all too much and I dunno how to handle any of it. Ryecroft, my dad, being banged up in this cell, all the stuff with my mum.

My chest goes tight and I suddenly feel like I can't breathe. Like I'm about to pass out. I go to the window and I try to breathe in some of the air from outside, but it ain't enough. My hands won't stop trembling and I just wanna get out of here. I just want it all to stop. I think about pressing my emergency alarm, but I know it'll just ring out. Especially now the wing's on lockdown. Besides, the last time I felt like this, they told me it weren't 'an emergency' and they just shut the hatch. And how can I tell someone what's wrong when I don't even understand it myself?

I go over to the shelf by the door, where my kettle is. I pick up the plastic container that I keep my teabags in and I reach my hand inside. I don't even have the crappy disposable shaver that they give you in my cell any more. Maybe cos part of me was always scared that I'd end up using it again. But, still, it's like I couldn't get rid of everything. Like I knew, somehow, that I'd always need it there. I pull out the broken bit from a metal aerial, as the alarms continue screeching around me.

8

It's been a week since the wing got locked down. I've got nine days till I'm released, and we're back in education now for another one of Malik's poetry workshops. We've only got one more session after this one, before we're finished completely, and even tho I don't want Malik's workshops to end, I'm still gonna keep writing. Oxy's out of seg, but he decided that he didn't wanna come any more. There's a few other people missing as well. That's just what happens in here tho. People drop out, or change their minds, or get into trouble. I'm looking forward to it and that, but I'm still feeling a bit weird after cutting last week. I just feel … ashamed. Especially after I'd gone so long without doing it.

The past few days, I've barely even left my cell. I ain't really been in the mood for talking. Not even to Dadir, and he's one of my closest mates. I've been reading loads, tho, and writing too. I've even finished most of the books I took out from the library as well – *Gold from the Stone*, *Rebel Without Applause*, *Poor*, *Adjusted*, *Search Party*. I even read *Poor* and *Search Party* twice. I can't believe I'd never even heard of Lemn, or George, or Caleb before. Their poetry's kinda like music, and I get why Malik mentioned rap and drill in our first session now too. All I've done is sit in my cell with their images and words, and in a way it's helped me to feel less alone. It's helped me to feel seen and understood, instead of pushed out. And even tho they ain't my stanzas, or lines, or words written in those books, it almost feels like I have a voice too. Like it's there, deep inside of me, and maybe I can use it as well. Even tho I ain't felt too good, writing's seemed to help a bit, somehow. Which is funny, cos that was the thing I hated the most at school. This is different tho.

I lean back in my chair while we wait for Malik to come in, and Dadir reaches over and nudges me.

'Yo, Ty,' he says, and even tho it's noisy, he lowers his voice. 'You all right? You've been proper quiet lately. You've barely even spoken . . .'

I nod. Even tho I trust Dadir more than anyone in the world, I can't tell him. I can't talk to him about the fact I cut myself. To be honest, I can't talk to anyone about it. Dadir knows that it goes on – everyone does, cos you see it. And I ain't just talking about the scars that people have up their arms or across their chest, either. Sometimes you see people self-harming on the wing, and even tho it happens loads, no one ever really speaks about it.

'Yeah, I'm fine,' I lie, and I straighten myself up. 'I've just been a bit distracted, that's all. Y'know, with getting out and all that stuff. I'm good tho . . .'

Dadir stares at me and I can tell that he ain't convinced. With Clinton and Shaun and that lot, I could tell them any old bullshit and they would just buy it. Not Dadir tho. It's only been eighteen months, but he knows me better than any of my old mates. He can tell that something's up, but he knows not to push it too much as well.

Dadir nods. 'All right,' he says. 'But you do know you can talk to me?' he adds. 'I mean, I might not give the best advice or nothing, cos one time my little sister asked me if she should shave off her eyebrows and I was, like, "Yeah, why not?"'

I splutter. 'You didn't?' I reply.

'Don't know why she asked me that question,' Dadir continues. 'I swear, she looked like a thumb, bruv. Then she started crying cos she had to draw them on, and they just came out wonky all the time. My mum was *mad*! It was worth it tho . . . So, yeah, my advice ain't too great, but I'm a good listener. I mean it.'

I laugh and it feels good, cos it's the first time I've done it all week.

'Appreciate it,' I tell Dadir, and I know he ain't just saying it, either. It makes me wish I could open up to him, but I guess I wouldn't even know where to start. And even tho I know Dadir won't judge me, part of me feels so ashamed for even doing something like that in the first place. So it's easier to just keep it all inside. Like I've always done, I suppose.

Malik comes into the room with one of the screws, and he gives us a wave.

'Morning,' he says. 'How you all getting on?'

A few people respond, and even tho I'm still thinking about the other week, I get lost in the session. Malik starts talking about meter and a type of poem called an elegy, which has no rules, but is often written in mourning about sadness and loss. Then he gives us an exercise to do. Malik's barely even finished talking when I pick my pen up and start to write. I dunno if it's cos I've been feeling so much over the last few days, but it's like I can't stop the words from pouring onto the page. And I can't explain why, but I instantly feel better. I don't feel as embarrassed, or ashamed, or angry, or any of that stuff. It's like everyone around me just fades away and the only thing that matters is me and these words.

Once I've finished, I start moving some of the lines around, or crossing out some of the words so I can find ones that work better. I'm so absorbed in what I'm doing that I don't even notice that Malik's come over. He crouches down beside me.

'How you getting on, Ty?' he asks.

I'm pretty much done, and I've already read over it a couple of times as well. Everyone else is still writing tho.

I nod. 'Yeah, good,' I say. 'I think I've finished.'

Malik gives me a smile. 'Can I have a look?' he says.

I shrug. 'All right,' I say, even tho I'm nervous. I still don't even know what he thinks of the poem I gave him last time, yet. What if the only reason I've finished so quickly is cos I've done it wrong? I'm suddenly worried that it's probably a load of rubbish, so I try not to look at Malik as he picks up the piece of paper and starts reading it. I feel myself shaking again as I stare down at my hands.

'Wow,' Malik says, and he puts the poem back on my desk. 'This is incredible. It's so powerful and I love this line here . . .' He points to the second line down, and I can hardly believe what I'm hearing. Malik actually likes it. Not just that, but he said it was 'incredible' as well. It feels amazing, cos not only have I done something right for once, but I might have found something that I'm actually good at too.

Malik points to another bit of the poem. 'And this line too. Honestly, Ty . . .' He shakes his head. 'I read the other poem you gave me last week as well. I've written a couple of suggestions on it, of things you could tweak or change, but that was brilliant too . . .' He pauses. 'Whatever happens, even after these sessions finish,' he continues, 'you need to promise me that you won't ever stop writing. Cos I'm telling you now, you've got a gift.'

I feel myself staring at Malik, and part of me wants to ask him to repeat what he just said, cos it don't seem real. It feels like some sorta dream. A gift? *Me?* A tiny part of me wonders if Malik is just saying it, but I try to push that to the back of my mind.

'I won't,' I say, and I shake my head. 'I've been practising and that,' I say quietly. Cos I don't really want anyone else to hear. 'Took some books out the library. I actually finished most of them. I read more of Caleb's poetry as well. Even read some of the books more than once. I ain't never done that before, y'know, read a whole book.'

Malik smiles. 'That's amazing!' he says. 'I can give you a list of some of my favourite poets if you want?'

'Yeah,' I say. 'I'd really like that.'

Malik taps my poem. 'Speaking of reading, tho,' he continues, 'd'you wanna share today?'

My heart starts to race. 'Yeah, I dunno about that,' I say, and Malik laughs.

'Okay,' he replies. 'Like I said, I'll never force you to do anything you don't wanna do. But you never know, these guys might get a lot out of hearing your work. And you might get a lot out of reading it.'

I stare at him. But I still ain't sure. Not just of the poem, but of myself too. Then Malik picks up my pen and scribbles some things on the page.

'It's amazing,' he says. 'But if you do want to read it, I'd finish it here. It's even stronger that way. And I'd maybe find a different word to use here. It'll be perfect then.'

I nod. 'Thanks,' I say.

Malik smiles, then heads over to Lewis, and I make the changes to the poem. And then Malik goes:

'All right, if I can get you to put your pens down. Does anyone want to share?'

Pretty much everyone puts their hand up, and then people go round reading their poem out, and we all clap. Dadir's the last one to read, and once he's finished, Malik says, 'Anyone else want to share?'

I dunno if it's cos Malik said that my poem was good, or if it's cos he said I might get something out of reading mine out. But today, I put my hand up.

'I'll go,' I say, and my voice is already trembling.

'Yes, Ty!' Dadir cuts in, and Malik smiles wider.

'Whenever you're ready, Ty,' Malik says.

I suck in a sharp breath, and for a second I think about backing out and saying that I've changed my mind, but that'll only make me look like more of an idiot. I'm starting to sweat, but I keep my head down, and I don't look at anyone while

I read. I'm shaking, and even tho it goes by in this blur, it feels good to read the words I've written out loud. I don't know what it is, but it makes them seem . . . different. More powerful, maybe. When I've finished, I glance at Malik and he gives me a nod.

Dadir's eyes widen. 'I didn't know you could write like that!' he says. '*Jeez!*' Then everyone claps. Malik claps the loudest and he has a big grin on his face. Even tho I was nervous, I'm glad I did it, cos Malik was right. There's something kinda special about reading your work out loud. And for the first time ever, I don't feel ashamed of something I've done. I actually feel proud.

Birds

They name the wings after birds

Kingfisher, Quail, Ibis, Jay
Cos maybe a place that keeps you caged
Doesn't sound so bad if it's named after something
that's meant to fly
But only in the darkness do you hear the cries

Of boys with broken wings
Feathers plucked torn
Who just want to go home.

9

I'm still on a high from Malik's poetry session when I get back to my cell. Malik even wrote down that list of his favourite poets like he said he would too – Jay Bernard, Roger Robinson, Zena Edwards, Nick Makoha, Patience Agbabi, Zaffar Kunial, Malika Booker, Solomon O.B. Spider had taken the food off my tray at lunchtime again, but I decided to just let him, cos I was so close to getting out and would only be here for another eight days. I wasn't gonna let him piss me off, and I defo wasn't gonna do anything that might put me at risk of getting additional days added. Or having something planted in my cell. Not when I can almost taste my freedom as well.

It's association now, so all the pads are unlocked and I'm

sitting on my bed, trying to write another poem. Dadir's got a meeting with his solicitor, so I've decided not to bother going onto the wing. Which I'm kinda glad about, cos it means that I can write some more. I'm trying to do that thing that Malik taught us about in the second session, where you try to find the beauty in the ordinary things around you. I figure that if I concentrate on poetry, then it stops me from thinking about anything else.

I glance up towards the window from my bed, and I write a few words down. I try to describe what I can see through the bars. The rest of the prison building, the bit of light. How one time, this small bird just came and sat on the ledge on the outside of the window. Then, when it flew off, it left behind this tiny brown feather. I'm partway through a line, when someone comes into my cell. I expect it to be Dadir, cos his meeting would've finished by now, and there's still another hour of association left. When I look up, tho, I see that it's Spider, Jason and Kofi. Spider smiles and he's got this glint in his eye.

'What's up, Forrester?' he says. 'Got you a leaving present, innit!' I look at Spider's hand and notice that he's holding a sock. By the way that it's weighed down and the shape at the bottom, I can tell that there's something in it. Spider clocks me looking.

'Told you we'd have a game of pool before you go,' he says with a smile.

I jump up off my bed and Kofi slams my cell door shut. My

heart starts to thump hard against my chest and I feel the blood rushing through my body. There's three of them and only one of me. I should've known that Spider wasn't gonna be content with just winding me up with little comments. I should've known that leaving here wasn't gonna be this easy. I quickly look around my cell – I got nothing to defend myself with. There's an emergency alarm by the door, and if I can get to it, it'll start going off, and one of the screws will come to see what the problem is.

My eyes dart towards the alarm and I go to make a run for it, but Jason grabs hold of me and Kofi punches me hard in the stomach. I double over in pain and I try to shout for help, but the whole place is so loud, I don't think anyone can hear me.

Spider laughs. 'D'you really think I was all right with what you did?' he spits. 'You disrespected me and I ain't gonna let that slide.'

I shout again and the words get caught in my throat, but Spider just laughs again. 'They can't hear ya,' he says. 'Don't you get it? No one hears you in this place, and even if they do, they don't give a fuck. D'you think any of them screws are gonna be bothered whether you make it out of this place or not? You won't be seeing your release date – I'll make sure of that.'

I shout louder, even tho I know that no one is coming, and I don't care about trying to look like a big man any more. I'm scared. You might be 'safely' locked up away from everyone else, but in here, there ain't no such thing as being safe. There's tears running down my face now, and I'm screaming, but I'm cornered in my cell. No one can hear me. And Spider's right, even if they can, they don't care. I hear myself begging Spider to leave it, but he just laughs louder.

'Who the fuck do you think you are, Forrester?' he says. Then the next minute, he hits me hard in the face with the sock that's got the snooker balls in it. I yell out in agony. I've never known anything like it. I'm on the floor and I hear something crack, then feel a gush of warmth, and I know that it's blood. Spider's on top of me and I try to cover my head, but he carries on hitting me, again and again. Kofi and Jason are getting punches in too and someone is holding me down. I try to shout for help again, but my voice cracks and the word gets stuck in my throat.

My vision is blurry, but I can see the outline of Spider on top of me and I hear him laughing. My screams are barely even a whisper now cos I know that no one's coming. I look up at the ceiling and I feel another blow to my head and I think that this is it. I'll never get to see Kias, or my mum, or Isiah. I won't even make it to the end of my sentence. I'm just gonna die, right here, in this cell.

And then everything goes black.

10

I open my eyes and it takes me a minute to realize where I am. I blink and everything gradually comes into focus. I'm in a tiny hospital room. It don't look like the hospital wing in Ryecroft, either. I hear the low beeping sound of a machine and see that there's wires and equipment attached to me. The pain hits me all at once and I let out this sound that's halfway between a cry and a whimper. It's the worst pain I've ever felt in my life and, on top of that, I feel tired and out of it. My throat's dry and I suddenly realize I've got tears running down my face, cos I thought, for sure, that that was it. I was gonna die. I suck in a sharp breath, then quickly wipe away the tears with the back of my hand.

Then I turn to my left. There's two police officers sitting

beside the door, and that's it. Even tho I know that I wouldn't be able to have my family around me, it still doesn't make it any easier. I'm still a criminal, and maybe that won't ever change. One of the police officers says something about going to get the nurse and disappears out the door. And even tho I'm seventeen – and I'd never admit this to any of my mates, not even Dadir – I just want my mum. Not just her, but Kias and Isiah too. The police officer comes back in, followed closely by a nurse, and she gives me a kind smile.

'Tyrell,' she says. 'It's good to see that you're awake. You might feel a little groggy because of the pain relief that you're on, and there will be quite a bit of discomfort while your injures heal, but I can up your dosage now that you're awake.'

I nod. 'Thanks,' I say.

'I'll just need to do some more tests as well. To check that there's no permanent damage. I'd like to keep you in for one more night or so, before we get you discharged. Okay?'

'Okay,' I say.

'You're very lucky, you know,' the nurse says. 'You've got some bad bruising and you had mild concussion, but you'll be okay. That was a really close call, though.' Then she gives me another smile and says something about going to get some pain relief.

I realize that I don't know how long I've been in hospital for, or why Spider and that lot even let me live. Not when they wanted to hurt me so badly as well. The last thing I remember is Spider saying, '*You won't be seeing your release date. I'll make sure of that*,' and I'm suddenly frightened, cos I can still hear his voice, sharp and clear, and I feel like I'm about to throw up. Surviving this is one thing, but what's gonna happen when I go back on the wing? What if Spider and that lot try to finish the job?

I sit up and try to eat some food, but my whole body hurts and my face is still too swollen to chew without pain. I manage to get myself out of bed, but it takes a long time to get to the sink to splash cold water on my face. It stings, but it seems help a little bit at least. I've been back on Jay for a couple of days now. I really didn't wanna come back, cos I was frightened of what Spider and that lot might do. They've been put on seg, tho, so at least I don't have to worry about running into them. Especially as I'm getting out tomorrow. Even tho I know that Spider and Jason and Kofi ain't on Jay right now, tho, I keep looking over my shoulder. It's, like, I'm constantly expecting someone to attack me again.

I stare at my reflection in the cracked mirror. I can just about make out my brown eyes and my 'fro is proper big now. It's doing that thing where when it gets to a certain length, the curls just look funny. Other than that, I barely recognize myself. It turns out, I had two fractured cheekbones, a broken nose, a couple of bruised ribs and a busted lip. I'm lucky none of my ribs got broken, even tho everything hurts like hell. My face is still black and blue. Tho it don't look anywhere near as bad as it did a couple of days ago, it's still a mess.

Dadir was the only reason Spider and his mates stopped beating me up. He heard my screams when he went back to his cell after his meeting, and he raised the alarm. I owe that guy my life. If Dadir hadn't gone and got the screws, then I would've just ended up as a statistic in some report. Cos people die all the time inside, either by killing themselves, or being killed by other inmates. Sometimes people are just found dead in their cell as well. No explanation or nothing. Stuff like that hardly ever makes the news tho. Cos who cares if some seventeen-year-old who's locked up for committing a crime dies?

After Dadir went and got help, one of Spider's friends who was acting as lookout let them know that the screws were on their way. Spider and Jason and Kofi got off before they could be caught beating the crap out of me. But they were seen on CCTV going into my cell. So, even tho there's no cameras inside the pads, it didn't take a brain surgeon to figure out who'd done this to me.

I've got a meeting with the governor in a minute, cos Spider and the rest of them are gonna have to have a judiciary hearing to see what their punishment will be. The last time I had one of those hearings was when I had that fight with Spider on the wing. My face is still throbbing, and I know that if Spider saw me like this, he'd be proud of his handiwork. I move away from the mirror, cos I can't stand looking at myself like this any more. I know that this probably sounds stupid after everything that's happened as well, but I'm gutted that I never got to go to Malik's last poetry session. It was yesterday, but I was in so much pain that I could barely leave my cell, never mind try and write something. And, yeah, I know that I'm lucky to be alive, but Malik's workshops felt like more than just some random classes. It was like for the first time in so long, someone had given me some hope. This feeling that I had something to look forward to, and I hate Spider for taking that away from me.

I didn't even get to show Malik the other poem I was working on, and it ain't like I'll ever see him again, either.

Davidson unlocks my cell.

'Forrester,' he says; then he looks at my face. He doesn't even hide the fact that he's trying not to laugh. 'Made a right mess of you, didn't they?'

I don't say anything, but I shuffle after him out of the cell.

'That's twice you've almost ended up dead now,' he says. 'If there's going to be a third time, make sure it's done properly.'

I stare at him and I think, *This fucking idiot.* I've never wanted to punch someone more in my life, but I just glare at him instead. They're always making jokes like that in here. He said something similar when I tried to kill myself at the beginning of my sentence. I'd even heard him ask someone who couldn't stop cutting themselves if they were 'ruining their cell again'. No wonder you feel like your life ain't worth shit. We head down along the wing, and then Davidson unlocks a metal door, then another one, then another. I can't wait till I can just walk around on my own without having someone escort me everywhere. I can't wait to be able to take a fucking shower whenever I want. We walk down this long corridor in this part of the prison that you never really go in. It's where the governor's office is.

Davidson knocks on the door and then we head inside. The governor's sitting behind this desk and there's a load of papers out in front of her. Her dark hair is scraped back off her face. She ain't really old or anything like that, and her features are pointy and sharp. There's a chair just in front of her too.

'Tyrell,' she says. 'Hi.'

I nod. 'You all right, miss,' I say.

She smiles and gestures to the chair. 'Please sit down.'

I lower myself into the seat and wince, while Davidson stands by the door. I sit there as she flicks through the paperwork. Then she clears her throat.

'As I'm sure you're aware,' she says, 'the nature of this meeting is to determine what happened on the twenty-sixth of April, when you were assaulted in your cell. The information that you give us will be used in the judiciary hearing, which is due to take place next week. Would you like to shed some light on what happened?'

I look right at her and I almost want to laugh. I might have been beaten to a pulp, but there's no way I'm gonna grass, so I just shrug.

'Don't remember,' I reply.

She pauses and she almost looks frustrated, but what the fuck does she expect me to say? She knows what happens to grasses in here. But even if I weren't inside, I still wouldn't grass anyway. She puts the pen that she's holding down and sighs heavily. It's all right for her. She gets to come in, sit in this office, then go home. She don't have to deal with being in here properly, like the rest of us.

'Tyrell,' she says. 'I can understand that you probably don't want to say, but as you know, the CCTV footage does show Wesley Adebayo, Jason Dwyer and Kofi Osei entering your cell shortly before the attack, then leaving it right before you were found unconscious. We're trying to figure out if one individual was more involved, or if they were all equally involved, so we can decide on the correct punishment. I know you've had some issues with Wesley in the past . . .'

I stay silent. She must realize that she ain't getting anywhere with me, cos then she goes: 'Look, Tyrell, you're being released tomorrow, so if you're worried about any possible repercussions, you don't have to be. Wesley, Kofi and Jason will be kept on seg for at least another week. We could always put you on another wing for your last night too?'

I stare at her. Spider knows a lot of people in here. If I snitched on him, he could quite easily get someone to hurt me even more. Moving wings won't make a difference, either. He could just get a new kid to do it who's got something to prove. Besides, I couldn't even be kept 'safe' in prison. Somewhere that's got cameras everywhere and countless screws and locks on every door. How the hell am I meant to be safe when I'm on the outside? Does she not think that Spider's got friends out there too?

I look at her like I've got no clue what she's even going on about. My face is throbbing and the pain is really getting to me now. I've had nightmares pretty much every night since it happened as well. Thinking that Spider had somehow managed to get back in my cell. But if Spider, Kofi and Jason end up with extra days added to their sentence, then it ain't gonna be cos of me. It ain't gonna be cos of something I said.

'Tyrell?' she presses, and I shake my head.

'I told ya,' I reply. 'I don't remember. Can I go back to my cell now?'

When I get back to my cell, I pick up the poetry books that I borrowed and decide to go to the library. It's association now, and I ain't really been out my cell since Spider's attack. Even tho I haven't wanted to go back on the wing, being stuck in my pad ain't been any easier. If I ain't having nightmares, then it's flashbacks of Spider beating the crap outta me. I hold on to the books, and tho it takes ages cos of my busted ribs, I make my way down the stairs and across the wing. My chest is tight and every movement is agony, but I try to concentrate on just getting to the library and nothing else. It feels way further than I thought it was, tho, and there's loads of people out, shouting down from the landing or mucking about on the wing.

I wanna look over my shoulder to make sure there's no one behind me, but twisting round is impossible. Every single noise puts me on edge and I'm starting to sweat. My whole body is trembling. I just wanna get off the wing and go back to my cell, cos there's too many people about. But then the library door comes into view and I feel myself calm down a little.

I manage to turn sideways a bit and push it open with my arm, and I'm relieved to see that there's only a couple of people in there. Gareth's sorting through some of the books that must've been brought back, cos he scans them into the computer. He glances up when he hears me come in and this look flashes across his face. I can't quite work out what kind of look it is at first, but it's like a mixture of shock and pity. I clock a few people staring at me and I know it's cos of the state my face is in and cos I'm moving proper weird.

Gareth smiles. 'Tyrell,' he says, and I'm surprised he even remembers my name, considering we only spoke once. 'It's good to see you back again,' he continues. Then he lowers his voice. 'I heard what happened. Are you okay?'

It catches me off guard, cos Gareth actually seems concerned, but the truth is, I can't remember the last time I properly felt okay. And I ain't just talking about those few hours when I'm writing poetry, either. I shrug and I swallow hard.

'Yeah, I'm all right. It's just one of them things, innit,' I say, even tho I don't really mean it. In some ways, it is 'just one of them things', cos what happened to me happens all the time in here. But I guess that still doesn't make it any easier. I clear my throat and I ain't sure if Gareth's convinced, cos he gives me a sad smile.

'Anyway,' I continue, and I put the books down on the desk. 'I just wanted to bring these back. I read all of them, apart from that Kayo Chingonyi one, but I'm getting out tomorrow and I didn't wanna forget.' I don't tell Gareth that since being attacked, it's been hard for me to really concentrate, which is why I haven't read Kayo Chingonyi's book. 'I really liked the ones I read tho!' I blurt out. 'Like, each collection was so different, but I got something from every book. Part of me felt kinda sad every time I got to the last poem on the last page as well ...' I pause and I sneak a look at Gareth. I suddenly feel proper embarrassed and wish I hadn't got so carried away. 'Does that make me sound weird?' I ask, and Gareth laughs.

'Not at all,' he says. 'You're speaking my language! What did you think of *Gold from the Stone*?' he asks.

'I loved it!' I say. 'I won't lie, I weren't too sure I'd even like it at first, but once I started, I couldn't put it down. D'you know he's got a poem in there about Manchester Piccadilly? And a couple about Moss Side too? Straight away, I felt at home, cos it's my ends. A book's never made me feel that way before.'

'I thought you'd like it!' Gareth says. 'And I know that poem quite well. Manchester's actually covered in Lemn Sissay's poetry. It's on the side of buildings and on flagstones on the street.'

'Swear down?' I say, and it comes as a shock. 'I never knew that,' I add. It's kinda mad to think that I've probably passed those words a million times before, maybe even walked on them, and I've never even noticed.

'You'll have to look out for them the next time you're around there!'

'Yeah, I will do!' I say. Then, before I can stop myself, I add: 'Like, even those Casey Bailey poems … Those books just made me feel understood –' I shrug – 'for the first time in my life.' Saying that out loud seems strange, cos how can a book understand you? It's true tho. It weren't just Lemn and Caleb who got me; it was Casey too. He wrote about feeling low and not understanding why, no matter how hard he tried. About numbness and loss and giving up on hope. But it's kinda about new beginnings amongst all that pain too. I don't say none of this to Gareth, tho, cos I'm still aware of the other two guys in the library. But maybe I don't have to.

Gareth smiles again and he starts sorting through the pile of books that I brought back.

'I'm so pleased to hear that, Ty!' he says. 'I really am. Did you say it was Kayo Chingonyi that you didn't get chance to read?'

'Yeah!' I go.

Then Gareth pulls *Kumukanda* out the stack and holds it out to me. I ain't sure why he's giving it back to me at first and I must look confused, cos he lowers his voice and says: 'We're technically not supposed to do this, but I've got a spare copy. It would be a shame if you didn't get to read this one too. Call it a leaving gift.'

I stare down at the book in his hands, at the illustrated cover inside the plastic sleeve, and I'm almost too scared to take it, cos apart from my mum, no one has ever given me anything before. I don't even own a book, and this one looks so new. I take it from him and I feel this rush of emotion, cos this is probably the nicest thing that anyone's ever done for me. And even tho I'm locked up, Gareth ain't treating me like I'm some waste-of-space criminal. I struggle to get the words out cos I'm feeling pretty overwhelmed, but I finally manage to say:

'Thanks, yeah. I really mean it. I'll look after it for ever.'

11

There's only fifteen minutes of association left, so I go to Dadir's cell and pray that he's in there. The last thing I wanna do is go searching for him on the wing or by the pool tables, where everyone will be. I felt calmer for those few minutes I was in the library, but now I'm back on the wing, I feel proper nervous again. I head into Dadir's cell and I'm relieved to see he's there. He's sitting at the crappy little table, writing something down on a scrap of paper, and his face lights up when he sees me.

'Yo,' he says. 'I went to try and find you before, but you weren't in your pad.'

'Was at the library!' I reply, and Dadir raises his eyebrows.

'You?' he says. 'Library?'

'Yeah, I know,' I go. 'I never even stepped foot in a library before I come here.'

Dadir smiles. 'Well,' he says. 'You've got no excuse now. Especially with that poetry you've been writing ... bare talented and shit!'

I laugh, but I can't laugh too hard, cos my face still kills. Dadir mentioning the poetry workshop just reminds me how I gutted I am that I missed it all over again. I'd tried asking Dadir in the servery at lunch, what they covered in the last session but he just said 'some free verse and sonnet shit'. He didn't exactly explain it the way that Malik would've done.

Dadir stares at me and he screws up his face. 'I'm sorry to say it, bruv,' he continues. 'But it's like the more I look at it, the worse it gets. They proper mashed up your face.'

'Yeah, I know!' I reply. 'This is nothing compared to what it was like before tho. *Trust me!*'

Dadir shakes his head. 'I thought you were gonna be getting all the girls as soon as you left here, but you ain't getting no one now,' he says with a laugh.

'Shut up, man,' I say, but I can't help but smile. Even that hurts tho. I swallow hard and there's so much I wanna say to Dadir, like how I couldn't have gotten through my time here without him. Or how he's been there for me, more than he'll ever know. More than any of the so-called 'mates' I had on the outside as well. Not just that tho. I wanna tell him that he can't give up, either. No matter what happens with his appeal, or the rest of his time inside, he's gotta keep fighting. He's gotta survive.

'Dadir,' I start. 'Thank you . . . You saved my life. If it wasn't for you, I could've been dead.'

'You don't have to thank me,' Dadir says. 'We're brothers, you know that. I'm just glad you're all right and that the screws got to you in time. Besides . . .' He pauses. 'You've saved my life in here too. You might not know it, but you have. Just having a mate like you has made all this bullshit more bearable. I'm proper gonna miss you, bro.' He rubs underneath his eye. 'Who am I even gonna talk to?' he continues. 'Everyone else in here pisses me off! And you know the older wing's gonna be ten times worse. Never thought I'd be spending my eighteenth birthday in prison . . .'

Inside I shudder. He's only got a few more days before he turns eighteen and he's transferred to the older wing at Ryecroft and then when he turns twenty-one, he'll be shipped off to adult prison, either in this country, or, in Somalia, and I know he's proper scared. I wish I could stop it somehow, or that there was something I could say to make him feel better. I used to think that justice and the law were the same thing, but coming here has made me realize that they ain't. The law doesn't always serve justice, either.

146

'You'll be all right,' I say, even tho my voice comes out weak and it doesn't feel like anywhere near enough. 'If you can handle this place, at sixteen, you can handle anywhere. Besides, the way you took Jacino out in the showers that time when he tried to go for you, I know you'll be fine.'

'Ha! Maybe,' he says, but he doesn't sound too convinced.

I gesture towards the scrap of paper in his hand.

'What you writing?' I ask. 'Poetry?'

'Nah,' he says. 'I'm leaving that to you. I'm writing some new bars tho,' he replies. 'I'm working on a new track, innit. Spoke to Johnson, like you said, and he said that as long as I stay outta trouble, I can work on it in the studio.' He shrugs. 'After that session with Malik, I just thought that this place has already taken *so* much from me. It's already taken my future and my life, I can't let it – won't let it – take music too. It's the only way I'm able to really express myself.'

I nod. 'I'm glad,' I say.

We both go quiet for a minute, and knowing that I ain't gonna see Dadir again, I suddenly wanna tell him that part of me is scared. Cos I just don't know what it's gonna be like when I leave here. What my mum and Isiah are gonna be like. What I'm gonna be like. What if Davidson was right and I do end up back here again? In another cell, just in and out of prison, like my dad. I ain't like Isiah or Kias – I'm not smart, or special. It's like I got the bad genes of our family and all I do is mess everything up.

147

Even tho I don't mean to. I can't say none of this to Dadir, tho, cos even tho I'm gonna be on licence, I'll have something he doesn't have. *Freedom.* I know that Dadir would take having a curfew and being on tag a million times over being locked up in here, so it don't feel right for me to say anything about how worried I am.

I know that association is gonna be over soon, and then we're all gonna get banged up. Part of me doesn't wanna go, cos I don't wanna say bye to Dadir. As soon as I leave, I won't be allowed to see him again, cos that's part of my licence condition too. The next time I'll be able to see him is when he's released, and even then he might not be in the UK. They might not even let him come back here.

'I'll write to ya,' I say, and I can feel my heart breaking. 'All the time ... and you need to make sure you phone me as well.'

'I will!' Dadir goes. 'You better make sure your probation worker don't find out tho!' he adds. 'The last thing I need to be seeing is your ugly mug back here!'

'She won't,' I reply. Then I add: 'I've left some stuff in my cell for ya. Johnson said he'll bring it to you once I'm gone.'

'Appreciate it,' Dadir says. Then he stands up to give me a hug.

'Better not,' I tell him. 'My ribs are proper hurting still.'

'Oh shit, yeah. Sorry!' he says, and he puts a hand on my shoulder instead, and gives it a kinda squeeze. Feeling it there, I wanna cry. I still can't believe I ain't gonna see him again. Dadir pushes me away playfully.

'Now piss off, bruv,' he says, and I hear his voice crack. 'I fucking hate goodbyes.'

It's late and I'm back in my pad, trying to get to sleep. Every time I close my eyes, tho, I get flashes of Spider and his mates attacking me on the floor. So much has happened in here already, and I can't help but wonder who they'll move in next. The usual night-time racket starts up again and I hear Oxy, who's back on the wing, screaming and banging against his cell door. My heart starts to race, cos even tho I know that Spider and that lot are still in seg, I'm proper shitting myself that they'll somehow find a way to get to me. I turn over and I try to block out all the noise. Then I stare up at the ceiling and I hear someone shout:

'Yo, Forrester. I heard Spider proper did you in! Heard he's gonna come and finish the job . . . I'd sleep with one eye open if I was you, Forrester!'

I try to ignore it and take in deep breaths. I dunno why, but the noise seems even louder than it did on the first night I was here. Oxy's still banging and shouting for someone to let him out of his cell. And I hear whoever it was from the other cell go: 'Oi, you listening? I said, you listening, Forrester? You fancy another game of pool . . . ?'

There's laughter and jeering and I can hear more people

shouting. Not just at me, but arguing and swearing at each other from across the wing. Some new people must've come in off the induction wing, cos there's loads of banging against the cell doors and I hear: '*Oi, what you in for? What you in for?*'

Across the landing, Oxy's still screaming to be let out of his cell and his emergency alarm goes off. I hear him say that he ain't had a shower in five days, and what sounds like Davidson saying: 'That's not an emergency, Oxy. Carry on making all this noise and it'll be another five.' Then I hear the sound of the metal shutter slamming and Oxy kicking off even more.

'You can't fucking treat me like this,' he screams, and it sounds like he's starting to trash his cell. The noise is so loud and I wanna press my hands over my ears. Just to try and block it all out. But my face is still hurting and I force my eyes shut, willing sleep to come, but all these memories hit me at once. One after the other ... The screws beating the shit out of Oxy and pressing his head to the floor. Lewis shouting for help and saying he 'doesn't wanna live any more', but just being ignored. One of the screws cutting the bed sheet off from around my neck. Shaun on the night of the robbery. Davidson telling me to make sure I 'do it properly' next time. Spider's fists coming down on me in this cell. Thinking I was never gonna see my mum, or Kias, or Isiah again. And my dad kicking my mum on the kitchen floor, when I was too scared to even do anything. Too young to even try and help. I can feel my heart pounding in my chest.

I try to suck in some more deep breaths. Usually, this would be when I'd cut myself, to try and make it all stop. But this time, it's like I can't even move. The air feels thick and heavy and it catches in my throat. I can't stop shaking and I feel like I'm about to pass out. I let out this cry, loud and hollow, and I just lay there, curled up on my side, with my hands pressed to my ears, and tears and snot running down my face, trying to make it all go away.

12

I don't know what time it is exactly, but I can tell by the light coming through my window that it's still proper early. I feel like crap. I couldn't sleep at all last night, and I don't really get what happened to me, either. Why, all of a sudden, I felt like that. All of Kias's drawings have been taken off the walls and all my stuff is in one of those clear plastic bags. Not that I've got much anyway. My breakfast's still untouched on the floor by my bed. It always gets brought to you the evening before, but I just don't feel hungry. I just feel this weird mix of emotions. I'm tired and nervous and happy and scared. I've thought about this day so many times, imagined it even, but I ain't bursting with excitement like I thought I'd be. It's weird cos it's, like, one of the best days of my life has finally arrived and it don't feel any different, really. Not like I thought it would. I just feel tired and drained.

I hear the sound of the key in my door for the last time and I just hope that it ain't Davidson. Even if I am getting out, I can't be bothered with his comments today. The door opens and I'm relieved that it's Johnson at least. I suppose, out of everyone, he's one of the safest screws in here.

'You ready?' he asks.

'Yeah,' I reply, and I grab my plastic bag. 'Will you defo make sure that Dadir gets that stuff tho?' I say, and I gesture towards the teabags, some packets of food and a couple of shower gels on the shelf.

Johnson nods. 'Yeah,' he says. 'I'll take it over to him later on. I don't think he'd appreciate being woken up at this hour!'

'Nah,' I say. 'He wouldn't. Thanks.'

Johnson nods. 'It's all right,' he says.

We head out onto the wing and I follow him onto the landing. The prisoners who get released are out way before everyone gets up, so I ain't used to how quiet it seems. I look around at the endless rows of cells as we make our way down the stairs. I catch a glimpse of the ground floor of the wing and the pool tables. Johnson unlocks a heavy set of doors. We're in a part of the prison that I ain't been in since I first got here. Johnson points to my bag.

'We've just gotta get you searched,' he says, 'before we

can get you processed. Someone needs to check through your belongings as well. Then you'll need to see the nurse and sign some paperwork before you can head out. You got your property card on you?'

They made a note of all the items they took off me when I got arrested and wrote them down on this crappy piece of card.

'Yeah,' I say.

He nods, then lets me through another door. There's only two other people being released the same time as me. I've heard that if there's loads of you, then it can take *ages* and you have to wait around for time. Imagine that, when all you wanna do is get out. I go through into this room and I'm strip-searched. Even tho they're kinda careful, I try not to show how much pain it's causing me. More than that, tho, I forgot how humiliating it is and how when I first got here, I tried to tell them I wasn't doing it. That didn't go down well. Then they go through all my stuff, even tho I don't know what they're looking for.

When I go to see the nurse, she checks my weight and my temperature and that; then she looks over my injuries. She asks me bare questions, like if I've been feeling dizzy, or if I'm on any medication, or if I'm hearing voices, or have I thought about hurting myself. I dunno how she can just ask stuff like that, like it's nothing. I say no to all of them, altho a small part of me wonders what would happen if I'd answered yes?

She goes through this other sheet and ticks loads of boxes

off, and then I'm put in *another* cell. This time, it's a holding one. Along with the other two inmates. If you thought being released was a quick ting, like how it is in films and that, you're in for a shock. There's no going out your cell and straight to the gates. I'm in there for what feels like hours and I regret not eating my breakfast now. Then finally, Johnson comes back. He takes me to reception and I hand over my property card so I can get all the stuff back that they took off me.

One of the screws gives me bare papers, stapled together. 'You just need to sign this release document,' he says. 'And the Firearms Act. Along with your licence agreement.'

I scan over it proper quickly, cos with the way it's written, I don't even understand it properly, and I ain't about to waste any more time in here trying to read through five hundred pages. Besides, I get the main gist of it. *I can't own a gun, and if I break any of my conditions, then I'll be recalled straight back here.* I see a few lines about how long I'm on probation for – *eighteen months!* But I don't bother to read the rest. For all I know, I could be signing my life away, but I scrawl my name on the page anyway.

That same officer gives me an envelope with my discharge money in it – £46 – then he hands me back another clear bag with the stuff I was wearing when I got arrested. It's just an old hoodie and a chain. They took the hoodie off me cos you ain't allowed to wear anything that you could use to hide your face inside. It feels strange, seeing the last thing I wore before I came here. It wouldn't even fit me now. Not that I'd wear it anyway. Cos all it is is a reminder of being in Ryecroft. I shove it inside the bag with all my other shit.

'Here's your copy of the licence document,' he says, and he hands me another piece of paper. 'It's got all your terms on there that you would have agreed to in your probation meeting. You need to make sure you go straight there as soon as you're released. If you don't, then that's a breach of your agreement. D'you know where you need to go?'

'Yeah,' I reply, then take the licence thing and shove it in my bag too.

The officer grunts, and then Johnson gestures for me to follow him, and we go through another set of double doors. Then we're outside and it suddenly hits me how bright everything is. I ain't never seen this bit of the prison before, either. I don't even remember seeing it when I first came in here. Probably cos they brought me in round the back and it was so dark by the time we got out of the prison van. It's mad to think that you can be somewhere for eighteen months, 548 days, and still have no idea what it really looks like.

I follow Johnson and I suddenly feel this rush of emotions now, cos I'm finally out, and for *so* long, I thought that this day would never come. I definitely didn't think it would after what happened with Spider in my cell, either. Part of me still doesn't believe that's happening and I start to feel this panic rising in the pit of my stomach. Every time I've started to have a tiny bit of hope in this place, it's just been snatched away.

We carry on walking down this path and I just wanna hurry up and get through the gates in case someone realizes that they've made a mistake and they try to send me back. I half expect it to happen, for Johnson to get a call through on his radio, but he doesn't. We reach the gates and I turn and take a look at the prison building behind me. It's only now that I'm outside that I can properly see how big it is. I stare at the different parts of the building and all the windows with the bars on and I wonder which cell's Dadir's and which one was mine? The gate opens and it's mad, cos it still doesn't feel the way that I thought it would. I hold tightly on to my plastic bag and Johnson holds out his hand.

'Well,' he says. 'Good luck, Tyrell! In the nicest possible way, I hope I never see you again.'

I stare down at his hand and I ain't sure what to do for a minute. It feels strange, shaking the hand of someone who's kept you locked up for eighteen months, but I take it anyway.

'Nah, you won't,' I say. 'You won't ever catch me in 'ere again. Trust me!' I dunno if I'm saying it for Johnson's benefit, or for my own. Maybe it's cos I still can't get what Davidson said outta my head, but I've never meant anything more in my entire life. I'm gonna do everything I can not to end up back here. I'm never stepping foot in Ryecroft again.

I let go of Johnson's hand and I take one last look around me. It's bittersweet and I feel a mixture of nerves and sadness and excitement now. Sadness for those eighteen months of my life that I wasted and cos I'm leaving one of my closest friends behind as well. But knowing that I finally got my freedom back, that I can at least start to think about some sorta future away from here, feels good.

I look up and I stare at the tiny speck of a bird disappearing into the vast sky. Then I head out through the metal gates and I don't look back.

13

I don't know where I expect to be when I walk out on the other side, but it ain't on a normal-looking street with houses either side. People must walk past here every day. I wonder what they think of everyone who's locked up inside? Or if they even think about who's in Ryecroft in the first place. I stand on the pavement and I look around me for a minute. My mum took the day off work so that she could come and pick me up. It's getting even brighter now and I put a hand over my face to shield the sun from my eyes. I try to see if I can spot her, but I can't. I ain't got a phone on me, either, so it ain't even like I can ring her and I ain't sure what time it is. I think I'm out much later than I said I'd be, tho, cos of how long they kept me waiting. I'm starting to panic, cos I dunno what to do or how I'd even get home from here, when I hear her shout my name.

'Ty,' Mum calls. 'Ty!'

Mum gets out of a car from across the road and she comes running over. It's been a little while since I've seen her and I feel this tightness in my chest. I'm nervous for some reason. Maybe cos of how awkward our last phone call was, or how strained most of our visits have been. It's mad, cos Kias and Isiah look most like mum. They have the same soft features and round face. Kias even has this one random dimple that appears whenever he laughs like mum does too. I just look like my dad, everything sharp and severe, which I hate.

Mum waits for a car to let her cross and as she gets closer, I notice that she's crying. It catches me off guard, cos the last time I saw her cry was when she was begging me to 'just hold on' and not to try and kill myself again. I think these are happy tears tho. My eyes start to sting and Mum gasps when she gets nearer.

'Oh my god,' she says. 'Look at you!' She gently lifts my chin with her hand and she studies my face. 'They didn't even tell me you'd been in hospital until you were back on the wing. Even then, all they said was that there'd been an "incident" and you were "okay", but they wouldn't tell me anything else. I kept calling and calling the prison, but no one got back to me. I was so worried. I thought you'd ... What happened?'

I shake my head. I can see how worried my mum is and I feel bad. Especially cos the past year or so, I felt like she didn't care. To be honest, I didn't even realize that the prison had phoned her and let her know. I'd avoided ringing home as well, cos since Spider's attack, I haven't really felt like talking. Not even to Kias.

I try to keep my voice steady. 'Some guys just came into my cell,' I say, and I don't say anything else, cos I don't wanna talk about it, and I doubt my mum wants to hear all the gory details, either.

'And what's happened to the people who did this?'

I shrug. 'They got put on segregation. Might get a few more days added to their sentence.' I hope that she gets the hint not to ask any more questions, cos the last thing I wanna do is think about that day again. Especially now I'm out.

Mum shakes her head. She ain't stupid. She knows what happens to grasses inside – or just grasses in general – and she can probably tell just how scared I was.

'Oh, Ty,' my mum says. 'Come here.' And she brings me in for a hug. 'I'm just glad that you're out.'

It hurts so much, but I manage to put my arms around her. And even tho things have been awkward for so long, even tho there's been moments where I genuinely felt like she hated me, it kinda feels like the way it used to be. I think about how I very nearly didn't make it this far. Before I even realize what

161

I'm doing, I'm holding on to her tighter, cos I just wanna tell her how sorry I am. For all the times I went on rude, or didn't listen to her. But it's, like, I've done so many stupid things, I don't know where to begin.

'I never want to have to visit you in a place like this ever again, you hear?' my mum says, and she straightens herself up. Her voice cracks and it sounds more like she's begging me than telling me, cos I can hear the desperation in her words.

'You won't,' I say. 'I promise.' And I try to show her that I really mean it. Cos it ain't just that I never wanna go back to prison again. I don't wanna let my mum down again, either. I feel a tear slide down my face and I dunno why I'm crying. Maybe it's all the built-up emotion, or seeing my mum again. Or the fact that it felt like this day would never come. I sniff hard and I wipe it quickly away with my sleeve.

'Don't start, Ty,' she says. 'You're gonna set me off even more!' Then she gestures towards the car. 'Come on,' she says. 'Let's get this probation thing out the way, then get you home.'

The drive home is pretty long. I don't even know where we are, really, cos it ain't like they tell you in advance what prison you're gonna end up in. But we're a long way from Moss Side, that's for sure. I only found out we were going to Ryecroft when I heard other people in the sweatbox, which is this cramped van they take you to prison in, shouting that it was where we were

162

headed. Mum told me once that it was about two hours each way from where we live. We must be pretty far out, cos it doesn't look like we're even close to Manchester. All I can see is fields and the odd house. It felt proper awkward again when we got in the car and it was like neither of us knew what to say. I was about to tell Mum about the poetry sessions with Malik and how much I enjoyed them, but then she started talking about Isiah and how well he was doing at uni, so I didn't bother.

All I did was write a couple of crappy poems while I was locked up. How could I even compete with Isiah being at one of the top unis and getting high marks in all his exams? That's when I closed my eyes and pretended to try and sleep. I was still proper tired from staying awake the whole night anyway, but the last thing I wanted to do was listen to Mum bang on about how fucking 'great' Isiah is, like she usually does.

I actually manage to sleep for little bits, and by the time I finally open my eyes again, we're about to come off the motorway. I sit up and I stare out the window. I look at the buses and the McDonald's near the large petrol station. There's a mini Co-op there now that wasn't there before. I've only been gone eighteen months, but it feels like forever.

Mum turns down another street and I try to take it all in. The corner shops that I recognize or one of the buses that I'd jump on to go into town. It hits me all over again then. I'm home ... I'm actually out. I feel this sudden rush of excitement cos it means

163

that I'll finally get to see Kias, and I barely even notice that my mum has parked up. The probation centre is in this building that looks like an old church. I must've passed it a million times before, but I never knew that's what it was.

'You gonna be all right?' Mum asks.

'Yeah,' I say. 'I dunno how long it'll take tho.' And I genuinely don't. Especially after they took their time getting me processed and released.

Mum nods. 'That's all right,' she says. 'I'll just nip to Asda. Then I'll come back and wait in the car. If I'm not back by the time you've finished, just stay here, okay?'

'Okay,' I reply.

I get out the car and I suddenly feel embarrassed, cos what if everyone else knows that I'm about to go into probation? A couple walking past stare at me as I head towards the building; then they quickly look away when they catch my eye. There's a college a bit further down on the other side of the road, and it must be near lunchtime, cos I see loads of teenagers around my age heading out of the gates. I turn away, and I dunno why, but I can't help but feel all this shame creeping up inside me. It's embarrassing having to go to probation. Not just that, tho, but everyone's gonna look at me and think the same: *criminal*.

I make my way up the stairs and towards the entrance, then head inside. The building is dark and dingy, and even tho it ain't a church any more, it still smells like one, dusty and damp.

There's a few chairs and posters around, but it still looks kinda depressing. There's a woman at the main entrance bit when I come in and she looks me up and down. Her eyes glance over my busted-up face and I can just tell that she's judging me. She shifts over in her chair and it's almost like she doesn't even wanna look at me, let alone speak to me.

'Can I help you?' she says, and her voice is cold.

I pull a piece of paper out my pocket and pass it over to her. 'Err, yeah,' I say, and I clear my throat. 'I've got a meeting with Becky.'

She gestures to a hard-looking wooden bench that's close by. 'Sit there,' she says, and then she turns and picks up the phone.

I sit down and I put my head in my hands. Everything about the building is so dark and depressing. There's quite a few other rooms as well, which I'm guessing is where the other probation meetings are. I glance up and I see a few guys older and younger than me come in and out of some of the rooms. I don't make eye contact tho. I just carry on staring at the floor. I dunno how long I'm waiting for, but it feels like *ages* and I wish I at least had my phone to distract myself with. I just wanna go home now, cos I'm tired and proper hungry by this point. If walking out wouldn't be breaking my licence conditions, then I'd leave right now.

After a bit, Becky comes over to me. We managed to have one more meeting before I was released, but cos of Spider's attack and how long I was in hospital for, we had to do it over the phone. Even tho Ryecroft had told Becky what had happened and she'd asked if I was all right when we spoke, she still looks kinda shocked for a minute when she sees my messed-up face.

'Are you all right, Ty?' she asks. 'It's good to see you!'

I nod. 'I'm fine,' I reply. Then before Becky has chance to say anything else, I go: 'Don't worry, it ain't anywhere near as bad as it looks!'

Becky doesn't seem convinced, but I still can't tell her that ever since Spider attacked me, I've been having nightmares almost every night. Or that it was proper hard for me to go back out on the wing and be around people. I don't tell her about that weird thing that happened last night when I was in my cell, either. When I'd tried to block all those memories about my dad and everything else out. Maybe it's cos I don't know how to say it. Or maybe it's cos I still don't really understand it myself. Why I started feeling that way.

Becky smiles and she genuinely looks like she cares. Even when we had our probation meetings inside, I'd get this feeling that she actually wanted me to succeed and not to end up back in Ryecroft again. Like Becky thought there was more to me than the stupid shit I'd done. It felt good to have someone believe in me for the first time in so long.

It's weird, cos Becky's white and middle-aged and probably pretty posh, but she's always just treated me like I'm a normal

166

teenager. She's never once made me feel like a criminal or just a prison number, either. Which is so different, compared to all the other people I've come across.

'Well, I'm glad you're okay,' she says. 'Although it's a right work of art,' she teases. 'Come on, we're just over here!'

'Funny!' I say, as I follow her into one of the small rooms. 'If probation don't work out for you, you could go into stand-up!' I add. I can't help but laugh tho. I don't mind Becky saying something like that, cos I know she's only messing about, and there's a difference between the way that she says stuff and the way that some of the screws would. We go into the room and it's even more depressing than the rest of the place. There ain't no pictures on the walls or anything like that, and there's a plant in the corner that looks like it's dying, and a tiny window on the far side of the room with only a little bit of light coming through.

'Not the most inspiring of places, I'm afraid,' Becky says. 'Sorry about that!'

She gestures towards a seat in front of a desk that has even more paperwork on it. I'm sick of just sitting and signing shit and waiting – feels like I've been doing it all morning. The next few minutes are just the same as well. Becky goes through my licence conditions *again*, and I try not to switch off. I know I can't see Clinton or Abass or Shaun. I can't associate with any 'serving prisoner', and I need to stay out of my exclusion zones. I nod, but I can't look her in the eye, cos I feel a bit guilty that

I'm already in Dadir's phone pin list under a fake name.

What if Becky somehow guesses that I'm planning on staying in contact with him? She doesn't, tho, cos she obviously ain't a mind-reader. Then I sign even more shit.

When she gets to another bit in this stack of papers, she says: 'This part is nearly over, okay, Ty.' Then she adds, 'But as well as your curfew and being on tag, you'll need to make sure you attend all your probation meetings with me so that we can work through your sentence plan.' She pauses. 'I can't stress how important this is, Ty. You can't miss a meeting. *Understood?*'

It all feels a bit overwhelming now, and even tho Becky is still talking to me in the way she usually would, I can hear the firmness in her tone.

'Yeah, understood,' I say, nodding like I'll do whatever I need to, tho I'm still taking in what I can and can't do.

'The only circumstances where you'd be able to not turn up to a meeting,' Becky continues, 'is if there's a serious emergency. But if there is, you have to phone me and let me know. Otherwise, you'll be classed as an unauthorized "no show" and you could get recalled right away.' She pauses. 'I know neither of us wants that to happen.'

'No way!' I say, and Becky gives me a small smile. 'Just make sure you know your licence conditions inside out and stick to them,' Becky says. 'Even the slightest breach could have serious repercussions, Tyrell.'

'Okay,' I say. 'I get it, I do!' I think about telling Becky that she's starting to go on like my mum, but I know that she's just trying to get me to see how important it is that I stick to all the rules that have been laid out. It's mad, cos even tho I'm technically 'free', I don't really feel it. Not with all this hanging over me. I can't stay out when I want. I can't even go to north Manchester if I want to, either, cos that's where the jewellery shop was. And if I so much as put a single toe outta line, then that's it. I'll be right back to where I was eighteen months ago. I slump back in my chair.

'I'm sorry,' Becky says, even tho I don't get why she's apologizing. 'These first sessions aren't always the most exciting, and I like to get that bit out of the way.'

I smile. 'It's all right,' I say, and I just hope that now that we've been through all that, she'll say that we've finished and let me go.

'Anyway,' she continues, 'now that's done, shall we move on to something more positive? Have you thought any more about what we talked about, in relation to your sentence plan? What you want to do? Are you going to look into getting some work? You will be entitled to benefits until you can find a job. Or I know you were maybe thinking about enrolling at college?'

I rub underneath my eye. I *was* thinking about college when I was inside. Actually, getting a few qualifications made me think that maybe I could give it a try. And in a weird way, Malik's poetry sessions made me feel like that too. Hearing him say that I have a gift and I'm good at writing made me think that maybe some sorta future might actually be possible. Now that I'm out, tho, the thought of it is scary. More than scary, if I'm honest ... It's actually terrifying. I wouldn't have GCSEs like most people in college – I only have Functional Skills English and Maths – and it's the first time in my life that I'd be doing something on my own. Properly on my own, without my mates there. And I know that I spent the last eighteen months inside, without Clinton or Abass or Shaun, but this is different. Before we got locked up, we'd do everything together. They were sorta like family to me. And now, I don't have any other friends on the outside, really. Not just that, either, but what if it's like school all over again? I'm just gonna end up feeling thick – and who's gonna talk to me? Especially when I'll be wearing a tag ...

'I think I do wanna go college,' I say finally. 'But what am I supposed to tell them when they ask why I ain't got no GCSEs? Or where am I supposed tell them I've been for the past eighteen months?'

Becky's face softens. 'Well, you don't have to tell strangers anything you're not comfortable with. But we would have to let the programme leader or whoever it is at college know. You'll have to declare it on your application form, as your conviction isn't spent yet. It won't be for a few years ...' She pauses. 'Besides, it's important that the college knows so that they can support you in the best way possible.'

I stare down at my hands. I guess I was concentrating so much on actually leaving prison that I didn't think about what would happen afterwards. I already knew that I'd be on the police's radar even more now, cos I've actually done time, and that I'd have to tick the box that says I've got a conviction if I went for a job. I didn't know I'd have to do it if I was applying for college too tho. I'll never be able to forget it, or escape what I've done. And a small part of me thinks that's what I deserve.

'Am I gonna have to go over it all again and explain it?' I ask Becky. 'Like, why I was in prison?'

'Possibly, yes,' Becky says. 'They might just want a bit of background information around your conviction, but if you do decide to go down that route, I can talk to the college for you and explain.'

Right away, I think of Dadir. He'll be inside for nineteen years, and when he eventually does get out, he'll have to declare that he was in prison for murder. No one's gonna ask him the details, or whether or not he even did anything. They probably won't even question the whole joint enterprise shit, either. They'll just see that he was sent down with a life sentence and that'll be it. He'll be written off. Ibrahim Saleh's killer won't have to deal with that, cos even tho he admitted to killing him, he got acquitted. Besides, his family is so rich and powerful that the charge he'll have for lying to the police and carrying a knife won't really matter anyway. He'll still be able to get a good job.

171

He'll still be able to have whatever future he wants.

It's mad that you're just supposed to tick one box. One tiny little square that doesn't tell you shit about someone's life. Or how they even ended up in pen in the first place. I put my head in my hands and I'm suddenly mad at myself for getting into this mess in the first place. For throwing away my life, like all my teachers said I would do. 'Maybe I don't wanna go to college any more,' I say finally, but Becky can see right through me.

'Not everyone will have a problem with it, Tyrell,' she says. 'Some people might be more understanding than you think. You'll actually be surprised by how many people have convictions. People from all different walks of life too. I can understand that it's scary as well. But sometimes being scared or uncomfortable isn't a bad thing.'

I shrug. 'I suppose,' I say, tho I ain't sure I really believe all that stuff about people being understanding. If someone sees that I was inside for armed robbery, are they really gonna trust me? Could I even blame them, either, tho? Becky gives me a sad smile. Most of the time, you're used to seeing people who really ain't got a clue about your life, or what you're going through. Teachers at school and all those support workers in the different types of PRUs and provisions I've been in. Then those judges and barristers. I still remember the way the jury looked at me when I was on trial. Like I was scum. Something rotten that was stuck to the bottom of their shoe.

There was another look, tho, that properly got to me. I could see it on most of their faces when the barrister read out the bit about my family background. It's almost like they were saying I was destined to end up in Ryecroft cos my dad's an addict who's been in and out of jail, and I'm from a 'deprived' area. That's what they said about me and Abass and Shaun. Like, just being who we are is the reason we ended up in court in the first place.

Becky's life is absolutely nothing like mine. I can tell. But she at least tries to understand. Which is why we've always got on, I guess.

'You don't have to make any decisions right now,' she says. 'It's a lot, I know. Maybe go home and have a little think about it? And if it's something you do want to do, we could go and check out one of the colleges and get you enrolled?'

'What am I supposed to say?' I reply. 'When we turn up together? That you're my mum?'

Becky laughs. 'You care too much about what people think!' she says. 'I don't have to go in with you. I can just get a form and help you fill it in. I just wanted to let you know that I am here if you need help.'

I nod. It feels weird to have someone in my corner who ain't Mum, or Isiah, or Kias. Even tho Isiah gets on my nerves pretty much most of the time, when push comes to shove, or if anything bad happens, he's always there. My family ain't perfect, but we look out for each other. But I ain't really used to complete strangers offering to help me or anything like that. It's unfamiliar, but knowing that someone's got my back makes me feel . . . I dunno. Like I ain't so worthless after all.

'Thanks,' I say to Becky. 'I'll think about it, yeah? Seeing as you're being so safe and everything tho. Do I really have to come here every week? Can't you just sign me in if I stay out of trouble and that?'

Becky laughs. 'Yeah, nice try, Tyrell!' she says. 'That definitely won't be happening. I'll see you next week!'

14

When we get home, Mum ushers me into the living room, which looks completely different compared to the last time I was here. She's moved stuff around and there's a new table as well. I take it all in and it feels strange to be standing here. Somewhere that feels both like my home and nothing like it, all at once. There's loads of pictures up on the wall above the gas fire. Of Isiah and Kias and some of me as well. I dump my bag down on the floor.

'You moved everything around?' I say.

'Yeah,' Mum replies. 'I needed to make space for the table. Your room's still exactly how you left it, though. I haven't touched anything in there. Well, apart from the sheets, and the rest of your bedding, and I might have tidied up a little bit. But that's about it . . .'

I smile. 'Thanks,' I say.

'You hungry?' Mum asks. 'There's some food in the fridge. I didn't know what you wanted, so I just got all sorts . . . There's some stuff in the Asda bags as well. Oh, crap!' she says, and she glances at her watch. 'I can't believe that's the time already . . . I'm going to have to pick Kias up from school, but help yourself, okay? I'll be back soon!'

'Okay,' I say, but my mum's already out the door.

I wish I could've gone with her, cos then that would mean even less time that I'd have to wait to see Kias, but I'm supposed to wait in till my tag's fitted. I look around the living room and it feels weird being in here on my own – in the last room I was in before the police came and took me away. My stomach is proper grumbling now, and I'm just about to head into the kitchen, when something catches my eye. Our front window looks out onto the street that curves into a U-shape. It's a cul-de-sac and all the houses have pretty much identical painted doors and tiny gardens. I spot a girl walking down the street with a guy. They're both chatting and laughing, and it takes me a minute to properly work out if it's her or not.

They stop just outside the house that's directly opposite mine, and it's only then I realize that it's *definitely* her. Elisha.

I stop, cos it feels like it's been forever since I last saw Leesh,

176

and some of my happiest memories were hanging around with her when I was younger. Last time I saw her, I was with Shaun and Clinton and that lot, and I acted like a total nob. We'd had a massive row the day before, cos she'd said that Shaun and Clinton and Abass weren't my real friends. Just like my mum and Isiah said too, and I guess I didn't wanna hear it. I told her that she didn't know what she was talking about and who I hung around with was none of her business. Then I said that she was just jealous, cos it's not like she had any other mates.

I'd never spoken to her like that in my life, and even tho I knew she was upset, I never said sorry. I never once tried to put it right. That's not the way you're supposed to treat your best friend. We promised when we were really little, like, in primary school, that we'd always have each other's back and never let anything come between us. But I did. Just cos I was too bothered about what Shaun and that lot would say too. Whenever they'd see Leesh, they'd just ask me what I was doing 'hanging round with a girl' – especially if there was nothing going on between us.

Looking at her now, her loose curls are slicked back into a side ponytail, and this guy she's with must be her boyfriend, cos she reaches up and wraps her hands around his neck.

Suddenly, before I know what I'm doing, I'm out the door and halfway down the garden path towards the gate. And just as I'm thinking this is a bad idea and what if Elisha don't wanna see me, the guy that she's with spots me. He says something to her;

then she looks in my direction. I see all these emotions spread across her face and I can't tell if she's happy to see me or pissed that I'm here. But then she says:

'Oh my god. Ty!'

And even if I wanted to turn away before, it ain't like I can do anything now. You'd think that eighteen months is nothing really, but people can change a *lot* in that time. I think I probably still look the same, apart from my busted-up face and the fact I've had a growth spurt. Elisha seems so different, tho, and I ain't just talking about the way she looks, either. Even the way she's standing has changed. It's like everything around me is different in some way, but I've just stayed the same. The world and everyone in it has moved on and I'm just . . . *stuck*. Which makes me think back to using that exact same word in Malik's session . . .

'You all right, Leesh?' I say, and it feels weird, cos I ain't called her that in so long.

I suddenly feel embarrassed, cos I notice the guy she's with staring at me. He's Black and he's got a baby face. I notice that he's got a fresh trim, new clothes and decent trainers too. Everything I ain't got. He probably already knows where I've been just by looking at me. That's if Elisha ain't already told him. I notice him staring at my jogging bottoms that are way too small for me and then at my battered-down trainers as well. Like he's judging me. I feel ashamed, but also mad, cos I don't know this guy from Adam for him to be looking at me like that.

'You good?' I say, when he catches my eye.

He must be able to tell that I don't like him, cos he looks proper awkward and mumbles a *'You all right?'* before pretending to glance at something on his phone. All the fear and worry I had about seeing Elisha again quickly vanishes when I see a smile spread across her face. I dunno how I expected her to react, but it wasn't like this. I notice that her braces have gone too and her head doesn't look as big. She looks ... pretty.

Elisha comes over to me and, for a minute, it's almost like nothing's changed. Like we never had that fallout and stopped talking in the first place. She's still the same Elisha I'd race my bike down the street with. She throws her arms around me, and it takes loads of effort not to wince cos of my ribs. I want to hug her back, and it somehow feels different to the times we've hugged before. Maybe it's all in my head. Or maybe it's cos so much time has passed and we still ain't properly cleared the air since we stopped talking. I probably stink too, cos I've been up since proper early and I weren't allowed a shower before I got let out. I'll still have that nasty prison smell on me as well, but she doesn't seem to mind.

It suddenly feels awkward then, and I clock her boyfriend glaring in my direction. Maybe he thinks I fancy her or something. I feel like telling him that it ain't ever been like that between us, but it's kinda fun seeing him sweat. I notice Elisha looking at my face.

'I didn't know you were out!' she says. 'I mean ... I knew it would be soon, cos your mum and Kias said, but I didn't think you'd be out already!'

Already.

If only she knew that it doesn't feel like that. It feels more like I've been waiting for this day to come my whole life.

'Got out today,' I reply. 'Literally a few hours ago. Mum's just gone to pick Kias up and that.' Leesh glances at my face again, and before she even says anything, or asks if I'm all right, I add: 'It's nothing, y'know. You should see the other guy! He got off way worse than me.'

I don't even know why I'm saying it, cos the lie sticks in my throat. Maybe it's cos her boyfriend is here and I don't want him thinking that I'm pathetic for getting jumped. Or maybe it's cos part of me doesn't want Elisha's pity, either. She gives me a sad smile and I dunno if she believes me. She used to just know when I was bullshitting, or lying about being all right and stuff. But I ain't sure if that's still the same now.

I suddenly wanna ask her how she's been. I wanna find out everything that's gone on the past year and a half that I ain't seen her. Even more than that, I wanna find out about all the stuff that's happened since we stopped talking. I dunno why, tho, but I can't seem to get the words out and I just go quiet instead. Maybe if this eediat weren't here, it would be easier. I look down at the ground. She must notice

180

how awkward it's suddenly gone, cos she goes:

'This is my boyfriend, Anton. Anton, this is Tyrell.'

Anton slides his phone in his pocket. 'Safe,' he grunts, eyeing me like he doesn't like me, but he's wary cos I just got out of prison. Not just that, but he thinks I beat someone to a pulp while I was in there too. It feels weird, seeing Elisha with the guy. I've never even known her to have a boyfriend before. I'm sure she could have her pick, any guy she wanted, so I dunno why she's gone for this fool.

Elisha looks at me, then Anton, and then she says, 'I just come home to dump my college stuff. We're on our way into town ...'

'Yeah, yeah,' I say, and I take that to mean that she don't wanna be stood here talking to me any more.

I ain't surprised she's at college, cos Elisha's always been proper smart and had her head screwed on, unlike me. Hearing her saying it out loud, tho, just reminds me again how much everything's changed. For her, anyway. Maybe she was just trying to be nice or whatever when she was making out she was happy to see me. I suddenly feel para, standing here in my scruffy clothes and trainers with holes in and that. Maybe she's embarrassed to even be seen talking to me in the first place.

'It's cool. I gotta get off anyway,' I lie. 'Just thought I'd come over cos I saw you over the road. I'll catch you in a bit, yeah?' I reply, and before Elisha even has time to answer, I turn and head off.

I sit in my room and I suddenly feel more alone than ever before. All the friends I made when I was at the PRU, or even people I used to chat to when I was with Shaun, who told me they would be there to 'celebrate with me' when I got out, ain't nowhere to be seen. The only one of my friends who even wrote to me and tried to stay in touch was Leesh. I look around my room. It feels like the only place in the house that ain't changed. Isiah would kick off if he knew, but I went in his room, and that looks completely different too. He's still at uni, Mum said, but he'll be back in about a week, which I ain't looking forward to. The last thing I need is Isiah going on about how 'great' his life is now that he's in London. He should just stay there then, if that's the case.

I gaze at the Marvel and football posters stuck to the walls. I have a look through some of my hoodies and old clothes and stuff, and I try a few things on, but everything's really small now. I've got the few clothes I wore when I was inside, just the same couple of tracksuits, but I need some new stuff. I open the plastic prison bag and go through my things, just for something to do. Then I pull out the book that Gareth gave me and make some room for it on one of the shelves. I'm just trying to kill some time until Mum and Kias get home, but I sit on the bed and I notice my phone on the little table next to it. I root around in the drawer for my charger, and then I plug it in. It takes a little while for my phone to even come on, cos

I ain't used it in time, but as soon as the screen lights up, bare messages start to come through.

There's a few from some of the kids I was in the PRU with, asking if it was 'really true' about me being sent down? Which is dumb, cos they would've seen it in that article that the *Manchester Evening News* wrote. Not just that tho. If they thought I was in prison, how did they expect me to reply to my WhatsApp? On this same number as well? There's still a few more messages coming through and I see one from Elisha:

> I know u won't c this, but ur mum told me wot happened. Thinking about u, Ty. Hope ur okay! xx

She'd sent it the day I'd gone to Ryecroft. Me and Elisha weren't really talking then. She saw the police drag me off, cos the whole street was out that night, but my mum didn't tell anyone when the court dates were, or anything like that. Probably cos she was so ashamed. We weren't even friends then, but knowing that Elisha still sent me that message – that she said she was 'thinking about' me – makes me wish I'd replied to her letter even more. That one she sent me when I first got banged up. The one I tried to reply to. But I couldn't find the words.

I stare at her message and I think about sending her one back. About telling her I've only just seen it. Or maybe saying it was good to see her instead and making some joke about the fact she's finally grown into her face. But we ain't joked like that in ages. Besides, she'll still be with Anton, and replying to someone after eighteen months is an absolute piss-take. Even if I was inside.

I'm just about to click off WhatsApp when I get three messages through from a number I don't recognize. There's a video as well. I click on the video and it takes me a minute to realize that it's from someone's Snapchat. There's loads of people I don't recognize at first, drinking from plastic cups and passing a bottle around, and then I see Clinton. There's music blasting loudly in the background and people are laughing and joking. It looks like there's a proper party going on for him. The caption on the video says: *Fresh home!!*

I recognize a couple of other people in the video – Clinton's brother and his girlfriend – but there's loads of people I don't know as well. Clinton looks proper wasted and he says something to the camera about finally being out and how Fanmoore made it 'too easy' before the video cuts out. To be honest, when we all found out that we were being sent down, Clinton didn't seem too bothered. Maybe cos he'd been inside before. He'd told me that doing a stretch in prison would be a 'piece of piss'. I wish it had been like that tho. I suddenly realize that he's gonna know that I watched his video. I stare down at the messages he's sent me as well:

> Ty, we're finally out!! R we linking or wot??

> I've missed u, bro. Give me a bell ... Having a party round mine!!

> FREEDOM AT LAST!!!

I remember what Becky said about me not going anywhere near Clinton or Abass or Shaun, and I click off WhatsApp. If probation knew that I was chatting to Clinton right now ... that he'd messaged me, well, then we'd both be in some serious shit. They must've told him his licence conditions too. But maybe he just doesn't care. I go back on WhatsApp, and even tho I know I could risk getting recalled, a small part of me wants to message him back. Out of everyone in that group, Clinton was the one I was closest to. Even tho I did a lot of stupid shit when I was with them, there were good times too. There were times when Clinton was there for me, when he had my back. I don't exactly wanna be at a party right now, but it would be good to see a familiar face. Especially cos I ain't got no one around me now. No mates, nothing. And at least I'd be with someone who just understands what the past eighteen months have been like and who ain't gonna judge me, either. Not like Elisha probably was, or that Andre, or whatever his name was. I think about typing out a reply, but I suddenly panic, cos what if they're tracking my messages or something like that? I know I ain't some big time criminal, but it does happen.

Then I remember that I didn't just tell Becky I wouldn't be going back inside. I told Longman and Davidson too, and there's no way I wanna give them the satisfaction. Maybe I'm being para, but I delete the chat. I hear the sound of the front door opening, then footsteps running up the stairs and into my room.

'Ty!' Kias shouts. 'Ty!!'

I've only just got up off my bed when Kias charges straight towards me and throws his arms around me. He does it with such force that we both topple over onto the bed and his elbow catches me in my bruised ribs. It kills, but even tho I wince in pain, it's the best feeling in the world, seeing Kias again. I wrap my arms around him and he buries his face into my chest. He starts to cry, loud sobs, and I move my hand to rub his shoulder. He's holding on to me so tightly, tho, it's like he doesn't wanna let go. Almost as if he's scared that if he does, I'll suddenly be sent straight back to prison.

'It's good to see you, mate,' I say. 'I've missed you! I've missed you so much.'

My mum comes to the door and I don't even realize that I'm crying too till Kias finally loosens his grip, then reaches up and wipes some of my tears away with his hand. This time, I hug him tighter. My heart feels like it could burst with happiness, but at the same time, there's still so much pain and regret. If I'm honest, I ain't used to feeling good any more. I can't even remember what that's properly like.

Kias shifts over so that he's sitting on the bed. 'I've missed you too!' he says, and he holds his arms out wide. 'Like, this much, times this much, times this much!' He spreads his arms out wider and wider after each 'much' and I laugh. He's had a growth spurt since the last time I saw him.

'Wot happened to your face tho?' Kias asks. 'How'd you do that?'

'Nothing,' I say, and I put my arm around his shoulder. 'Just had an accident, that's all.'

Kias stares at me. 'Does it hurt?' he asks. 'It looks painful!'

I shrug. 'A bit,' I reply. 'Look at you tho,' I say, trying to change the subject. 'You've grown loads since the last time I saw you!'

'Two inches!' Kias says.

'Is it?!' I reply.

'Yeah!' Kias says. 'Mum made a mark with a pencil on the doorframe and she measured it. I'm almost the same size as you!'

I laugh. 'Not quite!' I say. 'You've still got a bit more growing to do before you catch up with me. You're almost Isiah's size tho.'

Kias giggles. 'D'you wanna come and see my Scalextric?' he says. 'Come and see it!'

He gently tugs me by my arm, but Mum steps in. She must be able to tell how tired I am, cos she says: 'Get changed out your uniform first, Kias, and do your homework. Ty can come and see it in a little bit!'

'Awww!' Kias says, but he doesn't argue back with Mum.

'Come on!' she says. 'Uniform, then homework first.'

Kias turns to me and hugs me again. 'I'm glad you're back!' Kias says. 'I don't ever want you to go away again!'

I hug him back and I glance at Mum over his shoulder. 'I won't!' I reply. 'I ain't going anywhere this time, *I promise*!'

I look Mum in the eye as I say it, so that she knows it too. So that, hopefully, she realizes that all that shit is behind me now. She gives me a small smile. I dunno if she believes me, but maybe it'll take time. Her trusting me. Things getting back to normal again. She holds her hand out to Kias.

'Come on,' she says again. 'Leave Ty to get some rest. You can pester him all you want in a bit!'

I suddenly realize how exhausted I am, and even tho it was amazing to see my baby brother, I'm glad that I can just have a minute to myself. Mum closes my door and I collapse onto my bed. I didn't have some big party like Clinton, and I ain't done any of the things I said I'd do as soon as I got out. I haven't gone to town, or got my hair cut properly, or gone and got a chickcn split. But I'm out at least, and even tho I'm proper tired and my eyes feel heavy, it's the best day I've had in years.

15

I wake up to the sound of the doorbell going. It must be about eight p.m. cos I can see from my window that it's dark outside. I fell asleep on top of my bed with all my clothes on. The doorbell starts going again and I go to look out the window. I don't know who would be coming here at this time. I'm suddenly panicked that maybe it's the police. That somehow they might have found out that Clinton sent me a message. But I didn't reply, so surely I can't be in trouble for that! Besides, I've never known the police to ring the doorbell in my life.

I hear my mum talking to someone and I make my way downstairs. There's this white guy standing in our hallway. He must be in his forties or something, and he has a black bag with him. I see him craning his neck to look around the house. He stares at the worn-down carpet and all of Mum's crap that's on the stairs, like he's judging us or something like that. I look at him and then back at my mum.

'Who's he?' I say. 'D'you know him?'

I don't like the way he's looking at me, either. It's the same way that woman in the reception of the probation centre was looking at me too. Like I'm scum. The guy raises his eyebrows when I say that, and he huffs underneath his breath. He clearly don't wanna be here, either.

'Are you Tyrell Forrester?' he asks.

'Yeah!' I reply. 'Who—?'

'I've come to fit your tag!' he cuts in before I can finish.

I glance at Mum. To be honest, even tho Becky mentioned it this morning, I'd completely forgotten about the tag. But I guess I've had a lot to think about since then.

The guy unzips his bag, but I don't move. I know that it ain't anywhere near as bad as being inside, but I really don't wanna walk around with this thing strapped to my foot. He pulls out what looks like a Wi-Fi box with a phone attached to it.

'Can we go in the living room?' he says to my mum. 'I'm gonna need to install this.'

'Yes,' my mum says. 'Of course.'

She glances at me, and I see it then on her face. That same embarrassment and shame that she had the day that I was up in court. She gestures towards the living room and this guy follows her inside. I hear her moving stuff about and saying something about making space and I feel … hurt. Sometimes I feel like she wishes that I'd never even been born. I walk slowly down the last few steps and I head into the living room. The box thing has been put on one of the shelves on the bottom corner of the TV unit. Almost like she's trying to hide it away.

'I'm gonna need you to come here, Tyrell,' the guy says. 'Take one of your shoes off and roll up the leg of your jogging bottoms for me.'

I make my way towards him, then kick my left trainer off. I regret choosing that foot straight away, cos it's the sock that's got a hole in, and I feel the tops of my ears go hot. He looks down at my toe poking out the hole in my sock and he pulls a face. He obviously knows I've just come straight outta prison tho. He pulls out the tag, which looks a bit like a watch, and he fastens it to my ankle.

'This isn't the first one of these I've fitted around here, I tell you!' he says, and he adjusts it a bit too tight. 'And I'm pretty sure it won't be the last one, either!'

'You what?' I say, and I look at my mum. I'm proper angry, but she shakes her head to tell me to *leave it*. I know the last thing she wants is me kicking off. I stare down this guy as he moves the tag around, but he doesn't even seem to notice.

'And what's that supposed to mean?' my mum says.

He looks up. 'Nothing,' he replies, although it's obvious what he's trying to say. That cos we live on a council estate, it's full of people who've been inside. My mum looks pissed. She folds her arms across her chest and I see her giving him daggers. Even tho he didn't say it, as far as he's concerned, I'm a criminal. Is that all I'm gonna be seen as from now on? No matter how long I'm out. Is that what Elisha was really thinking when she spoke to me in the street earlier? The thing is, there's loads of people who break the law all the time. Politicians and people like that, but they barely get arrested, never mind having to wear a tag.

The guy snaps my tag into place.

'Ouch, man!' I say. 'That's too tight! You're cutting off my circulation – can't you loosen it up a bit?'

He stares at me. 'Well, we need to make sure you can't slip it off,' he says.

I kiss my teeth and, I swear, if he don't get out my house soon, recall or no recall, I'll kick him out myself. Now that he's installed it, I think that's it. But then he makes me walk around the whole of the house to set the perimeters or whatever. After he's done telling me where to walk and stand, which he looks like he's enjoying a bit too much, he goes:

'If you're not in your house by ten p.m., this alarm will go off and it will alert your probation worker and the police. The same thing goes for if you enter any of your exclusion zones.'

'Right,' I say.

The guy stares at me like I'm a piece of crap again, then heads out the house. I look at my mum and she shakes her head.

'The cheek of that man,' she says under her breath. 'Coming in here, saying stuff like that. I'm in two minds about whether to complain or not ...'

She trails off and I raise my eyebrows. Even my mum must know how pointless that would be. Who's she gonna complain to? And what's she even gonna say? '*My son who's just got outta prison had to deal with some rude man who was fitting his tag*'? Yeah, right ... I can't see them giving a toss about that! But, still, it feels kinda good to have my mum on my side for once. To know that she's trying to look out for me at least.

She glances down at the tag on my foot and I see her furrow her eyebrows. I know she finds it hard, cos she always brought me and my brothers up to know right from wrong. Even when I was running around with Shaun and that lot, before we did the robbery or any of that stuff, I knew deep down that it weren't right. But I still went ahead and did it anyway. I dunno why, really. Maybe it's cos Shaun and them lot felt like family to me, and it felt good having people around me who bigged me up. When I was with them, it weren't about all the things I'd done wrong, and no one was comparing me to Kias or Isiah. I could just be me.

Even if that version of me wasn't who I really was. It's, like, the more I hung around with Shaun and that lot, the more

I wanted to impress them. I'd go along with things just cos they were doing them and I didn't wanna feel pushed out, cos that's how I felt at home.

My mum stares down at my sock.

'For god's sake, Tyrell,' she says. 'You could've made sure you put some decent socks on!'

I pull a face. 'I've just come outta prison. Where am I supposed to of got these "decent" socks from? Everything I've come out with has got holes in . . .'

I know it ain't really about the socks, which is why she's suddenly switched on me. It's cos I've embarrassed her yet again. I've been embarrassing her for most of my life. My mum's always had this thing about us acting right. Staying out of trouble and behaving properly. She used to go on about it all the time – maybe cos she didn't want any of us to end up like my waste-of-space dad. Isiah and Kias listened, but I guess I never did.

'You've got a room full of clothes upstairs!' she replies.

'None of that stuff fits me any more,' I snap back. 'It's all the shit I was wearing when I was fifteen—'

'Watch your mouth!' my mum says. 'I don't care where you've been for the past eighteen months – I'm not having you speaking like that while you're under *my* roof. Do you understand me? And I'm not having you running around doing all sorts again, Tyrell. Do you hear? Bringing the police to my

194

door . . . stealing . . .' She pauses. 'I raised you better than that!'

She moves a hand to rub at her temples, like just looking at me is stressing her out, and I feel bad, cos she did. My mum's only ever tried to do her best for me, Kias and Isiah.

'I don't think you realize that it doesn't just affect you,' Mum continues. 'Even when you weren't here, the police were still kicking down my door. Searching my house and dragging Isiah off because there'd been a robbery or a break-in someplace or the other. And Kias didn't speak for weeks when you were gone. He's had to deal with people saying all sorts to him at school. Half of his friends aren't even allowed to come here any more . . .'

'What?!' I say, and I'm genuinely surprised, cos she's never mentioned anything about this before. I feel even worse now, cos my actions haven't just impacted me. They've impacted Kias and Isiah too. Kias, who'd always had loads of mates at school; and Isiah, who'd never even had a detention in his life. The thought of him being involved in a robbery is ridiculous. It also makes me want to laugh. But I don't, cos I can imagine how upset and scared Isiah must've been. Besides, my mum's already pissed, and I know that if I suddenly start laughing in her face, she'll probably chuck me right out the door.

'I didn't know,' I say finally. 'You've never said anything to me about this before.'

But my mum just sighs. It's a joke: the police can come busting down our door to drag Isiah off for something he didn't

195

do, yet the time I phoned them when my dad was laying into Mum and I genuinely thought he wouldn't stop, they didn't even bother to show up. Then there was the time Dad turned up again with a can full of petrol, after she had kicked him out, and threatened to burn the house down with us all in it. The police just asked my mum if he'd actually done anything and to call them back if he did. What good's that gonna do? What's the point in someone coming to 'help' you when it's too late? I really thought Dad would actually do it that night too.

I stare down at my hands cos I feel too guilty to look my mum in the eye. I hate that I've caused all this, yet again. It's like the only thing I'm good at is ruining everything.

'I'm sorry,' I say, and I hope she can see just how much I mean it. 'I really am. I never wanted Isiah to get dragged into any of this. Kias too . . . And I'm sorry that I embarrassed you as well,' I blurt out. I sneak a look at my mum. It's the most honest I've been in ages, and it's the first time I've actually tried to say sorry for everything as well.

My mum's face softens. 'I know you didn't, Ty,' she replies finally. 'We love you, and that day, you didn't just lose your freedom. I lost my son, and Kias and Isiah lost their brother. I was worried sick, not knowing if you were really okay in there. I used to wake up with this fear every single morning that, one day, I'd get a call from the prison and they'd tell me that something terrible had happened to you. That I wouldn't just lose you to this system, but that I'd lose you for good. D'you know how terrifying that is?' she says, and she gently lifts my chin with her hand.

Hearing this shocks me too, cos I had no idea that my mum felt this way. That all the time I was in Ryecroft, she was worried that I might not actually make it out alive. I'm even more thankful for Dadir now. My mum pauses for a minute, like she's thinking carefully about what to say, and then she adds:

'This is a fresh start, Ty. But you're going to have to try even harder now that you've got a criminal record. Ten times harder than before. I don't want you to end up back in prison again. I just . . .' She pauses. 'I've seen how easy it is for people to end up right back there and I don't want that to be you. This system is designed for certain people to be able to go on and live their lives and for others to fail.'

Her words hit me hard, cos I think about what Dadir said about people spending their lives in and out of jail. Or the amount of times I've seen it myself. People who were serving short sentences being released, then ending up right back inside again, not long after they've left. It ain't always cos they've committed another crime, either. It can be over the smallest thing. I think of Morgan, who'd been in care and got recalled cos he had no fixed address and couldn't find anywhere to live. It would be hard enough finding a place anyway, never mind when you've just spent a few years locked up. Or there was a

197

guy on Wren, who got sent back cos they told him he couldn't visit this part of Manchester, and that's where all his family lived. So he obviously broke his licence conditions and went to see them. The thing is as well, until you've been to prison, you don't realize just how easy it is to end up back there.

I nod. 'I know, Mum,' I say, and I'm already scared about the way people are gonna view me for the rest of my life. A criminal and nothing more. Maybe it's thinking about all of this, or actually hearing just how worried and upset she was when I was locked up, cos I say: 'I've been thinking about what I'm gonna do. I wanna try and go to college, maybe get my GCSEs or something. Then, who knows ...'

I trail off, cos I ain't really sure what I'm gonna do after that, but I know that I wanna do something decent with my life. Even if I'd stayed on at the PRU, I still wouldn't have been entered for all my GCSEs anyway. They were only gonna let me sit three or four. But maybe, this way, I'll at least be able to get five. Even if I will be so much more behind compared to everyone else.

My mum's face lights up and she pulls me in for a hug.

'That sounds like such a good plan,' she says. 'I love you so much, Ty.'

'I love you too,' I say.

And for the first time ever, even tho I'm standing here with a prison tag around my ankle, I've never seen her look more proud.

16

I'm back inside my cell. I feel the weight of Spider on top of me and I can't breathe. He's got his hands around my throat and I try to prise his fingers off of me, cos I'm choking, but he just laughs. *'You won't be seeing your release date,'* he spits. *'I'll make sure of that!'* I try to scream ... to shout for help, but I can't get any words out. All I can hear is Spider's laughter echoing around me again and again. I can feel the air slowly leaving my lungs. Then the next minute, Spider lets go. I splutter, gasping for breath, and I try to shout for help, even tho I know that no one's coming. I beg Spider to leave me alone, but his hand's already raised and he's got a glint in his eye. I see the sock weighed down with the pool balls in it. *'D'you really think I was all right with what you did?*' he says. '*You disrespected me and I ain't gonna let that slide.*' I can't breathe. '*Stop!*' I try to croak. Then the next minute, his hand comes crashing down . . .

I sit up, clutching my neck, and it takes a few minutes for me to realize where I am. For everything to slot back into place. I ain't still in Ryecroft on Jay Wing. I'm back home, in my room. My heart's racing and I feel this sharp pain in my chest. Even tho Spider ain't here, it's like my body don't get that, cos it won't stop trembling. I'm sweating and I can't breathe, which makes everything even worse, cos I feel like I'm having some sorta heart attack. I'm hyperventilating and I fumble around in the dark until I find the switch on my bedside lamp, then flick it on. My room floods with light, but it doesn't make me feel any better. It doesn't make me feel safe. I keep getting flashes of Spider and all the other shit I've seen at Ryecroft, but I can't block it all out. I'm hot and I desperately just need some air. I climb out of bed and make my way to the window on the other side of the room. Then I move the curtains out the way and heave the window open.

My breathing steadies as the cool air hits me in the face and I start to calm down a little. But even tho that pain in my chest ain't nowhere near as strong as it was, it still feels like there's too much going on. Like my head's crammed with all this stuff and I just want it all to go away. I just want it all to stop. I go over to my bedside table and I move all this shit around in the drawer.

But I can't see anything in there I can use. I don't understand it, either, cos I'm out now. I shouldn't be feeling like this. I thought that leaving Ryecroft would make everything better. That being released would fix everything, somehow. But for some reason, it's like all the thoughts and memories and flashbacks are even louder now. Maybe cos there ain't the noise of the wing to drown it all out.

My fingers wrap around an old lighter and I pull it out. Cos I don't know what else I'm supposed to do. I don't know how else I'm supposed to cope. Then I break off the plastic safety bit at the top so that the sharp metal underneath is exposed.

Afterwards, I feel ashamed and disgusted, like I always do after I cut. In Ryecroft, it made me feel a bit better at first. But now, it's almost like it ain't enough. I try watching my telly on low, so that it won't wake my mum or Kias up, but I can't concentrate. I dunno how it's possible to feel both numb and like I'm in so much pain, either.

After a bit, I give up trying to force myself to go back to sleep, so I turn on my big light instead. I'm not really sure what else to do, but the Kayo Chingonyi book that Gareth gave me catches my eye, so I pick it up off the shelf. I start reading *Kumukanda*, and I dunno why, but it helps to calm me down pretty much right away. Kayo speaks about being from two different worlds. What it's like for a kid being born and growing up in Zambia, then moving to the UK, and the difference between the way that people see him and who he actually is. He even talks about being a poet and how he isn't sure what his dad will think, cos he, Kayo, is talking in this other language that isn't really his.

And even tho the only time I've ever left Manchester was when I got sent down, I can relate to it, cos I feel like I'm trapped in two worlds too. The one where I'm back at Ryecroft, and the one I'm in now. The one where I'd do all this shit with Clinton and Abass and Shaun, and the one that's full of poetry and books and words. I guess I dunno which one I belong in.

I stay up all night till I finish the book, and it reminds me how much I enjoyed Malik's sessions. How good it felt when I was writing … How writing felt exciting and made me feel like I could escape. Not just that, but like I could actually get everything out of my head. Like I had a voice for once as well. So, I find a pen and an old blank exercise book from school, and it's like my brain has woken up and I just start to write. I don't even know if any of it makes any sense, but I don't really care, cos it makes me feel … *good*, and I just get lost in the words.

I ain't even sure how long I've been writing for, but the next minute, I see the daylight creeping through the curtains and hear my mum get up and go downstairs. Then there's a knock at my bedroom door and I hear Kias go:

'Ty? Ty? You up?'

'One minute!' I shout. 'Give us a sec!'

I scramble around till I find a sweatshirt, then pull it over my head to cover my arms. The last thing I need is Kias, Mum or anyone else knowing what I've been doing. I get my sweatshirt on just in time and I'm just about to tell Kias that he can come in, but he's already charging into my room. I lean back against my pillow and Kias jumps onto my bed. He's still in his pyjamas and I wrap an arm around him.

'What you doing in 'ere so early?' I ask, and Kias looks up at me.

'Just checking you ain't gone,' he replies. 'Cos you could've just disappeared in the middle of the night!'

I laugh, but it hurts, because my little brother is only eight. He shouldn't have to worry about that shit. Anyway, even if I did wanna disappear, it's not like I can with a ten o'clock curfew. I wrap my other arm around Kias.

'I told ya,' I say. 'You ain't never getting rid of me again. You don't have to worry. You're gonna be sick to death of me in a couple of days.' I tickle him playfully.

Kias erupts into fits of laughter. 'I'll never be sick of you!' he says between giggles. 'Mum, maybe, and Nan. Sometimes I get sick of Isiah cos he eats all the good cereal when he comes home. But never you.'

I smile. 'I'm glad!' I say.

Kias points to the open exercise book that's still on my bed.

'What's that?' he asks. 'What you writing?'

'It's nothing,' I reply, and I reach over and close it quickly.

'Can I see?' Kias says.

But I shake my head. Even tho I was proper nervous, it felt amazing reading that one poem out in Malik's session. I don't think I'll ever do that again, tho, cos these are just for me. Not anyone else. And even tho Kias is my little brother, I suddenly feel embarrassed. I can tell how much he wants to see what I've been writing, as he tugs gently on my sleeve, but I shake my head.

'You've gotta get ready for school,' I say, and he looks disappointed. I feel bad, but I'm not ready to bare my soul yet, even to my little brother.

Kias folds his arms across his chest. 'Awww!' he complains sulkily, just as Mum pushes open my door without even bothering to knock.

'There you are!' she says to Kias. 'I've been shouting you. Come on, you need to get a move on. Get washed and brush your teeth!'

'Can't I stay home with Ty?' Kias begs. '*P-leeeas-e!*'

'No!' my mum says. 'How many times have I told you, school's important. You can see Ty when you get back. Go on. Bathroom ... *Now!*'

'Okay,' Kias says, but he sounds disappointed. Then he leans in and gives me a hug.

'Bye, Ty!' he says.

'See you later,' I reply, before he slumps off.

Mum gives me a smile. 'You gonna be all right today?'

'Yeah,' I say. 'I'll find suttin to do. I might look up college courses and that online.'

Mum nods. She almost looks like she's about to leave; then she stops herself and adds, 'Have you spoken to Elisha since you been back?'

It kinda takes me by surprise cos, for some reason, that's the last thing I expected her to come out with. She never really knew exactly why Leesh had stopped coming round, why we stopped talking. I don't wanna say why, either, cos I know that it'll just be *another* thing that I got wrong. That Mum can blame me for.

'I saw her yesterday,' I say, and I don't say anything about how awkward it had felt. Or how it was almost like Elisha didn't wanna be seen talking to me, either. I shift over in bed, cos I don't blame Leesh. I feel guilty about how I just sacked her off as soon as I started hanging around with Clinton and Shaun and Abass and that. 'Why'd you ask?' I add.

Mum hesitates. 'Because while you were at Ryecroft, every time I saw Elisha, she'd ask me how you were doing, without fail. Which is more than any of your other so-called mates did. I don't know what's gone on between you two, but she was a really good friend to you, Ty.'

'I know,' I say, and I feel even more guilty, cos we promised we'd always have each other's back. Before I got sent down, I'd always have loads of people coming to the house. Mates I'd made at the PRU or from the estate or just Abass and Shaun and Clinton and that. Mum was right tho, not one of them wrote to me or asked her how I was, and I know that she'd bumped into a few of them, cos she'd told me. It's true what they say. Nothing teaches you who you can depend on like getting locked up.

I shrug. 'Leesh is going places,' I say. 'She's at college. She'll probably be going to uni soon, like Isiah. Why would she still wanna be mates with me?' It hurts to say it out loud, but it's true. Maybe we started off in the same place – on this estate, going to the same primary then secondary school – but our lives are completely different now, and I'm just so far behind.

Mum gives me a sad smile. 'Do you know how hard it is to find real friends … good friends that you can rely and depend on at that. Friendship isn't always about agreeing, because the people who really love you, who care about you, will *always* have your best interests at heart. Even if you can't see it. The same way that I do.' Mum shrugs. 'I just think that some friendships are worth fighting for.'

Mum finishes, and I nod. She's right. And Elisha tried to tell me about hanging around with Clinton and Shaun and that in the beginning, but I didn't wanna hear it then. And sometimes it's easier not to bother with stuff, cos at least then you won't end up being hurt.

'What if she don't wanna know?' I suddenly blurt out. 'What if she don't want nothing to do with me?'

Mum pauses. 'Well, at least then you'll have your answer,' she says. 'Don't you think that's better than not even trying?'

I shrug. 'I suppose,' I say.

The conversation goes back to feeling a bit strained again; then Mum gives me a smile.

'I better go and check on Kias,' she says. 'That boy will do anything to avoid school!' She pauses. 'I was thinking as well that maybe we could go and get you some new clothes? I know the ones you've got are a bit worse for wear. Besides, it might be good to throw them away? Have a fresh start . . . ?'

'Yeah,' I say, and I can tell that she's properly trying. 'I'd really like that. Thanks.'

Mum nods; then she heads out and closes the door.

I think about Elisha. It had been so good to see her yesterday, and those few moments where it felt like nothing had changed just made me miss her even more. I reach for my phone and I go to the last message she sent me. I dunno what to say at first and I think about going over there, but I don't just wanna turn up at her door. Especially if she don't wanna know. So I type:

Was good 2 c u yesterday, Leesh. Wot u up 2?

I think about saying that I've missed her, but I chicken out of doing it, cos maybe I should wait till I see her face-to-face. I suddenly feel para that I replied, cos she messaged me eighteen months ago, and what if she's changed her mind now? What if she don't want anything to do with me any more? But Leesh comes online and she replies right away:

Was good 2 c u too! Nothing … Do u wanna cum rnd?'

It feels strange standing outside Elisha's house. I ain't been over here in *so* long. Even tho it's only across the road and it's Leesh, who I've known for pretty much my whole life, I feel nervous. I knock on the door, and I dunno why, but my heart's proper pounding in my chest. Or maybe it's just cos I ain't really used to being back outside yet. Even going across the street feels like a big deal. I notice that I'm sweating and it ain't just cos I'm nervous. It's kinda warm outside and I've got one of Isiah's thick hoodies on, cos it was the only thing I could find. He'd have a fit if he knew I was wearing it, but the clothes I come out with ain't been washed yet and they've all got holes and stuff in as well. Not just that tho. I had to try and find something that covered the scars on my arms. I ain't just talking about the old ones, either, cos there's the fresh ones from last night too.

I look around me and suddenly feel like I wanna go back home. We've never even spoken about the robbery or anything like that. I start to feel that same panic from the other night again, tho, and I don't wanna see Leesh any more, or even talk to her. I don't wanna see anyone. I think about getting off and just messaging her to say I can't come round any more, but the door opens before I can even move. My legs won't stop shaking, either, even tho it's just Leesh. She's wearing a T-shirt and jeans and she gives me a smile. And even tho she ain't got her braces on any more, it's still one of those goofy ones.

'Hey!' she says, and she looks like she doesn't know whether to hug me or not.

'You all right?' I reply, but the words catch in the back of my throat.

Elisha opens the door wider. 'Come in, come in!' she says, and I follow her inside.

It hits me all at once, standing in Elisha's hallway, and all these memories come flooding back. Waiting around for Leesh so we could walk to school together. Running in and out of each other's houses on birthdays and Christmases. Riding our bikes up and down the street. Me sitting with Leesh while she cried in the living room cos she was upset about her mum. Me coming over here with Kias one time when it kicked off with my dad . . .

We go into her living room, which still looks exactly the same.

'D'you want a drink?' Leesh asks. 'Don't know how you're not baking in that hoodie!'

'Am all right, y'know,' I say, and I try to laugh it off. 'Am still on that prison temperature . . . I ain't adjusted yet. Probably won't for a long time, to be honest. I'll have a drink, tho, please. Only if you're getting one anyway tho . . .'

Leesh nods. 'Be back in a sec,' she says, and she disappears out the living room.

It feels weird being so polite, cos I remember when I used to come in 'ere and help myself. Elisha's was like my second home. My house was like that for her too. But now, it's almost like we're strangers.

I look around. There's a picture of her on the mantelpiece from what must've been prom, cos she's wearing a long blue dress and a tiara. She looks proper pretty as well. I got kicked out of school way before I had a chance to even think about going prom. They don't do shit like that when you go to a PRU, either. They're lucky if people even turn up, never mind getting everyone together to go to some prom. Besides, you're hardly ever with the same kids that you started with, cos most people end up getting kicked out the PRU, or they decide to sack it off, or they end up going back to a normal school. So it seems pretty pointless anyway.

Leesh comes back and hands me a glass of orange juice.

'Thanks,' I say.

She sits down and I sit next to her on the sofa too. It feels proper awkward for a minute, cos there's so much I wanna say and ask her, but I don't know where to begin. I know I need to say something to fill the silence tho.

'So,' I say with a smirk. 'Anton, yeah? Guy's got a head like a fifty-pence piece . . .'

I dunno why that's the first thing to come out my mouth, but it's what I would've said to her before we stopped talking. As soon as I say it, tho, I wish I could take it back. It's obvious I don't like the guy, and I don't wanna cause another argument between us when we've only just started talking again.

Leesh shakes her head, but she don't look pissed or nothing.

'How did I know you were gonna start with that?' she says, but she's smiling. 'And there's nothing wrong with his head!'

I raise my eyebrows. 'If you say so!' I reply. 'Anyway, the last thing I knew, you were in love with Theo Kelly. You used to go on and on *and on* about him. What happened to that?'

Elisha blushes. 'I never used to talk about him that much,' she starts. She turns and catches the look on my face and she knows that she can't even try and lie about it. Not to me. She bursts out laughing and it feels good, hearing her laugh like this, cos it's almost like the old days. Almost.

'All right!' she says, and she hurls a cushion at me. I catch it just before it hits me tho. 'I used to like Theo, but . . .' She shrugs. 'The only person Theo likes, or should I say *loves* . . . is himself!'

'Yeah,' I reply. 'I could've told you that. Glad you've finally seen the light tho!' I pause. 'Well, kinda!' That last bit slips out, and Elisha pushes me playfully.

'Anton's all right!' she says. 'I really like him.'

The last few words come out quiet and she blushes again. It's strange, cos I've never seen her like this over a boy before. Well, apart from when she'd talk about Theo. And even tho she never said anything to me, I swear at one point she fancied Isiah, cos she'd just act proper odd around him whenever we were at mine and he came into the room.

'Okay,' I reply. 'If you say he is, then he must be . . . I swear, tho,' I continue, 'if he messes you about, or anything like that!'

Leesh rolls her eyes. 'Yeah, I can fight my own battles, thank you very much! Besides,' she adds, 'he wouldn't mess me about, cos I wouldn't stand for it! Anyway, Anton really ain't like that. You'd probably both get along if you gave each other a chance.'

'Maybe,' I say, even tho I don't mean it. I ain't got nothing in common with that square-headed idiot.

It goes really quiet for a moment; then Leesh says: 'What happened to your face? Who did that to you?'

I shift over on the sofa. I feel uncomfortable, and it ain't like I went into any of the details with my mum, or even Becky. I've always been able to talk to Elisha, tho, and even tho we ain't spoken in so long, that feeling's still there. If Clinton or Shaun or any of them lot asked me, there's no way I would've been able to tell them the truth. They would've taken the piss out of me for getting beaten up.

I shrug. 'Some guys,' I say. 'They jumped me in my cell. All cos I stood up to this one guy called Spider, who was giving me grief when I first got locked up.' I pause. 'I was shouting for help and that, but no one came. If it weren't for my mate Dadir, then I don't even know ... I probably would've been dead.'

I stop. It feels strange to be saying it so matter-of-fact like this. Especially when it was one of the most terrifying things that's ever happened to me. I put my head in my hands then, cos even just thinking about it, remembering being back in Ryecroft, feels too much. I'm shaking and Leesh puts a hand on top of my arm. I turn to look at her and she seems genuinely upset.

'That sounds so horrible,' she says, and she looks like she's holding back tears. 'Thank god for your mate!'

I nod, and as my brain and my body slowly start to calm down, I think about Dadir and wonder how he's doing. He'll still be padded-up right now, cos association ain't till another few hours.

'Dadir was my closest mate in there,' I say. 'It's mad, cos I never thought I'd miss anything about that place, or that anything good would ever come out of being there, but I miss him. That's crazy, innit?'

Leesh pauses. 'No,' she says. 'I'm glad you had someone in there.'

We both go quiet, and then the silence stretches between us, and Leesh shifts over towards me on the sofa.

'Ty, I'm sorry ...' she starts, but I shake my head.

'No,' I say. 'I'm sorry! I'm sorry that we had that dumb

argument and I went on like such a nob. I never should've put Shaun and Clinton and that before you, before our friendship. I've done some dumb fucking shit, Leesh, but losing you as a mate and that night of the robbery are the two things I regret more than anything. I don't expect you to forgive me, or even go back to being good mates with me, or anything like that. But I just wanted to let you know that I messed up . . .' I finish.

I sneak a look at her, and even if our friendship can't ever be fixed, at least I've told her how I feel. At least I've finally said sorry for my part in things.

Leesh's face crumples and it's hard to tell what she's even thinking at first, but then she says: 'Ty, you're my best mate. More than that, we're family. That never changed, even when you were acting like a complete nob . . .'

'Ha!' I say.

'But,' Leesh continues, 'you really hurt me and I didn't think you wanted anything to do with me again. We had that row and stopped talking – then the next minute, you were inside . . .' She pauses. 'I wrote you a letter, but I never heard anything back, so I just figured you were still mad.'

I shake my head. 'Nah!' I say. 'I was embarrassed, Leesh. Cos of how I'd gone on. Not just with you, but with the robbery and all that other shit as well. Besides, I didn't know what to write back.' I pause. 'I did try calling you one time tho,' I admit. 'About a week after I got sent down. Not just to say sorry tho.

I wanted to talk to my best mate again. It just kept ringing out, tho, which I figured was probably for the best, cos you would've just hung up on me anyway—'

'No!' Leesh says, and she says it with such force that it makes me laugh. 'There's no way I would've done that. No matter what, we've always been there for each other whenever things have got bad. You know that.'

'I know!' I say, and I feel so stupid now. Stupid that I even messed up our friendship in the first place. Or that I thought that Leesh wouldn't bother with me any more. I should've known better than that. It feels good to finally clear the air tho.

'I've missed you,' I say. 'I've missed not having my best mate around.'

Leesh smiles. 'I've missed you too, Ty,' she says. 'I proper hated it when we didn't speak.'

I feel a pang of guilt again, cos it was my fault that we didn't speak, and I hate that I hurt Elisha. That I wasn't a better friend. I push all that aside, tho, cos at least we've actually sorted it out now.

'Come 'ere!' I say, and I bring her in for a hug. Leesh hugs me back, and aside from noticing that my ribs don't hurt so much any more, it doesn't feel anywhere near as awkward as it did when I first saw her yesterday, when I'd just got out. It feels the way that it used to, and I'm glad that I actually listened to my mum for once. That I messaged Leesh back.

'All right!' I say, and I playfully push her away. 'That's enough of that soppy crap! I can't even call you bighead no more, cos you've actually grown into it!'

Elisha side-eyes me. 'Funny!' she says, but she's got a smile on her face. 'Wish I could say the same about you!'

I think about telling her that if anyone's got a big head, it's Anton, but I bite my tongue, cos I ain't gonna make the mistake of letting anything come between us again, and she obviously really likes the guy. Leesh smiles and nudges me gently with her elbow and it feels like things are right back to the way they used to be.

'What you gonna do now you're out?' she asks me. 'D'you know?'

'I'm thinking about going to college and that,' I say, and I can't look her in the eye cos, even tho I know she'd never do something like that, a tiny part of me expects her to laugh. Maybe cos the thought of someone who's been kicked out of every school and PRU going to college, trying to get some GCSEs, is actually a joke. Not to mention the fact I've spent the past eighteen months inside as well.

Leesh doesn't laugh tho.

'I'm glad!' she says. 'That sounds like a good idea, Ty. Don't be doing any more of that stupid shit tho! Cos I might have to whack some sense into you!'

'I won't,' I say. 'Not this time. Anyway, I promised my mum. She'd switch if I ended up back there.'

Leesh laughs. 'I mean, I know you've just got out, but your mum can be pretty terrifying too. Remember that time we accidentally spilled a whole bottle of cherryade on her carpet ... ?'

I shake my head. 'She *still* goes on about that to this day!' I smile, but I ain't even joking. Mum can be the calmest person ever sometimes. But when she needs to, she can be proper strict – I've probably seen that side of her the most, cos I was always the one running around and getting into trouble. My life wouldn't be worth living if I actually ended up back in Ryecroft. It ain't just cos of my mum and the fact I promised Kias that I'd be sticking around either tho. It's cos I actually wanna try and do something with my life.

'What's happened with Clinton and Shaun and that lot?' Leesh asks. 'You spoken to any of them?'

'Nah,' I say. 'Shaun and Abass are gonna be in for a while – they got life. Clinton got out, but I can't chat to him or nothing like that cos it's against my licence conditions.'

I dunno know why, but I don't tell Leesh that Clinton messaged me. Maybe cos I don't want her to worry. Or maybe cos I know how much she hates Clinton. And even tho I made some mistakes and did some dumb things when I was with him, he was still my mate. We still had a laugh and could joke around, but there were times when he really had my back as well. Like when I got into a fight with some guy at my PRU who came back with his older brother to try and beat me up. Clinton threatened to take them both out, and they got off. Not just that, tho, but Clinton told me that him and his sister had been taken into care cos their dad used to hit their mum. I guess we both know what that's like. We both know how it feels to hate someone you're supposed to love and to be afraid of them too.

Leesh shrugs. 'Probably for the best,' she says.

'Yeah,' I reply, although I ain't sure I fully mean it. At least, not when it comes to Clinton anyway. I ain't even sure what I'm gonna do after college. I guess I've never even thought that far ahead, cos for ages it's felt like my life has been prophesied for me – PRU, prison – and no matter how hard I try, I won't ever be able to escape that. Cos that's my fate. Pretty much everyone and everything has made me feel like that anyway. I can't really see beyond college right now, but I do know that I wanna carry on writing. I think about how much I loved Malik's poetry sessions. How everything just seemed to make sense when I was writing. How much better I'd felt last night after writing some more of my own poems too.

'When I was inside,' I tell Leesh, 'we did these poetry workshops with this guy – Malik, his name is. I never thought I'd like any of that stuff, cos Isiah's always been the one that's into reading and that, but it was really good. For the first time, I actually found something that I like doing. That I'm interested in … I even went and got some books out the library and everything. We had this one session, yeah, where I actually read something out that I wrote. Even tho I was proper nervous and I couldn't stop shaking and that . . .' I pause, remembering that day on the wing and how I left Malik's session on such a high. 'It was one of the best feelings I've *ever* had. I never got to go to the last session, tho, cos that was a couple of days after I'd got out of hospital, and I was just in too much pain. I probably won't be able to do anything like that again tho, will I?'

I finish and it hits me again how disappointed I am that I didn't get to go to Malik's last workshop. That Spider snatched that away from me too. I turn to look at Leesh and she seems . . . shocked. I'm suddenly embarrassed that she thinks this poetry stuff is pathetic, but she goes:

'I've never seen you get excited like this about anything. Well, maybe football sometimes, but even then . . .'

'D'you think it's dumb?' I ask quickly, but Leesh shakes her head.

'No,' she says. 'You actually sound happy when you talk about it . . . What's his name again? The poet guy?'

'Malik,' I say. 'Malik Sabo. He's got loads of poetry videos online as well.'

Elisha grabs her phone. She types something in, then scrolls through it and turns the screen towards me.

'Is this him?' she asks.

I stare down at the photo of Malik. It's taken from a

performance he must've done somewhere, cos he's standing on this pretty big stage and one of his hands is reaching up in mid-air. He's talking into a microphone that's on a stand, and even tho it's only a photo, it's like you can feel his presence in the room. I wish I'd had the chance to hear some of his poetry in real life and not just in the videos that I've watched. The photo's been posted onto his Insta account. I haven't even reactivated mine yet.

I nod, and I think about his workshops again and how much I enjoyed them. 'Yeah, yeah,' I say, and I hear the excitement in my voice. 'That's him!'

Leesh scrolls through her phone for a minute; then she turns it towards me again. This time it ain't a picture of Malik tho. It's what looks like a flyer with loads of names on it.

'Did you see this?' she asks. 'He's performing at some spoken-word night in town next week. Do you wanna go?'

I've never been to a spoken-word night, but I know that I definitely wanna go. Not just to see Malik, but it'll actually be cool to hear people read out some poetry too. And after staying up reading Kayo Chingonyi's poems till the early hours of the morning, I kinda wanna be around other people who love words and poetry too.

'They do an open mic as well,' Leesh says. 'Half an hour before the main event. Says you've gotta sign up beforehand tho . . .' She's looking at me with this smile on her face.

I stare at her. Open mic – that's when you get to perform or read out stuff in front of strangers. The thought of reading my poetry out loud still makes me feel sick. At least in Ryecroft I was doing it in front of Dadir and that lot, but there's no way I'm reading anything out to a room full of people I don't know. I wouldn't even be able to get the words out.

I shake my head. 'I ain't doing no open mic,' I say. 'But I'll definitely be up for the spoken-word night.' Then my heart sinks. 'I've got a curfew tho,' I say. 'I'm on tag . . . I'll have to be back by ten.' I feel ashamed for a minute, telling Leesh I'm on tag. Cos it has a way of doing that to you, being convicted, of making you feel ashamed every time you're reminded of what you've done. Leesh looks taken aback for a minute, probably cos I never mentioned I was on tag, but then she gives me a smile.

'That doesn't matter,' she says. 'We don't have to stay for the whole thing. We'll have plenty of time to get back!'

'Yeah?' I say, relieved that I can go, even if only for a little bit. 'All right!'

Leesh grins, and I can't believe how in the time I've been here with her, my mood has changed. I feel excited because I'm looking forward to seeing Malik, but also cos I promised him I wouldn't stop writing poetry, and now I know it's something I still wanna do.

17

I stayed at Elisha's for hours, just chatting and catching up. She told me all about how she's doing A-levels at college and that she's applying to uni too, which I ain't surprised about at all. I probably ain't even smart enough to do A-levels. At least, that's how I've always felt anyway. Like, even if I did wanna go, would I actually be able to? You can't even move house when you're on tag. Unless it's 'exceptional circumstances'. Even then, I'd still have to have another meeting with Becky, and someone would have to come out and do all the security checks all over again, which is long.

Talking to Leesh made me feel good, but now that I'm back home on my own, I just feel . . . I dunno. Deflated and empty.

Don't get me wrong, I'm happy that Leesh has got this bright future ahead of her, but it's just brought it home that it ain't gonna be like that for me.

I'd be dumb to think that people wouldn't judge me, either, cos I've seen what happened to Clinton. He had a few minor convictions before we did the robbery. The first one was for theft when he was in care. He was living with some horrible woman who didn't feed him properly and didn't give him the money she was supposed to for food, so he took it out of her purse and she called the police. Then he ended up doing a short sentence at some detention centre, and when he came out, he kept trying to get a job. No one would give him one, tho, and even tho people don't say that having a criminal record is the reason they reject you, it blatantly is. And I don't want that to be my life, cos then what are you supposed to do? How are you supposed to start over if no one ever wants to give you a chance? It's, like, even when you're out, you're still stuck in it all. I guess I never realized that before.

I sit back on my bed and I reach for my phone. I've already seen the article that the local newspaper wrote about me when I got sent down, but I google it again anyway, cos even tho I ain't named, it won't be hard for people to put two and two together and find out what robbery I was involved in.

The headline says:

Manchester Gang Terror – Four Jailed for Armed Robbery

I stare down at the mugshots of Clinton, Abass and Shaun. They've used the ones the police took after we'd all been arrested. I'm just referred to as a *fifteen-year-old boy*, but they've put the streets that Abass and Shaun live on. Not me and Clinton, tho, cos we were both under eighteen. I don't even know why they do that. Maybe cos Shaun and Abass are from Hulme and Moss Side. The papers don't seem to care that their address is printed for anyone to see. I notice that they never did that with the student who stabbed her boyfriend and went to one of the top universities tho.

Sometimes I try to wrap my head around what goes on in court and how they decide who goes to prison for what. But the more I try, the more I don't understand. I look down at the comments and I see some guy called Geoff has written some whole fucking essay. I ain't about to read it, cos it's way too long, and I probably already know the kind of thing he's saying, but I see the words:

These people are a stain on society. Lock them up and throw away the key, that's what I say!

Then someone called Tracey has commented underneath:

To think I pay my hard-earned taxes so that people like this can doss about in a cushy cell, watch TV, play on a PS4 and get three cooked meals a day!! Bring back capital punishment!!

I click off the article, and I don't know why I even looked it up in the first place, cos now I'm fucking mad. Whoever that Tracey is has got no idea. You ain't allowed a PlayStation inside. And, yeah, there are a few people who find prison easier, cos they might not have anywhere to go, or their life on the outside might be just as bad. Some guy on Jay was homeless and ended up getting addicted to drugs. He didn't wanna leave Ryecroft cos he owed money to people and he didn't know what would happen when he got out. And maybe there's a few people like Spider who can cope with it all right. But for most people I know, it ain't cushy. It weren't cushy for me. Or Dadir. Try telling him that!

I don't wanna think about those comments right now, tho, so I grab my headphones and search for Malik's poetry videos on YouTube again. Me and Leesh watched a few when I'd been at hers. Even tho I really enjoyed his workshops and thought he was safe when he came into Ryecroft, actually hearing his words and seeing him perform makes me look at him even more differently now. I guess I'm even more in awe, knowing how talented he is. It's true, what Malik said, as well. Poetry is meant to be heard, and watching him perform actually makes me see that. He's powerful and everyone in the room is hanging on to his every word – you can just tell, cos of how quiet it is.

And the same way that Caleb's and Lemn's and Casey's and Kayo's words are like music, Malik's are too. Probably even more, cos I can actually hear the rhythm and the way that some of the words sound. A few of the lines seem like they could be straight off a drill or grime track. It ain't just that tho. It's the way that I feel seen in Malik's poetry too. The way that it fills me with so much joy and sadness and hope and rage. Just like all the books that Gareth recommended as well.

There's one poem that Malik reads about what his life was like growing up and the problems he had with teachers and him ending up in a PRU, or getting hassled by the police, or how he was constantly told that he'd never do anything with his life. He grew up on a council estate, like me as well. I keep listening to it again and again, but each time I listen, it's like I'm hearing it for the first time cos I notice something new. Something different he's doing with the way he says certain things. It ain't just that tho. It makes me think that if Malik and even Casey and Kayo and Caleb and Lemn can be from the same background as me, and go on to do what they do, then maybe my future isn't just destined to be a dead end. Maybe there's more for me than Ryecroft. Maybe I could even run sessions with kids inside, like Malik does, when I'm older too.

It must be my fifth time playing the video when I hear the front door open, then the sound of footsteps coming up the stairs, but I don't move. I'm getting towards the end of the poem when someone comes into my room. I expect it to be Mum telling me when tea's gonna be ready, or maybe Kias. When I look up, tho, I see that it's Isiah. I'm surprised cos I didn't think he was gonna be back so soon. I pull my earphones out.

'What you doing back?' I say. 'Mum said you weren't gonna be home for at least another week!'

Isiah comes towards me. *'Isiah! Nice to see you, bro – it's been ages!'* He puts on some dumb voice that's supposed to be me answering him back, and I pull a face. *'How you doing? Yeah, I'm good, y'know. What about you? Well, apart from this black eye I've got going on, I'm all right . . . I've missed you tho . . .'*

'You're an idiot, y'know that,' I reply. 'Why you got me sounding like one of Mum's friends? I don't even talk like that!'

'Yeah,' he replies. 'That's what you think!'

I shake my head, but I'm smiling and I get up to give him a hug. Me and Isiah fight like mad and he proper pisses me off sometimes, but that don't change the fact that I love him. Or that we've always been there for each other. No matter how much he likes to rub how smart he is in my face.

'I've missed you!' I say, and I bring him in for a hug.

Isiah holds on to me. 'I've missed you too, bro,' he says. 'It's good to see you. I'm glad you're out.'

227

'Yeah!' I say. 'Me too!'

We stand there for a minute, and even tho it stings to remember he stopped visiting me inside so much when he went off to uni, when I could've done with having my big brother around more, I push that to the back of my mind, cos it feels good to see him right now.

'Seriously tho,' I say. 'Why you back?'

'I'm only in two days a week, innit. Thought I'd come back and see my little bro!' he says. Then he looks at me dead serious for a minute. 'Mum told me what happened,' he continues. 'That you'd been in hospital ... You all right?'

'It's nothing!' I say, and I sit back down on my bed. 'It was just a dumb fight!'

I feel Isiah staring at me, but I don't meet his gaze.

'A dumb fight?' he says. 'And you end up looking like that ...? Jesus, Ty, you were in hospital!'

Isiah sits down next to me, and I dunno know why, but I don't tell him the truth. Maybe cos I still feel so let down by him. Or cos even tho I love him, it doesn't change the fact that we've drifted apart. We used to be dead close. It's mad, cos even tho Isiah's my big brother, I was always the one sticking up for him. At school when these kids tried to bully him, I came down and told them they'd have me to deal with if they didn't leave him alone. Then, when my dad would try to turn on Isiah, I'd stand up to him, cos I didn't want Isiah to get hit. I figured that it didn't really matter if it was me who ended up hurt. I tried to be there for my mum and Kias too. I guess, for a bit, it was kinda nice to feel needed. Like there was something I could do that Isiah couldn't. But I guess he doesn't need me now.

'Yeah, I don't wanna talk about it, so can we not. How's uni?' I ask, to try and change the subject. I dunno if I really care that much. I think I'm just saying it to make conversation and to avoid him trying to find out more about Spider's attack. Isiah doesn't press me tho.

'Yeah, it's good!' he replies. 'I'm enjoying it ... Some of the modules are pretty tough, but I like it. I do miss home tho!'

'You're mad!' I say. 'I wish I could go off somewhere! But that ain't gonna happen for a while. I've gotta be back in by ten p.m. every day.'

'Ten?!' Isiah laughs, and he shakes his head. 'That's only two hours later than Kias's bedtime!'

'Yeah, I know,' I reply. 'Don't rub it in!'

It goes quiet again which is probably cos neither of us knows what to say. Isiah stares down at his hands.

'Ty,' he starts, and I already know what's coming next, that he's about to give me the exact same lecture that Mum did. 'You need to make sure you stay out of trouble this time. Mum can't take it. It's been hard so hard for her—'

I turn to Isiah and I almost want to laugh. I feel the anger bubbling up inside me, cos he *always* takes Mum's side, and

Mum always takes his. It's been like that for as long as I can remember.

'Well, it ain't exactly been a walk in the park for me, either,' I say. I wanna tell Isiah that it's a bit late for him to start acting like my older brother all of a sudden, when all he usually does is run away, but I bite my tongue. Isiah clenches his jaw.

'You put yourself there!' he blurts out. 'You ended up inside cos of your actions . . . No one told you to go and break into that jewellery shop—'

'*All right!*' I say. 'Don't you think I know that? I made a mistake . . . I messed up, and I already told Mum that I ain't gonna do none of that shit any more.' I pause. 'We can't all be perfect like you, y'know,' I say, and that last bit just slips out.

Isiah shakes his head. 'It ain't about being perfect, Ty,' he says. 'It's about making the right choices.'

I stare at him. Isiah's proper clever, but he ain't got no clue sometimes. Like, Emmanuel did everything right his whole life – then one minor slip-up with some WhatsApp messages cos he was grieving over his friend who was murdered got him put behind bars. And what about Dadir? Not just that tho. How can you make the 'right choices' when you're in a situation where you've got hardly any? Or where your only two options are 'bad' and 'worse'. You carry a knife cos you're scared of being killed; then you get sent down for it. Clinton stole from his carer cos he needed to survive. He needed to eat. I would've done the same. I ain't never carried a knife, but if had to travel through certain areas and I was frightened, maybe I'd do that too. Isiah, tho, he made sure he never put a foot wrong cos he didn't wanna be like Dad. None of us are like him tho.

'It ain't that simple, Isiah,' I say. 'Thought you'd know that. Some people get more choices and more chances than others. Some people are allowed to make mistakes too, but it's never anyone who looks like me and you.'

Isiah shifts over from me and I know he hates it when he isn't right all the time. It's like he always has to be in competition with you to prove that he's the smartest. I see the vein throbbing in his right temple, which only happens when he's starting to sulk, but he doesn't say anything. Isiah stares down at the hoodie I'm wearing and he screws up his face.

Shit, I thought I'd gotten away with it!

'Yo, is that my hoodie?' he says. 'I swear, Ty, I've told you nuff times about just going into my room. Why can't you respect people's privacy?'

I wondered how long it would take for this to happen. For Isiah to start making a fuss outta nothing. Besides, it ain't exactly like I can tell him that I had to find something clean with sleeves to hide all the fresh cuts up my arms, is it?

'Chill out!' I say. 'None of my clothes fit me properly any more. I was gonna wash it and put it back anyway—'

'So you weren't even gonna tell me that you borrowed it?'

231

Isiah snaps. 'Typical. You always just do what you want, Ty . . .'

'Oh my days,' I reply, and I can feel the anger rising inside me. If it weren't for the fact that I don't want him to see the state my arms are in, then I'd rip the hoodie off right now and dash it at his head. 'Why you always making a big deal outta nothing?' I say. 'You can't like it that much, cos you didn't even take it with you. And why you always going on about people being in your room anyway? What have you got hidden in there . . . ?'

'Nothing!' Isiah spits. 'I ain't you!'

His words come out hard and cold, and out of everything I've been through – Spider, my dad, Ryecroft – this hurts the most. Maybe cos he's more or less saying what I've always known – that I'm the screw-up in this family. The problem, the burden, just like my dad. Isiah's words sting, but I try to push the pain to one side.

I'm angry, cos Isiah's always saying shit like this. 'What's that supposed to mean?' I say.

'Nothing,' Isiah replies, and I can tell he wants me to drop it, but I just wanna hear him say it. I want the words to come out of his mouth.

'Go on, what you trying to say? What do you mean, you ain't me?'

Isiah shakes his head. 'I said, *leave it*, Ty!' he says, but there's no way I'm letting him off that easy.

'Nah,' I snap. 'Go on!' I give him a little shove. 'If you're gonna open your mouth and say something, at least have the guts to say it with your whole chest.' I shove him again, and Isiah pushes my hand away.

'Move, Ty!' he says. 'I swear to god . . . why you like this—?'

'*Go on!*' I shout. 'Just say it, Isiah—'

'*All right!*' Isiah snaps, and he gets in my face. The vein is throbbing double-quick now and it almost looks like it's about to pop out of his head. If I weren't so mad, I'd probably find it funny. 'It ain't about the fucking hoodie!' he shouts, and I've never seen him look this mad. 'It's the principle, Ty! You don't give a shit about anyone but yourself. Every time there's some sort of trouble or mess, or Mum's upset, it's always to do with you . . .'

Isiah finishes and I can't even look at him. It feels like a punch to the gut. It's like the air has been knocked out of me. I feel myself shaking. All that stuff he said about me not giving a shit about any of them – it ain't true. I thought about them pretty much every hour of every day when I was inside. My family was all I thought about. Just like when Dad was around. Maybe Isiah's forgotten about that, but I haven't. It ain't just hurt I'm feeling now tho. It's disappointment, cos this is the first time we've seen each other in a long time and we're already arguing. The pain quickly turns to anger again, and before I know it, I'm charging at Isiah.

I punch him and he throws me off him. Then the next minute,

we're both rolling around on the floor. We knock into something and I hear it smash. Then my bedroom door comes crashing open. I hear my mum shout:

'*Enough!* That is enough! Pack it in, the pair of you!'

She pulls us apart and we're both a bit out of breath. I see that Isiah's lip is bleeding. He presses his thumb to his mouth, then stares down at the blood. I already know that I'm gonna get the blame for everything. My mum turns to me.

'What is wrong with you?' she snaps. 'I thought you were supposed to be turning over a "new leaf"? You've been out a day, Tyrell! One. Day. And *you*!' she says, looking at Isiah.

'What did I do?!' Isiah replies, and even he looks shocked that Mum's about to go off on him.

'You're supposed to be the eldest!' Mum shouts. 'You're supposed to be setting an example!'

'But he—' Isiah continues.

'I don't care what he did!' Mum snaps back. 'You rise above it, Isiah. I don't know what's wrong with the two of you, but I'm telling you now, if I have to come in here again . . .'

Mum glares at us. Then she gives me that familiar look, like it was only a matter of time before I'd ruin things again.

After Mum slams out the room, Isiah pulls himself up off the floor, then storms out too, wiping the blood away with the back of his hand as he goes. I don't get up tho. I just sit there. Maybe I *am* the problem. I put my head in my hands and I think about

234

what that Geoff guy said in the comment section of that article and what my own brother said too. Usually, I can block out that tiny voice inside me that says, *What if they're right? What if everything they've said about me is true, and I am a burden?*

But this time, that voice seems so unbelievably loud.

18

I'm up early. I didn't really sleep last night. Mainly cos of the
row that me and Isiah had. I just kept thinking about all the
stuff he said, about how every time there's some sorta trouble
or mess, or Mum's upset, that it's to do with me. I just needed
to take my mind off it all, so I wrote a few more poems. Some
of them were so I could get everything I was feeling off my
chest. But there were a few that weren't even about Isiah or
our row or any of that. And I felt like I could properly escape.
Like I didn't have to think about anyone or anything, cos all
that mattered was these lines and stanzas and words. It felt
good to get lost in them, and it definitely helped, but it's when
I stop that it all hits me. All the emotions and that. I write so

much that my old exercise book is almost full now.

I've got another probation meeting with Becky today. I get dressed quick-time, and when I go downstairs, Kias is eating breakfast and Mum's doing some dishes. Isiah must still be in bed. Tho I heard him go out last night and then come back in again, I ain't seen him since our fight.

Mum looks at me when I come in and I can tell that she's still pissed off. She has this way of not saying anything when she's properly annoyed, yet you can still feel it almost. I'd much prefer her to go off on me, tho, rather than it being all tense and strained. I pull down the ankles of my jogging bottoms. I've been trying to make sure my tag is covered, but I'm para that you can still see the shape of it underneath the material. It just makes me feel ashamed all over again and reminds me of what that Geoff guy wrote online about us being '*a stain on society*'.

I try not to think about it and I look at Kias, who's eating some dry Frosties out of a bowl, and I shake my head. 'You still doing that?' I laugh. 'Thought you would've stopped by now . . . How can you eat dry cereal?'

'I don't like it with milk,' Kias says, and he shoves a big spoonful in his mouth.

'Fair enough,' I say, and I give him a hug. 'Do what makes you happy, innit.'

Kias crunches loudly, making a big deal of showing me the chewed-up Frosties. Then he kisses his fingers like a chef would do when he's just made some proper amazing meal.

'*Mmm, mmmm!*' Kias says. 'Bon appétit!'

I laugh. To be honest, before Ryecroft, there's no way in hell I would've eaten a bowl of dry cereal. But after eighteen months of prison food, you can eat anything. I turn to Mum.

'I'm going to probation,' I say. 'I'll be back in a bit.'

'What's probation?' Kias asks.

I glance at Mum, cos I never know how much to say to Kias. He obviously knows I was in prison, but I don't think she ever really went into detail about why I got locked up. Why would she? He's only a kid. I'm glad about that, to be honest, cos I can handle some random stranger thinking I'm the worst person on the planet. Or Isiah. But not Kias. It would break me if he ever thought that.

Mum comes over to Kias. 'It's somewhere you have to go when you've been to prison,' she says softly. 'Once you're released. Ty will meet with someone there, and there's certain things he'll need to do. Rules he'll have to follow.'

'How long for?' Kias asks.

'Eighteen months,' I say.

'Eighteen months?!' Kias repeats, and his mouth falls open in shock.

I hate him knowing about this stuff. But I guess Mum's trying to help make sure he doesn't make the same mistakes as me. My dad used to boast about being able to do a stretch inside 'standing on his head'. Me? I was never scared of going to prison till it was too late, and I was in that sweatbox on the way there.

'All right,' I say, cos I don't wanna be standing around talking any more about this. Especially not in front of Kias. 'I'm gonna go, yeah?'

'Okay,' Mum says. 'You got your bus fare?'

'Yeah,' I reply, and she doesn't say anything else.

Kias has started singing now, cos he can never stay quiet for longer than two minutes. I love that about him tho. That he's constantly in a world of his own, that he doesn't care what anyone thinks. I hope he never changes. Mum starts drying the stuff on the draining board and I lean down and kiss Kias.

'I'll see you in a bit, mate!' I say. 'Have a good day at school, yeah?'

'I will! Bye, Ty!' Kias says.

Then I head out.

It's kinda warm outside, and I'm already hot in my sweatshirt. I make my way out the cul-de-sac and down the street. It's the first time I've been out on my own properly since getting out. I can't really count going to see Leesh yesterday, cos that was only across the road. There's quite a few people walking about and I start to get that heavy feeling in my chest again. The same one I got before I knocked on at Elisha's. I dunno why, cos it ain't like I'm even doing anything. I'm only walking to the bus stop. There's a few people heading towards me on the street and

I start to feel panicked. I cross over the road, to the side that ain't so busy, so I don't have to be near that many people.

But even after I've done that, I can't get rid of the panic feeling. I'm trembling even more now. I can hear my heart pounding in my ears and it's as if something is pressing down hard on my chest. I feel sick and my head is spinning and I just wanna get outta here. I just wanna turn around and run. Go straight back home, where I know that I'm safe. I can't move, tho, and I feel my whole body tense, cos it's like I'm getting ready to fight. Even tho I don't want to. Even tho I just wanna be left alone. I keep getting these flashes, one after the other: Spider in my cell; the screams of someone getting hot water thrown in their face; someone on the wing getting their head stamped on in the showers; hearing my dad hitting my mum … and no matter how hard I try, I just can't block it all out.

I'm proper hot and I move a hand to wipe away the sweat from my face. A bus goes past me, then another one, then another, but I don't stick my hand out. I just carry on moving. I keep going, even tho I'm finding it hard to walk.

I pass some sorta school, and then I'm by a brick wall and I just stop. Cos it's all too much and I don't know what to do. I hold on to the wall and I press my forehead into my arms. I shut my eyes tightly, and before I know it, there's tears and snot streaming down my face cos I can't move. My breath is getting quicker and I can't stop crying. I think I feel some people walk past me, but I ain't too sure. Then the next minute, there's a hand on my shoulder.

'Tyrell?' a voice says.

I recognize it right away. It's Becky. I don't look up, tho, cos I still can't move, and Becky rubs my shoulder gently.

'I was just on my way in when I saw you. It's okay,' she says.

I swallow hard, and I feel myself calm down a little bit cos Becky's here. She doesn't force me to move or anything like that. She just stands there with me, and rubs my shoulder.

'Come on,' she says after a minute or so. 'I've just parked up down the road. I'll drive you in.'

Even tho I ain't shaking anywhere near as much as I was, I still don't move. I feel embarrassed and I don't know what happened. One minute, I was all right. Then the next . . .

'Are loads of people staring?' I ask Becky. 'Are loads of people looking at me and that?'

'No, you're good!' she says. 'Come on. Just don't even think about anyone else. Keep looking at me if that helps. Not that you want to be staring at my mug!'

I feel myself give Becky a feeble smile. Then I shift over and I realize that my jogging bottoms have jacked up and that my tag is showing. Maybe that's why I felt people shuffling past without stopping. Cos who would wanna help a criminal?

'You ready, Ty?' Becky says. 'There's no rush, though.'

My breathing has pretty much gone back to normal now.

'Yeah,' I say, and I move myself away from the wall. 'Let's go.'

I'm sitting with Becky in the little room inside the probation centre. I take a sip from my cup of water and I feel a bit better now that I'm here. I still feel proper embarrassed tho. I don't say anything, but I reach for a chocolate Hobnob from the plate in front of me.

'That's my stress stash,' Becky says, and she picks one up too. 'It's a miracle there's any left, to be honest!'

I give her another small smile, and Becky takes a bite of her biscuit. When I've finished my Hobnob, she says, 'You don't have to talk about it if you don't want to. But do you want to tell me what happened out there?'

I shrug. 'I dunno,' I say, and I really don't. I stare down at my hands. Cos even if I don't understand it, it ain't like I can tell Becky that I cut myself. Or that sometimes it all feels like too much. It seems stupid, cos nothing's changed that much – not really. All that's happened is I'm back out and I should be able to handle it. I should be feeling happier than this.

'Ty,' Becky says softly, 'you can talk to me.'

And for some reason, I think of the questions one of the screws ticked off on my discharge board when I was leaving Ryecroft. Maybe it's cos he asked me in a completely different way to the way that Becky is asking me now. But it's like he just reeled off this list of things so matter-of-factly that I didn't really have a chance to think about it. He just asked if I was having hallucinations, or hearing voices, or felt depressed, or felt suicidal. Like he just wanted to get to the end of the sheet. And even when I saw the nurse before leaving, I still said that I was 'fine'.

Tho I suppose I didn't feel any of those things when I first got released, cos even tho I was a bit nervous, I felt excited that I was finally getting out. But, then again, even if I did feel any of that stuff, I probably wouldn't have said nothing, cos what if they would've tried to keep me in? It's, like, you have all this paperwork about your licence conditions. Everyone tells you what areas you ain't supposed to go to, what time you need to be home, what days you need to go to probation, how I can't associate with Dadir or Clinton or leave the country while I'm still on tag.

But no one ever tells you what to do when something like this happens. Or that there'd be a chance I'd end up feeling like this in the first place. In Ryecroft, when I cut myself, they'd just take everything I could hurt myself with out my cell. But it didn't really help anything, cos the feeling was still there. What am I supposed to do now that I'm on the outside?

I stare down at the floor. No matter how hard I try, it still feels like part of me is back there in Ryecroft. I don't get why I ain't as happy as Clinton was in that video. Yeah, I'm pleased to be home. But everything still feels so . . . tough.

'I don't know what happened,' I say finally. 'One minute,

I think I was all right. Then the next ...' I pause. 'Everything just felt too much. Like, there were so many people about and that. And I just ... I didn't feel safe.'

I shake my head, cos it don't make sense to me. Surely I'm safer out here than I am in Ryecroft with Spider and every other new person who comes onto the wing. It ain't just that tho. Maybe it's the fact that I still feel so stuck. Compared to Leesh and Isiah and everyone else. Or that everything's still so uncertain as well.

'I don't get it!' I say, and I'm surprised by how angry it comes out. 'People go prison all the time – I don't ever hear about anyone feeling like this. What – could I not handle it or something? Is there suttin wrong with me ... ?'

Becky shakes her head, but she gives me a small smile. 'It's not about being able to handle it, Ty,' she says. 'I've been doing this job for a long, long time. I've seen a lot of people come through these doors, and you're not the first person to feel like this, trust me. People cope with things in different ways. Have you ever heard of PTSD?'

I pause. 'What?' I say. 'Like, that thing soldiers get when they come back from war?'

Becky smiles. 'Soldiers do get it,' she says. 'But it's not just people who've fought in wars that suffer from PTSD. Any event that puts significant stress on your nervous system can cause that. You were sixteen when you were sent to Ryecroft,' she continues. 'That's terrifying. Prison is scary for anyone, never

244

mind a child. And the things that you think are "normal" on the inside, that you see every day ... are actually really traumatic. Your body would have been in constant fight-or-flight mode for the past eighteen months – hypervigilant to danger. Then, on top of that, you have to deal with integrating yourself back into the outside world again. A lot of people who've been to prison suffer from PTSD, anxiety, depression. Sadly, it's all too common.'

Becky stops and I try to let what she's saying sink in. I never really thought about all the stuff that happened being traumatic, but I guess she's right. I've pretty much spent the last eighteen months on constant alert. Never being able to forget where I am for one minute. But I guess, even before prison, that's how it was at home, with my dad.

'I suppose,' I say.

'You've been through a lot, Ty,' Becky continues. 'Don't be so hard on yourself. I know you saw the psych nurse a couple of times when you were inside. Have you thought about going to your doctor?'

'My doctor?' I reply. 'What's he gonna do?'

'They might be able to refer you for some counselling – talking therapy can really help. It's tricky, because some of the mental health services only work with young people if they are in full-time education.' She shakes her head. 'Don't even get me started on that. But we need to find a way to get you some support that isn't just about you taking a reoffending course.

Those are courses which look at things like, perspective taking, or problem solving, to help stop you from committing another crime and ending up back in prison.'

I stare at her. Talking to Becky does make me feel a bit better, but to be honest, I'd never even thought about going to my doctor or trying to tell him about what's going on. What would I even say? '*Sometimes it all just gets too much and I cut myself.*' Or, '*I have these moments where I can't breathe and I genuinely feel like I might be dying.*' Just the thought of talking to a complete stranger about all of that makes me feel sick. I couldn't even say any of this stuff to Dadir, never mind someone I don't know. In a way, I guess I've felt like this for so long that it just sorta feels normal now.

'Thanks,' I say. 'I'll think about it.' Tho I ain't sure I really mean it.

'That's all right,' Becky continues. 'Have you thought any more about going to college?' she asks. 'It might also be good . . . helpful, in terms of giving you some sort of routine. It could be something to look forward to as well.'

I nod. I'm so glad I've got Becky, cos if I had another probation officer who wasn't as safe, I dunno what I'd do, to be honest.

'Yeah,' I reply. 'I've seen some, like, GCSE resit course at South Manchester College.' I'd wanted to go to the same place as Leesh, cos at least then there'd be someone there that I know. But she's at one of those proper sixth-form colleges that only does A-levels, so I wouldn't be able to go there even if they'd want someone like me.

Becky nods. 'We can give them a call today if you like? Maybe see if we can get you enrolled?'

'Yeah,' I reply. 'I'd like that.' And even tho the thought of going to college is kinda scary, it feels good to actually be doing something about my future.

'You did some poetry sessions while you were inside as well, didn't you?' Becky asks.

'Yeah,' I say, and just the mention of poetry makes me feel that bit lighter. Just the thought of sitting in those workshops with Malik or writing stuff in my cell and in my bedroom fills me with joy. 'I've still been writing,' I say. 'I've got this old exercise book and it's almost full. I don't even know what I'm doing, really. I just know that I enjoy it ... More than that, I actually love it. It kinda makes me feel better as well, putting my thoughts down on paper and that.' I sneak a look at Becky. 'Does that make me sound weird?' I add.

Becky laughs and she shakes her head. 'No,' she says. 'Not at all. Writing and other types of art have often been used as a form of therapy. It can really help you to make sense of things and get all your bottled-up emotions out.'

I think about all the writing I did last night, after my row with Isiah, and about how Malik said exactly what Becky's saying now. Writing stuff down about how you feel, it does make sense, cos last night it made my head feel less full. Like I'd somehow got all of my worries out of my mind and onto the paper.

'I'm just still so pissed that I missed that last session when I was in Ryecroft,' I say. 'It was the one thing besides knowing that I was getting out that was keeping me going. It ain't like I can do anything like that now, is it?' The disappointment still stings, and Becky must hear it in my voice, cos she scrunches up her face like she always does when she's thinking.

'Hmmm,' she says. 'I'm not so sure about that. Leave it with me.' She pauses. 'I do still think you should look into making an appointment with your doctor, though, Ty. Writing is great as a coping mechanism, but sometimes you need a bit of extra help when you're suffering from trauma.' Her voice softens. 'Is there someone who could maybe go with you? So you're not on your own?'

I pause. I don't wanna say anything to my mum cos she's already got enough on her plate. There's no way I'd tell Isiah, either, cos it ain't like we're even close any more. Besides, we can't even be in the same room for five minutes without fighting. Then there's Leesh, but it ain't like she'd get it, either – not really. How can she, when the past eighteen months of her life have been so different to mine? I try not to think about the fact that I feel so completely alone, and I nod.

'Yeah, yeah, I'll look into it,' I reply, even tho I don't mean it. 'There's loads of people who could come with me too.'

19

I decide to walk home instead of getting the bus, just so I have some time to think about what Becky said about going to see the doctor. I know I ain't right, that these panic fits I have are almost worse than what I felt when I was in prison. Now I'm free, my brain has let loose on what I couldn't properly allow myself to feel when I was inside. Terrified, hopeless, and like I'll never stop looking over my shoulder. At the same time, the thought of telling some doctor about it fills me with shame all over again.

I'm calmer at least since seeing Becky, so I just keep my head down, as I walk home. On my way, I pass a row of shops next door to a Caribbean takeaway that's always heaving. It's one of the best in Manchester. I suddenly realize how hungry I am, cos apart from that Hobnob, I ain't had anything to eat all day. If I had some more money on me, then I'd stop and get something, but I only brought enough for the bus. That £46 I got when I was released needs to last me till I can sign on or get a job. I really don't wanna be asking my mum for money, either.

I see a group of guys queuing inside through the window and I feel myself tense up. Cos in Ryecroft, you're always on high alert for something that's about to kick off. I walk past, but I hear the noise of the shop bell go behind me as the door opens. And then someone shouts:

'Yo, Tyrell! Tyrell . . . Ty!'

My heart nearly stops, cos I recognize the voice. Only it's deeper compared to the last time I heard it. I turn, and before I can do anything, I see Clinton running towards me. *Shit!* I never replied to any of his messages, either. I don't even know what he's doing round here cos he's from north Manchester. Unless he came here to get some food? I kind of freeze, cos if they can tell that I'm in one of my exclusion zones from my tag, then surely they'll be able to see that me and Clinton are together? It ain't like I can see the outline of his tag from underneath his jogging bottoms tho.

'Long time!' Clinton says, and he brings me in for a hug, but even tho I'm kinda pleased to see him, I resist. What if the police or whoever have been alerted and they're on their way right now? I ain't even supposed to be in contact with anyone who's still locked up, never mind with Clinton, who's on my barred list. Clinton must see the fear on my face, cos he says: 'What's wrong with you? And why you looking at me like that?'

'Ain't they gonna be able to see we're chatting to each other?' I blurt out, and my heart starts to beat proper fast. 'Won't they be able to tell from our tags . . . ?'

Clinton shakes his head and he's laughing, which I don't understand. 'I ain't on tag,' he says. 'Are you?'

'Yeah,' I say, and I'm confused, cos how come I'm on tag and Clinton ain't?

'That's a piss-take!' he says.

'Why ain't you tho?'

He looks a lot bigger compared to the last time I saw him. He must've been hitting the gym hard inside. I feel a bit nervous in case someone sees us talking. Especially as the takeaway is on the way back from probation.

'I ain't got no fixed address, remember,' Clinton says with a smirk. He'd been in care since he was a baby, and just before we got sent down, he was living with a foster carer, and then he was homeless. 'It's like the one time in my life it's actually worked in my favour.' He cracks a smile and I can see that he's trying to make a joke out of it, but underneath, he seems scared. 'The hostel I'm in is tagged tho. They put me in some temporary probation one, innit. It's proper rank and there's some proper old people and all sorts in there. I've got a curfew and that, and they've given me exclusion zones and shit. I can't go anywhere near that jewellery shop. I can't chat to you or Shaun or Abass. But apart from that ...' He shrugs.

I feel relieved knowing that if they checked their system, they at least wouldn't be able to see that me and Clinton were in the same place. I feel Clinton staring at my face.

'Who did that to you?' he asks. 'Was it someone in Ryecroft? D'you want me to get them sorted out? One of my cousin's has just been transferred there, y'know. If you give me a name—'

'Nah,' I say quickly, cos the last thing I need is Clinton sorting stuff out for me. 'Anyway, you should see the other guy.' I hate myself for joking about it, but I can't exactly tell Clinton that I was jumped and that I have nightmares pretty much all the time. What would he think of me then?

'Ha!' Clinton replies. 'Well, I'm glad you figured out how to handle yourself in there anyway. I can't lie, I was worried about you. Especially when I got sent to Fanmoore. I heard Ryecroft was crazy, but Fanmoore was next level! The way I'm so glad that I never have to eat another mouthful of that nasty prison food again.'

I laugh. 'I know!' I say. 'I swear, those chips were so tough you could take someone out with them!'

'*Innit!*' Clinton says. 'And you only used to get about five as well – what's that about? And I definitely don't miss the way that people are *always* yelling at night either ...'

I shake my head. 'Don't remind me!' I say.

Clinton smiles, and in a way, it feels kinda good, knowing that we've both been through the same thing. That someone actually understands what it's really like.

'Y'see this,' he says, and he pulls off his cap and points to a random bald patch at the side of his head. 'That's the last time I let some amateur on B Wing near me with a pair of clippers. He told me he had a level-three in barbering ... Look at my hairline as well,' he continues. 'It looks like it's running away from my face ... *I swear*!' Clinton shoves the hat back on his head and I can't stop laughing.

'Yeah, I hear you!' I say between laughter. 'My hairline still ain't recovered,' I add, and I realize just how much I've missed Clinton and the feeling I'd get when I'd hang around with him and Abass and Shaun. Like I belonged somewhere. Like I didn't have to think about none of that other crap that was going on at home.

'I tried to message you a few times, y'know,' Clinton says, changing the subject. 'Had a party when I got released, wanted to see if you were about. You still on the same number, or—?'

'Yeah,' I say, and even tho one of the first things that Becky told me was that I can't have anything to do with Clinton, I feel kinda guilty that I didn't respond. 'It ain't that,' I continue. 'It's just ... it's against my licence conditions. I ain't supposed to talk to you, or Abass or Shaun.'

'So,' Clinton says. 'Who gives a fuck? I shouldn't even be talking to you now, but I don't care about none of that. I'm gonna do what I wanna do and they ain't gonna stop me. Besides,' he continues, 'they ain't gonna know. They can't keep track of what everyone's doing. If I wanna talk to my mates, I'll talk to them.'

'Yeah, I suppose,' I say, but even if Clinton don't care if he ends up back inside, I do.

'You worry too much, Ty,' Clinton says. 'You've always been like that tho. Proper sensitive, innit? You should chill out a bit. It'll do you good.'

'Yeah, maybe,' I say.

Then some guy comes to the door of the takeaway shop and shouts: 'Clinton, they ain't got any Rubicon – what d'you want instead?'

'Get us a ginger beer!' he shouts back. Then his friend nods and heads back inside the shop.

'What you doing now?' Clinton asks.

'Nothing,' I reply. 'Just on my way home. Why?'

'You should come hang out with us,' Clinton says. 'We're just gonna have some food and that.' I hesitate and Clinton must notice cos he goes, 'Come on, Ty, man. I ain't seen you for ages and it'll be good to catch up properly. Besides, you're kinda already here.'

I do wanna stay, cos being with Clinton actually just makes me feel normal. Especially after what happened on the way to probation this morning. Plus, I ain't really in a rush to get back home after my fight with Isiah and my mum going on funny too. Clinton turns to me, and I just remember all the good times we'd have hanging out after being at the PRU. Clinton's the only person around me right now who knows what it's like to be inside as well. I pause. *Maybe it wouldn't be such a bad idea?*

'If it's money that you're worried about,' Clinton continues, 'I've got you covered! I know the guy who works in the takeaway. He's *always* hooking me and my mates up with free food. He'll sort you out, no problem. *Come on, Ty!*' Clinton presses. 'It'll be just like old times . . .'

The words hit me – '*just like old times*' – and I suddenly come to my senses. Cos even tho I feel so alone right now and I desperately wanna be around someone or something that's familiar, deep down I know that I can't do what I've always done.

I swallow hard. 'I wish I could,' I say. 'But I really need to head back. I'll see you around, tho, yeah?'

And even tho part of me really wants to stay, I find myself walking away.

20

I'm at Elisha's, eating popcorn mixed with Smarties, Buttons, Munchies and Maltesers. Leesh has been mixing everything together like that ever since we were little. At first, I thought it was a bit weird, but now I can't imagine eating popcorn any other way. I don't say anything to Leesh about bumping into Clinton yesterday, or the fact that I nearly went and hung out with him and his mates. Mainly cos Elisha hates him. Plus, whatever it is she'll probably say about me getting into trouble, I know she'll be right. Especially as I've only been out for three days and have kinda, already, broken my licence conditions. Hanging around with Clinton would have felt good for a while, but then I would have started putting on a front, joking about prison and how it wasn't that bad, but that would have been a lie. And it's not like he'd understand about me thinking of going to college. Or that I'd been writing poetry. He'd have had a proper laugh at that.

I grab a handful of popcorn and shove it in my mouth.

'What's up with you?' Leesh asks. 'You're being proper quiet.'

I shrug. 'What if it's all a waste of time?' I ask her. 'College and everything else? Cos I've already messed my life up. I've been inside. Who's gonna want to give me a chance?'

Leesh shakes her head. 'People do still get jobs with convictions, Ty. Look at my brother.' She pauses. 'I ain't gonna sugar-coat it – some people will hold it against you. But I bet there's also going to be people who will give you a chance. Besides, what else are you supposed to do? Give up trying?'

'Yeah,' I say. 'I think you're right.'

Even when I was inside, there were people who didn't write me off then. Who showed me some sorta kindness and didn't just treat me like I was a criminal. Like Malik, and Gareth in the library. To be honest, I'd actually forgotten that Leesh's brother, Remi, had been inside too. It was over some madness, tho, when he'd been involved in a protest in Moss Side. Things kicked off and he got done for assaulting a police officer. The police were always giving him hassle long before that tho.

'There was this librarian at Ryecroft,' I say. 'Gareth, his name was … He recommended all these poetry books to me and he actually gave me one to keep as well. This one by Kayo Chingonyi.'

Leesh widens her eyes. 'I've heard of him!' she says, and she almost looks like she's about to die of shock. 'You always said that you hated reading . . . that you didn't like books!'

'I know,' I say, and I shake my head. 'I thought I didn't, till Gareth and Malik recommended me some. I really like all this poetry stuff tho.'

Leesh smiles; then she reaches over and playfully ruffles my hair. 'Look at you!' she says. 'All grown up!'

I laugh, but I gently push her hand away. 'Yeah, whatever!' I say, but it feels good to know that maybe I didn't completely waste my time inside.

I hear someone come down the stairs, and then Remi appears in the living room. Remi's a couple years older than Isiah, and I always thought he was cool. He can actually have a laugh and he ain't serious all the time like Isiah is. He's always there for Leesh as well, whenever she's upset, or has any problems, the way a big brother is supposed to be. To be honest, I always used to wish that Remi was my brother instead of Isiah. It's like everyone's got a better older brother compared to me. Remi rubs underneath his eye, and it's clear by the fluff stuck in his hair that he's only just woken up. He works nights doing security, so he's usually sleeping in the day.

Remi yawns and he comes over to give me a hug. 'Ty!' he

goes. 'I heard you were out! It's good to see you – it's been a while . . .'

'I know, yeah,' I say. 'It's good to see you too.'

He sits down on the sofa next to Leesh and he puts an arm around her.

'Move!' Elisha says, and she pushes him away. 'Have you even brushed your teeth yet? You've still got crud in your eye.'

'It ain't like I've got morning breath!' Remi replies.

'No, you've got afternoon breath,' Elisha says. 'Which is even worse!'

Remi shoves her playfully. 'Nah,' he replies. 'I can't wait till you go off to uni so I don't have to deal with this abuse! Ty, you hearing this? The next year and a half needs to hurry. I'm already planning on turning your room into a gym.'

'Yeah, I don't think so,' Leesh says. And you can tell just by the way she's smiling at him that she loves Remi. Like he loves her. Their mum left when they were both really young and it was their dad who brought them up, but they've always had each other's backs.

Remi moves over on the sofa. He scrolls through his phone for a minute, and then he shakes his head. 'Y'know that big case that's happening in Manchester?' he says. 'My mate's brother, Zion, is part of it.'

'What case?' I ask.

'You not heard about it?' Leesh says, and I shake my head.

I feel a bit stupid cos I've been so caught up in just getting used to being back out that I ain't even seen what else is going on.

'Eleven kids,' Remi goes. 'Going down for murder. All Black and mixed-race, and none of them have got anything to do with the guy who actually did it. They got sentenced at that super court today. Got about two hundred years between them. Thing is, this is the fourth case like this that's happened in Manchester as well. Why ain't no one talking about it? Where's the press coverage? Apart from them saying it was another "gang murder"?'

Leesh's face pales, and I feel angry and sick. It makes me think of Dadir and how he'll be waiting to hear back about his appeal around about now – that's if he hasn't already.

'Joint enterprise?' I say.

'Yeah,' Remi goes. 'You know about it?'

I nod. 'My mate Dadir got sent down for the same thing, all cos he nodded at this guy called Marlon who killed someone. They said Dadir was the "lookout" in some gang murder. Even used some of his drill music videos as "proof" that he did it. There was quite a few guys inside for joint . . .'

Remi shakes his head. 'That's what they did in this one too, used some drill music video that Zion had watched on his phone as part of the "evidence". I've been looking into it, and there's a case going on in Luton at the moment and one in Birmingham as well. And it's, like, they're locking up ten, twenty Black kids at once. They don't care. You've gotta ask yourself who is the law really serving when whole communities are being sent to prison. And the mad thing is,' Remi continues, 'you're supposed to foresee that someone is going to end up dead or hurt. How are you supposed to do that? It's impossible ...'

'That's crazy,' Leesh says, and her voice is shaking with anger. 'There's got to be something we can do?!'

I remember Dadir telling me about that whole 'foresight' thing as well, and I thought it was mad. How are you expected to know what someone else, a complete stranger, is gonna do? Yet when my dad was round threatening to kill us and my mum, it didn't count. It wasn't about foresight then. It was more, '*Call us back if he actually does something.*' I guess they didn't think she needed protecting.

'It ain't like we can change the law, is it?' Remi says, and I hear the helplessness in his voice. 'The thing is as well,' he continues, 'it's the fact that this whole gang narrative is so deeply constructed that all it takes is one liked drill music video, and that's enough. No one ever talks about that rock shit and some of the lyrics in that ... That's never on the news. And check it ...'

He pulls his phone out of the pocket of his tracksuit bottoms. He types something in and he brings up a video on YouTube. I get up and move closer to him and Leesh so that I can see it. He scrolls down and I see a few of the comments: *'disgusting'*, *'vile'*, *'promoting violence'*, *'no wonder they're all killing each other'* and all of that stuff.

'Every single one of these lyrics is from what one of them MPs or politicians has said, either in an anonymous briefing, or what they don't care about saying in public,' Remi says, and then he presses play.

We watch the video. I recognize the drill artist. All the stuff in there is a million times worse than what was in Dadir's music video, or don't even sound out of place to what I've heard before in other drill songs. I hear the N-word, lines about chopping a woman up and putting her in freezer bags, and about stabbing someone as well.

When the video stops, Remi goes: 'Imagine if it was you or me in a video, saying shit like that! It would be enough to get us what? Ten? Fifteen years?'

'I know,' I add, and it makes me think about what Malik said about how powerful language can be. How it can be used to break people. To tear them apart. None of those people who said those things in some 'anonymous briefing' will ever have it used against them in court.

Leesh is on her feet and she starts to pace the living room, the same way she does when she's thinking hard about something.

'We can't just be silent tho,' she says. 'Not when it's happening to so many teenagers in our own city. And everywhere else as well.'

'You're right!' I say, and I wanna do something even more cos of Dadir too. I just don't know what we can do? Part of me wonders if there's even any point in us trying anyway. Then I glance at Leesh and she looks ... determined. There's this fire in her eyes and I just know that she's thinking about everything we *can* do. That's one of the things I've always liked about her. How she always wants to speak up and try and make a difference whenever she sees something wrong or unfair happening in the world. No matter how big or small it might be.

I pause. I don't wanna put a downer on anything, cos I can see how excited Leesh is getting, but I don't know if this is just ... too big.

'What are we meant to do tho?' I ask. 'It ain't like we can change the law or nothing. We're just two teenagers, and this ... this is like a whole system, Leesh. Who's gonna listen to us?'

I can tell by the way that Leesh bites her lip that a small part of her agrees, but she shakes her head.

'But look at the things that *have* happened when people stand up for what they believe in,' she says. 'I mean, I ain't saying that it's just up to the two of us to change it all, but I'm hurt and I'm angry, and we have a right to be heard ... and so do all those other kids who might never be heard or listened to. Besides,' Leesh continues, 'maybe those boys in Manchester and wherever else will know that there's people behind them – who believe them – and it might help ...'

263

I nod. Leesh is right. I think about Dadir and how his story will probably never be heard. Not just him, tho, but Morgan and Cem, and all the other kids who've been failed and ended up inside. I think about how prison silenced me. So maybe it'll actually be good to finally use my voice. Not just good, but liberating and freeing too.

Elisha clicks her fingers.

'A protest!' she says, and she moves a hand to her forehead. 'Obviously, a protest – but maybe we can do it outside of that new super court, seeing as that's where those boys will be getting sentenced and where all of the joint enterprise cases are going to be. I can make up some banners and stuff ... and maybe get in touch with some charities. Oh, and I can put a poster together and message people on Instagram and stuff.'

I nod. 'That's such a good idea!' I say. 'I can help with the banners and all that stuff too.'

Leesh smiles and starts making a list of all the things we need to do in the notes app on her phone. I suddenly feel excited too, cos even tho there's so much that's out of my control, this protest is the one thing I can do. And maybe Leesh is right. Maybe it'll help in some way too.

21

Becky's waiting for me outside of the college. I got a message from Elisha last night saying that she did an Instagram post about the joint enterprise case and the protest, and how it was already getting loads of comments and shares. I couldn't sleep, so I just stayed up, thinking about this protest and writing poetry, and even when I'd filled up all the pages in the exercise book, I didn't wanna stop, so I went and got more paper. I kept thinking about what Malik said in our first session, about how words can also be powerful too, and so I went and found some poems online to help me feel inspired.

I read some by Saul Williams, Jay Bernard, Grace Nichols, Derek Walcott, Patience Agbabi, James Baldwin, Malika

Booker, Benjamin Zephaniah and Maya Angelou too. It also made me think of Casey Bailey, Kayo Chingonyi, Lemn Sissay and Caleb Femi as well. All of them have a voice in a world that wants them to stay silent, which I guess is a form of protest in itself. I couldn't get Dadir or that case in Manchester out my head, either, and it felt like there was so much I just needed to get down. I was feeling a bit scared about going to college too, cos I didn't want the same thing that happened to me on the way to probation the other day to happen to me again.

I seem to be all right now tho. I have good days and bad days, which I don't really understand. It kinda comes and goes, that awful feeling. Sometimes it's all right; and other times, it just creeps up on me and it all feels like too much. But I guess you can't just banish all that residual trauma from prison, like Becky said. Writing definitely does seem to help tho.

Becky smiles when I approach her, and even tho I made a joke out of her coming with me at first, I'm kinda glad that she's here. It feels good to have someone with me. Besides, I ain't stepped foot in school or nothing like that in years. The PRU doesn't really count, cos the way that some of the staff there were already acting like screws, it pretty much felt like being inside anyway.

This is completely different tho. The college building is kinda in the middle of nowhere, cos there ain't really any shops or anything close by. It looks new, tho, and it's massive. It's made up of mostly glass as well. There's a couple of people hanging around outside, but everyone else must be in their lessons already cos it's gone half nine. Which I'm glad about cos my face is still proper bruised and I don't wanna have to deal with everyone staring at me and wondering what happened.

'You okay, Ty?' Becky asks, and she gives me a smile.

'Yeah,' I reply. 'I'm all right. You?'

Becky nods. 'Can't complain,' she says. 'Come on, I think the main entrance is this way!'

We head through some gates and walk down this path. The building looks bigger the closer we get. It feels weird coming into a place like this. Especially after just leaving Ryecroft. Even tho I'm nervous, I start to feel a little bit excited, cos it feels like I'm at least taking a step forward. No matter how small that step is. We head into the main reception area and there's some big sofas and stuff.

'I'm just going to let them know that we're here!' Becky says.

'All right,' I reply, and I head towards the sofas and sit down.

I look around. There's some security barriers that only let you through if you have some sorta ID card. Past those barriers, tho, I can see a big open-plan bit, with computers and chairs and a canteen as well. There's loads of kids who look about my age, and some a bit older, hanging about in the canteen. Everyone looks like they've got friends as well. I see a few fit girls, and

I try not to look too hard, but I can't help it. Maybe college won't be so bad after all!

Becky comes back and sits down next to me.

'Can you see yourself being here?' she asks.

I shrug. 'Dunno,' I say. 'Maybe, yeah.'

To be honest, I've never really 'seen' myself going anywhere. Except maybe Ryecroft, like all my teachers used to say. So it feels weird trying to picture myself someplace else. Especially when for years I've been told that I'm the problem and that I'll never do anything decent with my life. Looking around, tho, I can actually start to picture myself here, and I like it.

A guy, who must be the person in charge of the course, comes over to us. He's wearing a suit, but he's a lot younger than I expected him to be. He already knows that I've been inside cos I had to declare it on my application form when I sent it off. I know that Becky's spoken to him about it too. I think about the way the woman who works in the reception of the probation centre looks at me and the things the guy who came to fit my tag said too, and I'm already expecting this guy to be an absolute bellend. He's probably wondering what I'm even doing here in the first place. Or thinks that it's a complete joke that I'm even thinking about college.

He holds his hand out when he reaches us. 'Becky, hi!' he says. Then he turns to me. 'You must be Tyrell. I'm John. I'm the programme leader for the GCSE resit course.' John shakes Becky's hand and then mine.

'You all right?' I say.

'It's great to meet you,' he says, and he sounds like he genuinely means it. I don't expect that, and it takes me a bit by surprise. John actually seems all right and I start to feel a bit more relaxed in his presence. We go through the security barriers and head along down this large atrium.

'So,' John says, 'Becky says you're thinking of doing Maths, English and Double Science?'

'Yeah,' I reply. I'm feeling nervous now, actually hearing someone say that out loud. I suddenly expect him to tell me that I'm aiming too high. Or maybe how, cos I'm already on tag, if I get involved in any fights, then I'll be straight out the door. He doesn't, tho, and it feels kinda nice that someone's actually giving me the benefit of the doubt for once.

'Look,' John says, and he gives me a smile. 'Becky's spoken to me about where you've been the past couple of years.' He lowers his voice, even tho no one's really in earshot. I know he's tryna be discreet or whatever, and I appreciate it. But the weird thing is, I suddenly don't mind him mentioning it. I've got to face up to it being talked about, gotta get used to it.

'But I want you to know,' he continues, 'that if you decide to come here, anything that you need, just ask. We'll be here to support you in whatever way we can. Okay?'

It takes me by surprise, but it makes me think about what Leesh said about some people being willing to support me, to give me a chance. And how not everyone will see me as a criminal, either. For the first time since I left Ryecroft, I feel like maybe it will be okay.

'Yeah, I will,' I say. 'Thanks, yeah,' I add, and he smiles.

'Do you have any questions, Tyrell?' John says. 'Anything you're worried about?'

I'm not used to this from teachers, either, being asked if I'm okay like this, and it takes me a second to reply.

'Nah ... I mean, no,' I tell him.

'Right, then,' he continues. 'Shall we show you both around?'

It ends up taking much longer than I thought at the college, cos I had to do all these things before I could even enrol, like a Maths and English test on the computer to check what level I'm at and if the GCSE course is the right one for me. I pass them both at Level 2, which I'm proper pleased about, and then I get an ID badge and a timetable. It's mad, cos the longer we're there, the more I see myself actually going to the college, and by the time we leave, I'm proper excited. Probably the most excited I've been in ages. I can't wait to tell Leesh and my mum about it when I get back. I know that it probably ain't as impressive as what Isiah's doing, but at least it's something.

When I turn onto the road that leads to the bottom of my street, I see that there's a police van outside my house. My heart starts to beat proper fast, cos what if they somehow found out that I'd hung out with Clinton? What if someone saw me talking to him the other day? Or they know that he'd messaged me on WhatsApp?

I speed up towards my house and my legs are shaking, cos even tho I'm scared of finding out why they're here, it's better than not knowing what's going on at all. I turn my key in the door, and there's four of them already in the hallway. I don't get why there's so many of them here. By the way that the house is all messed up, I can tell that they've searched it as well. I head into the living room. Mum, Kias and Isiah are there, and I can see that Kias is crying. One of his toy cars is broken on the floor. I'm surprised they're even here now, to be honest, cos normally when they search your house, they do it at some mad time in the morning. Probably cos they know you're likely to be asleep.

'What's going on?' I say, and I go over and put my arm around Kias. He reaches up and holds on to me as the officers carry on emptying loads of shit out onto the floor. Mum looks at me, and I know that even tho I told her I was going to college, a small part of her is wondering if I've done something wrong too. I catch a glimpse of it on her face. It stings, but I try to ignore it as this police officer, who looks like he's only a couple of years older than Isiah, comes sauntering over to me.

'Where've you been, Tyrell?' he asks me, and he seems so comfortable in my living room that anyone would think it was his house. That's the thing about being raided – it feels so violating and, at the same time, it reminds you that nothing's yours. Not really. Not your freedom, not your house – nothing.

'College,' I say. 'Why?'

'There's been a reported theft in the north Manchester area,' he says.

'What's that got to do with me?' I reply.

He doesn't say anything, but he looks pointedly at my tag. I dunno why there's four of them here. Four of them have come here to arrest me or whatever, but not one of them came when my mum needed help. I see Isiah glance at Mum; then a look flashes across Mum's face that says: *You better be telling the truth, Tyrell, or so help me, god!*

'I was at college!' I repeat, not just for this police officer's benefit, but for Mum's and Isiah's too. 'Ask my probation officer,' I continue. 'I was with her ... Call her if you don't believe me! And anyway, ain't that supposed to be the whole point of being on tag? So you can see where I am? Go on, check! I've been college and I've been home, that's it.'

'Calm down,' he says. 'No need to get so aggressive.'

'What?' I start, but I feel Isiah glaring at me. I glance at him quickly and he shakes his head. I know he's trying to tell me to shut the fuck up, but I'm mad. They're the ones who've come into our house and messed it all up. Who are already treating me like I've done something wrong. How am I ever supposed to put Ryecroft behind me if I'm still treated like a criminal

272

at every turn? I bite my tongue, tho, cos I really don't need to be getting into it with the police and giving them any excuse to recall me.

'Well, we're still gonna need to search you,' the police officer says.

'Why?' I start, but my words seem to vanish in mid-air. My voice goes unheard, like it always does. The policeman doesn't even acknowledge that I've said anything; he just manhandles me out the door.

'What you doing?' my mum shouts, and I can hear the fear in her voice. 'You don't have to touch him like that – he's capable of walking himself! Where you taking him ... ? Why can't you search him in here?'

Mum goes to follow us, but one of the other officers stands in her way. 'Can you calm down?' he says. 'It's protocol.'

Mum opens her mouth and I can tell that she wants to come into whichever room it is they're taking me in, but I don't want her there. When I was inside, Dadir told me that they ain't even supposed to strip-search you when you're under eighteen unless there's an adult with you. But it's humiliating enough having to do it at all, never mind with my mum there.

'Mum, it's fine,' I say. 'It's all right. I won't be two secs!'

She nods, tho I can tell she's still angry, and then I catch Isiah's eye. He looks proper worried too.

Two of the officers march me down the hallway into the

kitchen – into *my* kitchen. It ain't fine, tho, cos they shouldn't even be doing this in the first place. It just reminds me how powerless I am, even in my own home. They can come in here, fuck up shit, search me, and there's nothing – *nothing* – I can do. I've just gotta accept it. One of them starts to pat me down and he pulls the college ID card out my hoodie pocket. He tosses it on the kitchen table, and I already feel embarrassed and ashamed. Cos that's how being searched like this makes you feel.

I ain't in Ryecroft no more, but I might as well be. I feel myself trembling, but I don't want them to know how much it's affecting me. I don't want them to see how disgusting and worthless it makes me feel. One of them says something about removing my clothes, and I think back to Malik's poetry session. How powerful and important and alive it made me feel. How it felt like nothing else mattered in that moment, except those words. And I hold on to them. I hold on to the rhymes and the stanzas and the verses. I hold on to the image of that tiny bird, flying through the sky, and I try to block out everything else that's happening.

22

When I go back into the living room, I can see that my bag has been searched as well and that my college timetable's crumpled on the floor. They clearly ain't found any of the stolen items they're looking for. I can feel Mum looking at me, probably to check if I'm all right, but I don't meet her gaze. I just feel so upset and angry that they're even doing this. One of the other officers comes back into the room. He must've called probation while I was getting searched, cos he turns to the other officer and says, 'Probation have just confirmed that he was at the college. He wasn't anywhere near Cawthorne Street.'

I glare at them. They'd already assumed I was guilty before they even checked. I feel like asking them if they're happy, and telling them to get the fuck out my house, but I can't even speak. It's like I don't have any words. I think I see a look of relief flash across my mum's face, but it's so quick that I almost wonder if I imagined it. My mum looks angry now, tho, and I clock Isiah giving the officers daggers as well.

'I told you that's where he was!' Mum says, as the officers get ready to go. 'Are we not going to get an apology, no?' she adds, but they just ignore her, then head out.

I reach down and pick up my college timetable; then I look around the living room. It's a right mess. Isiah starts picking up some of the stuff that's on the floor.

'Unbelievable,' my mum says, and she starts tidying up too. 'It's bad enough that they do this in the first place, but they can't even give us an apology ... Look at the state of the place!' She turns to me. 'Are you okay, Ty?' she asks, but even if I wanted to, I can't get the words out.

Isiah comes over to me and puts a hand on my shoulder.

'Ty,' he says gently. 'You all right?'

But I just shake my head. Even tho I know I did nothing wrong, I'm too embarrassed and ashamed to tell them what happened in the kitchen. And, if I'm honest, I just wanna try and block it all out anyway. Even tho I ain't in Ryecroft any more, even tho I've been out for four days, I'm still sorta in prison, cos there's nowhere I truly feel safe. Not even my own home. There's nowhere I can really be free.

'Is it gonna be like this for the rest of my life?' I finally manage to say. 'It's, like, I'm trying *so* hard to put all this behind me, to go to college and do things right – but nothing I do is enough. It's like they never want me to forget that I was inside . . .'

Mum comes over and she wraps her arms around me. 'Hey,' she says, and she lifts my chin up. 'I know you're trying. I really do. We can all see that, and I want you to know that everything you've been doing isn't a waste of time. You've come so far, Ty, and this is all going to have a positive impact on your future.' Mum pauses. 'But the way that this system is designed, it's so easy to get into, but much harder to get out of. Especially if you're Black and don't have a lot of money. It is possible though,' she continues. 'You'll just have to fight extra hard, I'm afraid. But I know you've got it in you – and you've got us,' she finishes.

'Mum's right,' Isiah says, and I'm surprised to have them both on my side for once.

It suddenly hits me just how tough it is. How it's so much more complicated than just doing your time and being released. I feel so lucky to have Mum and Becky and Isiah, cos there's plenty of people who don't have that, and I can't even imagine how tough it is for them. And even tho I'm still shaken up and angry from before, my heart swells a little.

'Thanks,' I say, and knowing that they both have my back helps to take some of that pain away.

*

I help Mum and Isiah tidy up the living room, and even tho we manage to get it looking the way it was before it got searched, it still don't feel the same. I can't stop thinking about what happened or the fact that I'm constantly gonna be treated like this by the police for the rest of my life. The helplessness and shame I felt from before quickly turns to anger, and I go up to my room to write a few poems in the notes app on my phone to try and get all my feelings out. It helps a bit, but it's like I've still got all of these emotions bottled up inside. I pick up my phone and make my way back downstairs. I just need to get out this house. At least for a little bit.

'I'm going to Leesh's!' I shout to Mum. 'I won't be long!'

And I head out before she has chance to ask me if I'm okay again. I'm about to go and see Leesh and tell her about everything that's happened, but then my phone vibrates in my pocket and I stop before I'm about to cross the road to her house. It's a message from Clinton:

U got off so quickly the other day. We cool? Wot u up 2?

I stare at Clinton's message, and I know that I ought to just ignore it and head over to Elisha's. But I still don't move. Maybe it's cos I'm so mad about everything that's happened, and deep down part of me thinks that if I'm gonna be punished like this for ever, then why shouldn't I just talk to who the fuck I want?

Cos maybe I don't wanna have to keep fighting for the rest of my life. Not just that, tho, but I do miss Clinton, and I wanna be around someone who gets what it's like. I type out a reply to Clinton, and before I know what I'm doing, I'm heading away from Elisha's and down the road.

I'm sitting in Clinton's room in the hostel in south Manchester. It's proper small and there's hardly anything in it, apart from a single bed and a couple of binbags full of Clinton's clothes. It smells of damp and mould, and it kinda reminds me of being back in my cell. Altho you at least had a window when you were locked up, and Clinton's room doesn't even have that. It's bare noisy too, and there's loud music coming from down the hall, and someone in the next room is shouting. Clinton looks like he ain't slept in years, never mind weeks. He's got these massive bags under his eyes. There's a loud scream from somewhere inside the building and it makes me jump.

'I don't know how you can sleep with all this noise,' I say, and Clinton shakes his head.

'I don't,' he replies. 'You think it's bad now, you should hear it at night ... There's people fighting and all sorts. It's actually worse than Ryecroft and Fanmoore put together. But it's, like, what other option do I have ... ?' Clinton shrugs, and he stares down at the spliff he's building in his hands.

I'm still mad at the system, but at least I've got a family

around me and I ain't stuck in this place.

'Mate,' Clinton continues. 'There's this one guy, yeah, who *always* stands in the hallway at six o'clock every night. He always stands directly outside my room as well, and he just starts shouting: "*The end of the world is coming! The end of the world is coming!!*" for about five hours. I swear, I wish it would come so I wouldn't have to listen to that shit every night.'

I laugh, but tho he's tryna make out that he ain't bothered, I know he is. I recognize it, cos it's the exact same way he used to go on when his foster placements would break down. Clinton lights up, even tho you ain't supposed to smoke in here. There's signs everywhere about that. Don't think it stops anyone tho. Clinton said that he could get hold of pretty much any drug easily if he wanted to as well.

'Still,' he continues, 'I've made some pretty good mates in here tho. One of them, Dre, he got outta Fanmoore pretty much the same time as me.' Clinton holds the spliff out to me, and even tho I ain't done it in ages cos I don't really like how it makes me feel afterwards, I take a drag. Maybe cos I always used to smoke when I was with Clinton and Shaun and that lot. Or maybe cos I used to try so hard to fit in with them, and part of me still can't help but do it. Or maybe it's just cos I'm so pissed about everything.

'My house got raided,' I say to Clinton as I pass him the spliff back. 'Like, my whole house is a tip. They strip-searched me as

280

well ...' Even saying those words out loud makes me feel the humiliation and shame all over again. So when Clinton hands me the spliff back, I take another drag.

He shakes his head. 'That's fucking shit,' he says. 'I'm so sorry, Ty. The thing is as well, they shouldn't even be doing searches like that.' He pauses. 'Now you've been inside, tho, they'll just be raiding your house every time something happens. *Trust me!* They'd do it with me, and that was before I even got locked up. It happens to bare kids in care.'

'What you gonna do?' I ask Clinton. 'When you've gotta leave here?'

Clinton finishes his spliff. 'Dunno,' he goes. 'But I need to get some proper money, I'll tell you that.' He gives me a grin, but even tho the smile spreads across his face, it doesn't reach his eyes. He actually looks kinda sad. 'I'll probably end up back inside,' he says with a laugh. But his voice is hollow. 'Anyway,' he continues. 'Fuck it! I'm gonna do whatever it is I wanna do. I need to get out of this shithole. Dre said he's got a mate who could help me out ... probably selling or something. I'm sure he could help you out too?'

I lean back in the plastic chair that I'm sitting in. Clinton makes it sound so easy, and maybe it would be. Cos I'd be able to earn a lot of money and I wouldn't have to worry about applying for jobs and that or getting one when I'm older. Besides, if I'm already a criminal and everyone around me just expects me to end up back inside anyway, would it even make that much of a difference? In my heart, tho, I know that that ain't the life I want. And that I never wanna step foot inside a prison again.

'Nah,' I say. 'Am all right, y'know. I actually enrolled at college today and it was pretty good. There's loadsa fit girls there as well. It ain't just about that tho. I'm actually looking forward to learning something and—' I surprise myself by blurting all that out, but I guess the excitement about earlier is still there, even tho all that other shit happened when I got back home. Before I can finish my sentence, tho, Clinton starts cracking up like I've just come out with the funniest thing he's ever heard in his life. It pisses me off, but it also stings.

'What's so funny?' I snap, and Clinton wipes away some tears.

'You?' he goes. 'College?' And then he cracks up again. I can feel my anger rising and he must see it on my face, cos this only seems to make Clinton laugh even more.

'Nah, nah,' he goes, and he holds on to his side. 'I ain't being funny, but you ain't really the college type. I remember when we were at PRU, and you hardly ever did any work. Then there was that time the teacher tried to get you to read out loud, and you could hardly even say any of the words without stuttering.'

It hurts to hear Clinton laughing at the fact I wanna go to college and try and make something of my life. Elisha didn't do that when I told her, and I know for a fact that if I would've said the same thing to Dadir, there's no way he'd take the piss, either. If anything, he'd be encouraging me, just like Leesh was.

'That was ages ago,' I say. 'I got some qualifications when I was inside . . . and I met the programme leader today, who knew I'd been locked up, and he was actually pretty safe.'

Clinton shakes his head. 'Well, what you gonna do after that?' he replies. 'Go and get a job? Cos I can't see people queuing up to hire you when you've got a record. D'you think anyone's gonna trust ya when they know you've done an armed robbery as well . . .' He trails off. 'I love ya, Ty,' he continues, 'which is why I'm telling you all this. But things ain't gonna be that easy for me and you. All this college stuff, it's a waste of time.'

I feel deflated, cos I was actually starting to get excited. And even tho I couldn't see my whole future yet, I at least was starting to see the first step. Some kind of path. What if Clinton's right tho? What if it was stupid of me to even have some sorta hope? Cos look what happened today. The atmosphere in the room feels different now – heavy and strained – and I can't get Clinton's words outta my head.

'Yeah,' I say, and I hear my voice crack. 'You're right. It's probably a dumb idea.'

'See!' Clinton says, and he flashes me a grin. 'Stick with me – I've got your back, Ty. We've always been here for each other.'

'I know,' I say, and I force a smile. And maybe eighteen months ago, I would've sworn blind that that was the truth. But I really ain't so sure now.

23

When I get in, I head straight upstairs and make my way to my room. Kias is probably in bed cos it's gone half nine, and I think that Mum and Isiah must be in the living room cos I heard the sound of the telly when I came in. I stayed with Clinton for a while. Then we hung out with Dre and some of his other mates. All the time, tho, I just kept thinking how it didn't feel right. How I couldn't really be myself around them, and I just kept wishing that I was with Dadir or Elisha instead. Clinton even asked me if I wanted to hang out tomorrow, but I didn't wanna tell him that I was going to this spoken-word night, cos I knew he'd take the piss again. Same way he did when I told him about college. So I just made up some other excuse instead.

I push open my bedroom door. My room's a mess from where the police turned everything upside down looking for whatever it was that I was supposed to of robbed. I'm suddenly worried, cos I don't know where that exercise book is that I've been writing my poetry in, and I try to move some of the shit that's on the floor. And I dunno why – if it's cos of what happened earlier when I was searched by the police, or if it's cos of all the stuff that Clinton was saying about things not being that simple for me and him – but I start to feel that panic again. It hits me all at once and it's almost like my lungs are restricted, cos I can't breathe. I'm hot and my chest is hurting. I try to suck in air, but it's no use. The harder I try, the more I feel like I'm suffocating. I put my hands to my head to try and make it stop, but the flashbacks come, one after the other: Spider being on top of me in the cell; someone getting their head kicked in on the wing; my dad in one of his rages; being searched in the kitchen and knowing that I didn't want them to do it – that I just wanted them to fuck off, but having no choice. It's worse than it's ever been before and it's like everything's on loop, getting louder and louder.

I'm so hot that I pull my hoodie off and my T-shirt too, but it doesn't seem to make a difference. I can feel the tears streaming down my face and I think about trying to find something to cut myself with, to make it all go away. But I can't move. I think I hear my door knock, but I ain't sure, cos everything seems faint. But then the next minute, Isiah's here. He comes running over to me.

'Ty!' he says. 'Ty!' But his voice sounds proper far. He moves some stuff out the way; then he sits down next to me on the floor. 'It's all right!' Isiah says, and I hold on to him. 'It's all right, Ty,' he repeats. 'I'm here. Just breathe, all right. Just breathe ...'

I hold on tighter to Isiah and I cry into his chest. It makes me feel better, having my brother with me, knowing that I ain't completely alone. Isiah takes some deep breaths with me and he tells me to do the same. I do, and the pain in my chest starts to ease up. I feel my heart rate start to go back to normal too. I don't move tho. I just stay there for a minute. I don't know how long we sit there, but I suddenly start to feel awkward and embarrassed and I move away. Isiah looks proper worried; then he stares down at my bare arms. *Shit* ...

'Ty,' he says gently, and he takes in all the old scars and fresh cuts. 'What's going on? Talk to me, *please.* Has this happened before?'

I feel myself clam up and I think about lying, but I know that there ain't no point, cos even if I did try and make up some excuse, it's obvious what the scars are. That I did it to myself. I shrug cos I just feel defeated. There's so much that's gone on that I don't even know where to begin.

'Ty,' Isiah says again. 'You can tell me ... You can talk to me about anything, y'know that.'

I don't tho. I look at Isiah and part of me really wants to open up to him. Get it all off my chest, cos feeling like this and carrying all this shit around with me has been so heavy. I've felt so alone as well. But me and Isiah ain't spoken like this in years. The hurt bubbles up inside me, cos I don't really know how or why we became so distant. I just know that we did.

'I'm surprised you even care,' I blurt, and it comes out way harsher than I meant it to. I instantly feel bad that that's the first thing that comes out of my mouth, and Isiah looks stung.

'What?' he says, and I don't think I've ever seen Isiah this upset. 'I love you, Ty. I'm your brother. We might fight and shit, but that don't change the way I feel about you. I'll always be there for you, no matter what you're going through. I don't wanna see you like this. I don't wanna see you in pain.'

Isiah's words shock me. Maybe cos I ain't heard him say he loves me since we were really little. I can see how much he means it tho, and he gently puts an arm around me. It feels good to know that Isiah's here for me, and I just wanna let it all out now.

'Whatever it is,' Isiah continues, 'we'll get through it together, *I promise*!'

I nod, but I can't look at him cos I still feel so ashamed. 'It's happened before,' I say, and it kinda feels good to say it out loud. 'It started inside,' I add. 'It's just, like, I'd feel this panic out of nowhere, or things would happen on the wing, or I'd think about Dad and I'd just . . .' I pause.

'Go on,' Isiah urges, and even tho I can't meet his eye, I feel him looking at me like he's letting me know that he's listening. That he's still here, no matter what I say.

'It'd just get too much,' I continue quietly. 'So I started cutting to help me deal with it. I didn't wanna do it or nothing, but I can't explain it … It would just help. And it was, like, I had it under control. But then, when I got attacked and since being released and that, it's got worse …' I pause, and I wipe a tear away with the back of my hand. 'I dunno what to do. I dunno how to cope,' I finish. I sneak a glance at Isiah, and he isn't looking at me like I'm weird, or pathetic, or stupid, like I was scared that he might. He doesn't say anything about cutting myself not making any sense, like I thought he would, either. He just holds on to me tighter.

'Listen to me, Ty,' he says, and even tho his eyes are full of pain, his voice is firm and strong. 'It's going to be okay, d'you hear me? Everything's going to be all right from now on.'

I swallow hard, cos I didn't realize how long I'd been waiting to hear those words. How desperately I've wanted someone to say them to me. Not just now, but when I was in Ryecroft too.

'Thanks for telling me, yeah?' Isiah says with a nod. 'I'm proud of you. And, like, we'll make an appointment with the doctor and we'll get it sorted. But I want you to know, Ty, it ain't your fault. Don't feel embarrassed or anything like that.

You've been through a lot and you've just tried to find a way to cope. All right?'

'Yeah,' I say, and I feel so much lighter now that I've actually told Isiah.

'I'll come with you when you go to the doctor as well. But in the meantime, if you feel like doing it – if you get to a point where you wanna do that again – come and get me, all right? Or if I'm at uni, you can phone me. Any time, okay?'

'Okay,' I say.

'You thought about telling Mum?' Isiah asks.

'Nah,' I say, and I start to feel panicked again. 'Mum's already got enough to worry about. And, anyway, I don't want it to be *another* problem that I've caused. You saw how she was today.'

'It ain't like that,' Isiah says. 'She loves you so much as well – that's why she was so scared. Cos she didn't want you to be taken away from her again. I think you should tell her,' he continues, 'so that we can all be there to support you.'

I pause for a minute, cos maybe Isiah's got a point, but I won't even know what to say. My nose is running and I sniff hard.

'She won't understand,' I say.

'Well, you didn't think that I would,' Isiah replies. 'And I do.' Isiah nudges me playfully, and even tho I'm scared of what Mum might think or say, a small part of me knows that he's right.

'Can you tell her?' I say, and Isiah nods.

'Okay,' he says. 'I'll speak to her in the morning.' He goes quiet for a minute, like he's thinking about what to say, and then he adds: 'She can see that you're trying, y'know.'

'I know,' I say, and it makes me feel disappointed that I even have to win my mum's trust back like this. 'Guess we can't all be the perfect one,' I tease, and even tho part of me is winding Isiah up, I mean what I'm saying too. 'You don't know what it's like,' I continue. 'You've never had to deal with anything like this cos she's always so proud of you.'

Isiah's face softens. 'Mum's proud of you too!' he says.

'I ain't the one she'll be telling all her mates about tho,' I say quietly. 'You're the one at uni, not the criminal like me.'

'She's proud that you're trying,' Isiah says. 'That you're going to go to college. That you're sticking to your curfew, and things like that.'

I suddenly feel guilty, cos if my mum knew that I'd been with Clinton today and actually breached my licence conditions, I'm sure she wouldn't be so proud of me then. I look at Isiah, and I dunno if it's cos I've told him about me cutting and I've finally been honest, but I just wanna get everything off my chest. All the other things I wasn't able to say before.

'Can I ask you suttin?' I say.

'Yeah,' Isiah goes.

'Why didn't you come?' I ask. 'To Ryecroft? You barely came to see me and it was, like, as soon as you got into uni and went off to London, that was it. I know you're ashamed of me and that, but still—'

'Woah!' Isiah interrupts, and he genuinely seems shocked. 'Is that what you think?'

'Ain't it?' I ask.

'No!' Isiah says. 'Far from it. I can understand why you'd think that tho.' He looks down. 'I mean, don't get me wrong, I should've made more of an effort. I really let you down. I'm sorry, Ty. And I am ashamed, but not of you – of myself . . .'

I pause, and I wonder if I heard Isiah right, cos what does he have to be ashamed of?

'What?' I say, and I'm genuinely confused. 'Why? What have you ever done that's wrong?'

Isiah looks down at his hands. 'I'm the eldest,' he says. 'I'm supposed to be the one looking after you and Kias and Mum . . . and I couldn't even do that. I couldn't even do anything when Dad used to . . .' He pauses. 'You're the one who always stood up to him. Who tried to stop him from hitting Mum. You'd never even think – you'd just be straight in there. Even if it meant that he'd turn on you. You've always had that side to you. It's one of the things I admire most about you. Even if something scares you, you still stand your ground. You'd do anything to protect the people that you love. Even when I was getting bullied at school, it was you who stood up to them . . .'

Isiah pauses and I'm genuinely shocked, cos I've never heard him say anything like this before. I didn't think he remembered Dad kicking off and me being the one who stood up to him. All this time, I thought that he was embarrassed by me. Ashamed of me. When, actually, it was himself he was ashamed of.

'I'm sorry about what I said the other day,' Isiah continues. 'I didn't mean it! Maybe if I'd been there for you more, you wouldn't have ended up—'

'Nah,' I interrupt. 'I got myself in Ryecroft. That was my fault. I knew that what I was doing was wrong, but I still did it anyway.' I shake my head, and I can't help but laugh, cos it feels like a huge weight has been lifted and that we've finally cleared the air.

Isiah smiles. 'I wish we'd had this conversation ages ago,' he says.

'Yeah, I know,' I reply. 'Me too!'

'I love you, Ty,' he says again, and I nod.

'Yeah, I know,' I say, and I do. Maybe deep down, I've always known it, but I let all the other shit get in the way. 'I love you too,' I add, and then I pull Isiah in for a hug.

'It's all gonna get sorted, Ty,' Isiah says. 'I promise you, yeah?'

And for the first time in ages, I feel like I've finally got my brother back.

24

The next morning, I put off going downstairs for ages at first, cos I know that Isiah's probably spoken to Mum about what I told him. Even tho the conversation with my brother made me feel a lot better, what if she doesn't understand the way he did? I know that I can't avoid the conversation for ever, tho, so I pull on a hoodie and make my way downstairs. I head into the living room, and Mum and Isiah are both there. Kias is at school cos it's gone eleven, and I know that Mum usually has today off. They go quiet when I come in, which means they've obviously been talking about me.

But Mum and Isiah both smile.

'You okay?' Mum says, and she gets up to give me hug.

'I didn't want to knock on your door because I wasn't sure if you were still sleeping or not.'

'Only just got up,' I lie.

She looks proper worried, and I sit down in the chair opposite her and Isiah on the sofa. Mum hesitates for a minute; then she reaches forward and takes hold of my hand.

'Isiah told me what happened,' she says. 'What's been happening ... Ty, I'm so sorry. I didn't know. I didn't realize that all this was going on.'

I keep my eyes firmly on the ground cos I still can't help but feel embarrassed. But she gets up and comes and crouches down by the side of the chair.

'Look at me, Ty,' she says, gently lifting my chin up. 'It's not your fault, okay. It's nothing to be ashamed of. Now that we know, we can do something about it, okay?'

I nod, and it feels good that both my mum and Isiah are being so supportive.

'I just don't understand it,' I say. 'Like, some days, I'm all right. Then, others ... it just comes out of nowhere and it don't make sense. I'm out and I should just be happy and all of that stuff. So why am I feeling like this?'

Mum gives me a small smile. 'I don't know,' she says. 'I'm sorry. I wish I had the answers, but I'm not a professional. Don't put so much pressure on yourself, though, Ty. You've had a lot to deal with.' She pauses and she looks genuinely upset. 'I can't even begin to imagine what it was like in there,' she continues, 'but I know that it can't have been easy. Even before that, with things here, with your dad. I'm sorry . . .' she says, and she starts to cry.

Isiah comes over and wraps his arms round Mum, and I'm suddenly angry at my dad for everything he put her through. And the fact that it's her who's apologizing, not him.

'Mum,' I say. 'None of that was your fault. That was all Dad's fault, y'hear me? You've got nothing – *nothing* – to apologize for.'

Mum wipes underneath her eyes and Isiah nods.

'Ty's right,' he says, and he gives her shoulder a squeeze.

And in a way, although so much bad stuff has happened. I feel closer to my mum and Isiah than I have before. Isiah puts an arm around me too, and my mum sucks in a deep breath.

'I don't want you to just keep everything in, Ty,' she says firmly. 'Do you understand? After what happened last time . . . I want you to come to me or Isiah, okay?'

I nod. I know she's talking about the time I tried to kill myself during those first couple of weeks at Ryecroft. Maybe I felt like I wouldn't have been able to go to either of them then, but I don't feel that way now.

'I will,' I say. 'I promise!' And I actually mean it.

'It's ridiculous,' Mum says, and she shakes her head, 'that there's so many things in place . . . a curfew, probation. But there's nothing to help you with feeling like this. They must know!'

I shrug and I think of everyone else in Ryecroft. Of Lewis and Morgan, and all the people on the wing with scars up their arms. Or who have tried to kill themselves as well. All those thoughts and feelings don't just disappear once you're released.

'Isiah's already said he'll go with you to see your doctor,' Mum says.

'Yeah,' I reply, and look at Isiah. 'I'd like that. That's what my probation worker told me to do as well.' Mum seems a bit surprised when I mention that Becky knows too, so I add: 'I had a panic attack on the way to probation the other day. Becky saw me and helped me out and stuff, but I didn't really do anything about it cos I was embarrassed. Besides, I thought it would just go away on its own.'

Mum gives me a sad smile. 'I don't think it works like that, love,' she says. 'Ignoring things doesn't mean they go away.'

'I know,' I say, and even tho the thought of going to the doctor is still terrifying, it seems so much more doable with my mum and Isiah by my side. 'I'll give them a call this afternoon,' I say.

'I am so proud of everything you're doing, you know!' Mum says, and she kisses my forehead. My heart feels like it's gonna burst cos I've been wanting her to say those words to me for so long. And even tho I'm still so unsure about what's going to happen with my future and everything else, I start to feel hopeful, cos it's like I can see some sorta way out.

*

I'm in my room, trying to tidy up some of the mess after the raid yesterday, cos I couldn't be bothered to do anything last night, when there's a knock on my door. It's Isiah, and he's got some clothes in his arms. He comes in and chucks them down on my bed.

'I brought you these,' he says. 'There's a few hoodies and stuff in there, and a few sweatshirts and that. They'll just end up sitting in my wardrobe otherwise!'

I notice that one of Isiah's new hoodies is in the pile as well. He's clearly trying to pass it off as being one that he doesn't wear, but I don't say anything.

'Oh,' I tease with a grin. 'So *now* you wanna lend me your shit? Thanks tho.' I can probably wear the new one to the poetry event tonight. Especially since Elisha's gone and invited Anton as well. I don't want my clothes being *another* reason for him to look down his nose at me, like last time. I'm busy trying to put some of the stuff away in my bedroom drawers, so I don't notice Isiah pick something up off the floor.

'What's this?' he says, and I notice that he's holding the exercise book I've written my poetry in. I know me and Isiah have only just sorted everything out between us, but I swear I could kill him sometimes. He's always been nosy.

'Nah, it's nothing!' I say, and I try to grab it off him. 'Isiah, it's *nothing*. Give it here, I mean it!'

But Isiah holds the notebook away from me and starts reading it.

'Why you always in people's business?' I add. 'Anyway, it's just stupid—'

But Isiah turns to me. 'Did you write this?' he asks.

'Yeah,' I reply, and I feel my face get hot.

'Seriously?'

'Yes,' I say; then I reach over and snatch the exercise book out of his hands. 'Like I said,' I continue, 'it's nothing. I know – it's shit!'

'No,' Isiah goes. 'Ty, it's actually really good. Better than that. It's incredible.'

I pause, cos I don't know if he's taking the piss or if he's just saying it cos of what happened yesterday and he feels sorry for me or whatever, but he's not laughing. He actually seems dead serious. I clear my throat.

'You think so?' I say. 'You taking the piss, or—?'

'No!' Isiah says with such force that it takes me by surprise. 'Where d'you learn to write like that?'

I can't quite believe what I'm hearing. Apart from Malik and Dadir, no one else has ever said I could write for shit. Maybe Malik weren't just saying it was good cos he thought he had to. Isiah looks genuinely gobsmacked, and the fact that he actually thinks it's good means a lot.

'Inside,' I say. 'This poet came in and did some workshop

sessions with us and stuff, and I actually really enjoyed it. I've just been writing ever since I come out. I don't know what to do with them or nothing – or if I even want to do anything. But I just know that I haven't been able to stop.'

I look at Isiah and he shakes his head. 'I wish I could write like you,' he says. 'You ever thought about reading them out? Like, at an open mic or something?'

'*No way!*' I say. 'I did read out a poem in one of the workshops we did. But it was only a few people, and I kinda knew most of them anyway. I wouldn't wanna do it in front of an actual crowd. Me and Elisha are going to some poetry night later organized by the same poet who did the workshops while I was inside. But I'm just gonna listen, that's it ...'

'Maybe you should think about it,' Isiah says. 'I reckon you'd be really great!'

'Yeah, maybe,' I reply. But deep down, I know that ain't ever gonna happen.

Later, I knock on Elisha's front door and, while I wait, I pray that Anton's decided to stay at home and pull out last minute. But of course, when Leesh opens the door, Anton's there. I can hear him chatting to someone in the living room. I try not to show how pissed off I am, cos no one wants to be a third wheel. Everyone used to think that there was something going on between me and Elisha. Shaun and that lot thought it too, even tho I'd always tell them that we were just good mates. It's like they couldn't believe that we were just close friends without there being anything else. I wouldn't be surprised if that's the real reason why Anton's decided to come too. Especially after the way he was looking at me when I first bumped into the two of them. Not just like he was better than me, but also like he was a bit suspicious cos I was trying to get with Elisha or something like that. Leesh gives me a hug. She's straightened her hair, and apart from her prom picture, I've never seen it like that before.

'I've told loads of people at college about the protest, y'know!' she says excitedly. 'Everyone's proper mad and upset about the case, and I've seen loads of people posting about it on Instagram too. I think it could be a really good turnout! I've even been speaking to this woman from some charity – Smash Joint Enterprise, they're called. She said she'll be there as well.'

'Really?' I say. 'That's amazing!'

Leesh nods. 'I just want as many people to come as possible,' she says. Then she points to the living room. 'I'll be one minute, yeah? I'm just getting my stuff. Anton's in there!' And then she runs upstairs.

I really can't be arsed chatting to Anton with his square head, but I go into the living room anyway. I'm relieved to see that Remi's in there too. Leesh told me that he's gonna give us a lift into town.

'You all right, Ty?' he says when I come in, and he gives me a hug.

I glance at Anton, but he actually seems a bit nervous this time. Maybe cos Remi's here as well. I know that Elisha wouldn't want me and Anton fighting, so I at least try and make the effort for her. Even if I don't like the guy.

'You all right?' I say to Anton, and I give him a nod.

'Yeah. You?' he says.

I sit down and it feels proper awkward, cos neither me or Anton says anything else. Remi can clearly sense how awkward it is too, cos he looks at me then Anton with a smirk. We sit there in silence for what feels like forever. Then Remi goes: 'So, what's this thing you're going to? A poetry night?'

'*Yeah!*' me and Anton both say at the same time, and I side-eye him. I know that he's Elisha's boyfriend, but I still don't get why he has to be here?

I see Remi trying to hide another smile, and then he says: 'I mean, I was sneaking out to clubs at your age, but whatever floats your boat . . .'

Elisha comes into the living room. 'Yeah, they don't wanna be hearing about what you were doing fifty million years ago,' she says. 'Besides, you were *trying* to sneak into clubs, but none of them would let you in!'

'Oh, d'you wanna walk?' Remi replies, and Leesh pulls a face. 'Thought not!' he continues, and I see Elisha roll her eyes.

301

'You both ready?' she asks.

'*Yeah!*' me and Anton say at the same time, again, and Remi bursts out laughing.

'Oh shit,' Remi says. 'I wish I could come just to see these two there! You're like some sort of double act.'

'*Remi!*' Elisha says, and she punches his arm.

'All right, all right,' Remi continues. 'Just don't kill each other,' he says.

I wanna say that if there was a fight between me and Anton, I could take him out no problem, but I don't. Maybe it's cos I can tell how much Elisha likes him. We head out the door and towards Remi's car and, before we reach it, I already know he's gonna give us 'the talk'. Elisha's face goes red. We must've had this talk a million times before, every time Remi's dropped us somewhere. I can tell that Anton's never had it, but he's about to get it now anyway. Remi stops and Elisha moves a hand to her temples. She can't even look at Anton right now.

'Please,' she says. 'Remi. Just make this quick!'

Anton looks proper confused, but I shake my head.

'Awww, man,' I say.

Remi clears his throat. There's nothing in the world he loves more than Elisha, except maybe his car. I can tell that Elisha's dying of embarrassment and I'm cracking up.

'It ain't funny!' Elisha hisses. 'Why's he always gotta do this?

We should've just got the bus!'

'Firstly,' Remi says, and he looks at Anton. 'Before you even step foot in this car, there are some rules. Number one,' Remi says, and he puts a finger up, 'I don't want you eating or drinking in here—'

'We ain't even got anything to eat or drink!' Elisha cuts in, but Remi ignores her.

'Number two,' Remi continues, and he puts another finger up, 'you don't slam the door. You close it gently – *g-ent-t-l-yyy* – so there's a little *click*, almost like a whisper.' He unlocks the car, then opens the door and closes it to give us a demo. 'Like so. Number three—' Remi continues, but Elisha butts in:

'All right!' Elisha snaps, and she shoves Remi towards the car door. 'We can give him a rundown of the other eight once we get in!'

'*Eight?!*' Anton says.

'Yeah!' Elisha replies. 'Hurry up, Remi!' she snaps. 'We're gonna be late!

'All right, all right,' Remi replies, and he unlocks the car.

'Ty, you can sit in the front,' Elisha says, and I'm relieved, cos at least I don't have to be cramped in the back seat with Anton.

I climb in and I hear Elisha quickly telling Anton the other eight rules as we drive off. Remi starts playing the type of music my mum listens to, which is another one of his rules: if you don't like what he's playing, then tough. We drive through town, and then he parks up on a side street that doesn't look like there's much else on it, apart from a few abandoned buildings.

'Is this it?' Elisha asks, and she cranes her neck to look out the window.

'That's what it says!' Remi replies, and he points to his satnav. 'I'll meet you back here about half nine!'

'All right!' Elisha replies.

'Thanks,' I say to Remi as I get out the car.

'Gently!' he shouts as I close the door; then he drives off.

The place that we're at ain't really much to look at. We're by this alleyway, and I can't even see where this poetry thing is supposed to be. Elisha stares down at the flyer on her phone and she points to a doorway that I didn't even see. It looks abandoned and I'd be regretting coming if it weren't for the fact I wanna see Malik.

'I think it's in there!' Leesh says, and we head over.

We go through the door and there's a woman sitting at a table as we go in. She holds a clipboard out that's got a list of names on it. 'Are any of you signing up for the open mic?' she asks, but we shake our heads.

We give her three quid each and then we walk through into this back room. There's a stage right at the front with a couple of mic stands already set up. I look around and there's loads of people there our age or older. I ain't never been anywhere like this before. I scan the room to see who's about and I spot

Malik in the corner, talking to a small group of people. I wanna go over, but I feel proper nervous about just walking up to him. Besides, will he even remember me? I'm just some ex-offender he met when he was doing some workshops in prison. Anton says something about going to get a drink, then disappears to the back of the room. I nudge Elisha.

'There's Malik,' I say.

'Where?' Elisha replies; then she follows my gaze. 'You not gonna go over and say hello?'

'Nah!' I reply quickly. 'He ain't even gonna remember who I am. And anyway, what do I say?'

'Erm, *hello*?!' Leesh says. 'You could start with that. Tell him that you've been writing more poetry since you've been home as well ...'

I suddenly feel stupid. The stuff I've written is rubbish compared to Malik's poetry. Why's he even gonna care anyway? I shake my head and I just wanna go and sit down before he catches us staring at him.

'Nah,' I say, and I pull at Elisha's elbow. 'Let's just sit down.'

'Come on, Ty!' she says. 'What's the worst he's gonna say?'

Before I can answer, Elisha shakes her head and goes marching off into the crowd towards him.

Shit!

'Elisha!' I shout. 'Leesh!'

But she just ignores me and carries on walking. I'm gonna

305

look like even more of an idiot if she goes over to speak to him and I'm just standing there. Elisha makes her way through the crowds of people who are starting to come in and I follow her. It's getting even busier now, but I see Elisha tap Malik on the shoulder and say something to him; then he turns to look at me, and I feel my face getting hot cos I've got no choice now. But as I walk up to Malik, his face lights up and he actually looks ... happy to see me?

'Hey,' he says, and he brings me in for a hug. 'Tyrell, it's good to see you! How you doing?'

To be honest, I'm taken aback that he even remembers my name. I know that he did in the workshop sessions in prison, but he would've had a register or something then. I glance at Leesh and she looks me dead in the eye as if to say: *I told you so.*

I turn back to Malik. 'Yeah, I'm all right,' I reply. 'I mean, I'm out ...'

Malik nods. 'I can see that,' he says with a smile. He pauses for a moment and his grin vanishes. 'I heard about what happened at Ryecroft,' he says, and I know he's talking about Spider and his mates. 'The other guys told me that was why you couldn't come to the last session. I take it you're all good now?'

'Yeah,' I say, even tho that ain't completely true.

'You gonna be reading anything tonight?' Malik asks. 'I'm sure they'll still have space on the open mic ...'

'Nah,' I say quickly. 'I just came to listen and that.'

'He's been writing tho,' Elisha chimes in, and I die inside. I shoot her a look, cos I think that maybe Malik doesn't really care whether I'm writing or not, but he seems pleased.

'I'm glad,' he says. 'I meant what I said about you having a gift. I'm so glad you've carried on writing like you said you would.'

My heart nearly stops, cos even tho what Malik said meant everything to me, I wasn't sure if he was being serious or not. Speaking to him now, tho, makes me realize that he was, and I'm suddenly glad that I came.

'You got anything on you I can read?' Malik says.

'Yeah,' I go, and I unzip my bag and take out the exercise book. Leesh says something about going to find Anton cos he'll be on his own, and I hand the book over to Malik with trembling hands.

'There's a few in here,' I say. 'And there's a couple I started in Ryecroft that I finished when I got out . . .'

Malik nods and he opens the exercise book. It feels so personal, handing my poems over to him, and even tho I trust Malik, I shove my hands in my pockets and I notice how much I'm shaking.

'I know they ain't that good,' I say.

But Malik only shakes his head, his eyes focused, reading. He flicks through the pages, and it probably only takes him a few minutes to read some of the poems, but it feels like forever. I'm worried that he's gonna start laughing cos they're all rubbish, but he stops and hands me the notebook back.

'Wow,' he says. 'I knew you were talented, Ty, from the first time I read one of your poems. You should definitely read at the open mic.' He must see the look of horror on my face, cos he laughs, and then he adds: 'It doesn't have to be today, but honestly … people need to hear your words. People need to hear *you*!'

I stop for a minute and I can't quite get my head around what Malik's saying. That people need to hear me and my words. I can't help but smile, cos the last time I felt this good was when I was doing one of his sessions.

'Thanks,' I say. 'I ain't sure I'm ready to read yet tho.'

'That's okay,' Malik replies. 'But maybe one day you will be!'

I nod, and then I suddenly remember the protest, and I ain't even sure if Malik would want to come, but I go: 'Me and my mate Elisha, the one who came over with me before, we're organizing a protest outside the super court in town. You know, for that joint enterprise case that's happening in Manchester.'

'Yeah,' Malik says. 'I heard about that – it's fucking awful. And the thing is, it won't be the last one to happen, either. There's gonna be more and more cases like that. Good on the two of you for organizing something, though. Will you send me the details? I'd love to come. I know a few of my mates will wanna be there too. You on Insta?'

'Yeah!' I say. 'Well, I ain't reactivated it since I got out, but I've been meaning to do it.'

'Take my details,' Malik goes. 'Then just message me. I'll give you my number as well, just in case you don't end up going back on IG. I know what it's like!'

'All right,' I say, and I put Malik's number in my phone. I'm glad that he's gonna come to the protest tho. Cos even if there won't be a massive turnout, at least me and Leesh and Isiah and Remi, and Malik and his mates will be there. I dunno what else to say and I feel awkward for a minute, cos I still don't really know Malik that well. It's a bit weird too, seeing someone in a different place. Especially when the last time I saw him, I was inside ... I think about making an excuse and going back to Leesh, but then one of Malik's friends comes over.

'Sorry to interrupt,' he goes, and he gives me a smile. 'But, Malik, I think they're gonna start in a minute.'

Malik nods. 'All right,' he says, and then he turns to me. 'I'll catch you after the show, yeah, Ty?' And then he brings me in for another hug. 'It was good to see you tho. I mean it!'

'You too!' I say, and then Malik and his friend head off towards the side of the stage.

I look around me, and I suddenly realize how full the room is. It's even more packed than earlier, and I start to panic cos I can't see Elisha anywhere. I panic a bit more cos I'm just gonna be stood here, on my own, but then I catch sight of her in the crowd. Her and Anton are sitting to the left of the stage and he's got his arm around her. They're kissing, which is kinda weird to see, but as soon as Leesh clocks me, she pulls away and looks embarrassed. I knew I'd just be a third wheel. Leesh moves her bag off the seat that's the other side of her, and Anton looks pissed. Probably cos I interrupted them.

'How'd it go?' Leesh asks. 'Did you show him some of your stuff?'

'Yeah,' I go. 'He said I should read it out at an open mic some time.'

Leesh's eyes widen. 'You should, Ty,' she says. 'See, ain't you glad you spoke to him now?'

'Yeah,' I say. 'I am. Thanks.'

She smiles. 'No problem.' Then she hands me a can of Coke. 'Got you a drink!'

'Thanks.' I pull the tab to open it and take a gulp. I look around the room: it's even more full now. There's no seats left and there's people standing around the sides. I look away, cos thinking about the amount of people makes me nervous. Then the lights go down and a guy comes onto the stage.

'How's everyone doing?' he says, and there's a cheer from the crowd. 'For those who don't know me, I'm Darius, and I'm gonna be your host tonight.' There's more cheers from the crowd at that. 'We're going to start off with the open mic. So, first up, we've got . . . Khadija! Can you all give her a round of applause?'

The crowd claps, and a girl comes up. She looks around my age. She's got box braids and a nose piercing, and she's proper pretty. Khadija takes out her phone and I wonder what she's doing at first, but then she glances down at her poem and the whole room goes quiet when she starts to read. Khadija's poem is about identity and belonging, about finding a sense of home within herself. When she reads certain lines, people start to click. I can't look away, not just cos of her, but cos of what she's saying, and I feel myself holding my breath. I'm too scared to even move or blink in case I miss something.

When Khadija finishes, the crowd goes wild; then another guy gets up; then another. I see what Malik meant even more now, about the fact that poetry is meant to be heard. Hearing it in person is so different to just watching the videos on YouTube. It's like the atmosphere is electric. The last open mic performer finishes, and I'm just trying to take it all in, cos I've never been anywhere like this before. But even tho it's my first time, in a weird way, I kinda feel like I belong. And not just the way I'd try to feel when I was with Clinton and Shaun and Abass and that lot. Like I *actually* do.

Darius comes back on the stage and he says: 'I think you'll all agree that each and every one of those open mic performers was incredible. So let's give them another round of applause.'

The crowd cheers and shouts and whistles, and I do too. I glance at Anton, and even he seems to be having a good time.

'And next up,' Darius continues, 'let's welcome Malik Sabo to the stage.'

The crowd is deafening now, and Malik gets up, walks to the centre of the stage and adjusts the mic stand. He flips through a notebook.

'How you all doing?' Malik asks, and there's cheers and whoops from the crowd. 'Okay,' he continues. 'I'm going to read a few poems, and this one is called "Violent State of Mine".'

The room goes silent as Malik reads the poem. I know it. It's the one on YouTube that's got the most views. But it's different now that he's saying the words in front of us, in this tiny room. The poem's really clever, cos he starts off talking about young people and violence and knife crime, and you think it's just gonna be about that. But then it's like he expands the poem almost and starts talking about how violent the state is and how that trickles down. He talks about Grenfell, and the prison system, immigration, lack of opportunities and the police. It's like his words carry so much more weight. So much more power and pain and sadness. I hear the clicking that echoes around us and I feel Leesh stiffen next to me, like she's trying to take in everything that Malik says. I inch forward in my seat and I feel the goosebumps prickle my arms. And I just wanna stay here, listening to Malik's words and taking it all in, for as long as I can.

*

All the way home, I feel like I'm on cloud nine. I was gutted when we had to leave so that I can make it home in time for my curfew. I'm still on a high, tho, and I don't even care that I'm squashed in the back seat of the car with big-head Anton. Elisha said she wanted to sit in the front, which was actually fine by me, cos I didn't really feel like talking much. I just wanted to – I dunno – remember everything that happened and think about all the poems too. I'm gonna reactivate Instagram and follow Malik. I can't stop thinking about the fact he said that people need to *hear me* as well. That people need to hear my words.

Remi drops Anton off first and I even manage to mutter a 'safe' when he gets out the car. When we pull up outside Elisha's, Remi heads into the house and I turn to Leesh. I can't believe I didn't even want her to go and talk to Malik, and now I'm so glad that she did.

'Leesh,' I say. 'Thanks, yeah. There's no way I would've gone over to Malik tonight if it weren't for you. Never mind showing him more of my poetry.'

'I know,' Elisha says. 'I got you, Ty! And you must have made an impact, cos he remembered you. Besides, what kind of friend would I be if I didn't give you a shove when you needed it?'

I smile. I feel so lucky to have Leesh back in my life and I'm just glad that we managed to sort everything out again. I think of Clinton and how different I feel being around him, compared to when I'm with Elisha and even Dadir. I don't have to hide the things I like from either of them, and I know that they only want what's best for me too. I bring Leesh in for a hug.

'Thanks again, yeah?' I say, and then I add: 'Even Anton is getting more tolerable.'

'Wow,' Elisha says. 'That's actually progress. Before you know it, you two are gonna be best mates.'

'Yeah, I wouldn't go that far,' I say. Then I gesture towards my house. 'I better go,' I say. 'Curfew and that! I'll see you tomorrow tho?'

'Yeah,' Elisha goes. 'I'll see you tomorrow! Bye!'

25

When I come downstairs the next morning, Isiah's already waiting for me at the kitchen table. I was still on a high after the spoken-word night and I even did some more writing when I got back home too. But now that I've actually got to go and speak to a doctor, I ain't feeling that great. Mum's already left for work and Kias is at school. I ain't sure if having Isiah with me is supposed to make all of this seem easier, but it actually feels harder, somehow. Maybe cos I'm still so embarrassed and ashamed, and cos part of me thinks that no one will ever get it, no matter how much they pretend they do. Not even Isiah. I open the cupboard, but I ain't really in the mood to eat. So I just close it again.

'You all right?' Isiah goes. 'How was the poetry thing last night?'

'Yeah,' I reply. 'It was proper good, y'know. It's on every month as well. Me and Leesh are gonna go to the next one. You should've come instead of sitting at home revising!'

Isiah smiles. 'Final year and all that,' he says. 'Anyway, can you imagine . . . Mum'd go mad if I spent three years and all that money at uni just to not pass.'

'That's why you should be the one who messes up,' I tease. 'Like, Mum's expectations for me are in the gutter.' I'm half joking, but a small part of me thinks that I'm probably right, no matter what Mum says, and it stings.

Isiah must be able to pick up on the hurt in my voice, cos he goes, 'Ty . . .'

'I'm joking!' I say, even tho Isiah doesn't look convinced. He goes quiet for a minute and I can tell that he's thinking about what to say. I kinda already know what he's about to ask tho.

'You been feeling . . . okay?' Isiah asks finally, and I know by 'okay', he means have I felt like hurting myself. I did get a bit panicked by the crowd at the open mic night, but it wasn't nowhere near as bad as it has been.

I shrug. 'Yeah, I think so,' I say. 'I ain't felt like cutting, if that's what you mean. I've been all right.'

Isiah nods. 'You'd tell me, tho, wouldn't you?' he asks.

I pause. I'd like to think that I would, but the truth is, I don't know what I'd do. It ain't like I've been in that situation since Isiah found out a couple days ago, and when I'm in it, it ain't as simple as just asking someone for help. It's almost like it takes over. I don't wanna worry Isiah even more, tho, so I just nod.

'Yeah, I would,' I say, and I see a look of relief flash across his face. It still feels weird, talking to him about all this. Especially cos I ain't spoken about it ever, really. I can see how much Isiah is trying to be there for me tho – how much he doesn't want me to have to go through this on my own – and it feels good. Having someone there, for once.

'I appreciate it, y'know,' I say. 'You don't have to do all this.'

Isiah stands up and he puts a hand on my shoulder. 'Yeah, I do,' he says. 'I promised you that we'd sort it together, and I meant every word.'

I look down at the floor. 'What if I won't ever get better tho?' I ask, and I'm kinda surprised that I've said it out loud, cos it's something I've been thinking for ages.

Isiah gives my shoulder a squeeze.

'I don't have the answers, Ty,' he goes. 'I wish I did. But surely this can't make anything worse. And even if it does take a while, I'll still be there for ya. D'you hear? I ain't going nowhere this time. We'll sort it, together.'

I nod. 'Together,' I repeat.

Isiah brings me in for a hug and I hold on to him, my big brother.

'You ready?' Isiah asks, and he pulls away.

'Yeah,' I reply, and I suck in a deep breath. 'I am.'

We sit in the doctor's waiting room, and now it all feels so real. I haven't spoken the whole time we've been here, and Isiah keeps looking over at me, probably to check that I'm okay. Isiah keeps going on about something or other, but I can't concentrate. Still, I'm glad I'm not here on my own. My legs won't stop trembling and my palms are sweating cos I don't know how I'm even gonna begin to try and explain all this to a complete stranger. A doctor comes through a set of double doors and peers out into the waiting room.

'Tyrell Forrester?' he calls, looking around.

I glance at Isiah. 'Yeah,' I say, standing up, and Isiah gives me an encouraging smile.

The doctor is quite old, but he gives me a friendly nod. He holds one of the doors open for me and Isiah, and we follow him into a small room.

'Come on in!' he says. 'I'm Doctor Kaminski. Please, sit down.'

He gestures towards these two small chairs beside his desk. I sit down in one, and Isiah sits in the other. I look around the room at all these posters of the digestive system and the human body and all these tips on how to 'stay well', and I feel embarrassed and scared all over again. Doctor Kaminski brings up some medical records on his computer, and he glances at them for a moment before turning to me.

'What can I help you with today, Tyrell?' he asks.

I pause and my heart starts to beat hard in my chest. I look at Isiah, cos I can feel myself clamming up, and I suddenly don't wanna say anything. I just wanna get outta here. Cos how is this even gonna help? Isiah must be able to sense how I'm feeling, cos he puts a hand gently on my shoulder.

'Go on, Ty,' he says. 'It's okay. I'm right here with you, remember.'

I nod. Having Isiah here makes me feel that little bit braver. 'Err,' I start, and I can't meet Doctor Kaminski's gaze. 'I ... I don't really know how to say it or nothing, and I ain't even sure if it's anything you can help with, but ... I've been, like, cutting myself,' I blurt out. Saying it out loud makes me feel ashamed all over again, but I sneak a look at Isiah and he gives me an encouraging nod.

'I don't mean to do it, or nothing like that,' I add. 'But sometimes everything just feels like it's too much. Like it's all just getting on top of me and I dunno what to do. Cutting myself feels like the only way I can cope, and I'm scared that I won't ever be able to stop,' I finish quietly.

It takes me by surprise that I was even able to say all that. If Isiah wasn't here, I probably wouldn't have been able to. I glance at Doctor Kaminski, and he doesn't look at me like I'm weird, like I thought he might. Instead, he gives me a reassuring smile.

319

'I can't imagine how difficult that was for you to say, Tyrell,' he replies. 'You should be really proud of yourself, and I want you to know that this step you've taken is huge.' He glances at his computer screen. 'It says on your records that you spent the last eighteen months at Ryecroft Young Offenders, is that right?'

'Yeah,' I say.

He nods. 'Have you had any other symptoms?' he asks me. 'Trouble sleeping, or any feelings of anxiety or overwhelm?'

'Yeah,' I go. 'Sometimes I find it hard to sleep cos of these flashbacks, and I have these episodes where I panic and I get really hot or I can't breathe properly, and sometimes ... sometimes I feel like I'm gonna die.' I pause. 'Does that sound stupid?'

Doctor Kaminski shakes his head. 'No,' he says. 'It doesn't at all. In fact, I'd be very surprised if you didn't have any of those symptoms, given how traumatic an experience prison can be for young people.' He pauses. 'Have you felt depressed? Or suicidal?'

I hesitate, and I feel Isiah tense next to me at the word 'suicidal', almost like he's scared for me to answer cos of what I might I say. Especially cos he knows that I've felt that way before.

'I did when I first got sent to Ryecroft,' I say. 'I tried to ... kill myself. But since then, nah. I ain't felt nothing like that.

It just feels like I don't know how to cope with it all, and sometimes I feel ... unsafe. Like I'm still back in Ryecroft, even tho I'm out.'

Doctor Kaminski nods. 'Well, it would be good to get you referred to and seen by a mental health professional, so we can get to the root of the problem and offer you the appropriate help. One of the things I'd recommend to help with the self-harm is talking therapy. Have you ever done that?'

'Nah,' I say. 'Never.'

'I can refer you for some counselling,' he says, 'if you'd like that? It can help you to process a lot of the things you've been through and also identify your triggers ... find new ways to cope.'

I pause. 'Yeah,' I say. 'I'd like that.'

Doctor Kaminski nods. 'It might take a bit of time, Tyrell,' he says. 'But you'll get there. You just need to be patient with yourself. The most important thing is that you've made the people around you aware and you've taken those first steps towards getting help.' And I feel like for the first time in forever that I've actually been heard.

When I get back, I'm still a bit overwhelmed by all the stuff Doctor Kaminski said, but I'm glad that I went. He printed some information off for me and even gave me a couple of numbers to call in case things get really bad too. I do feel a bit better now that everything's out in the open tho. It's almost like a weight's been lifted, even if I'm only at the beginning of trying to sort all this out. I'm in my room now, and I reactivate my Insta, then search for Malik and give him a follow. He follows me back almost right away.

My phone pings. Elisha's messaged me on WhatsApp. Something about this big organization that's meant to be joining the protest on Saturday, tomorrow. I'm just about to respond, when I hear my mum calling me from downstairs.

'What is it?' I shout back.

'Someone's on the phone,' my mum replies. 'Dadir . . .'

I'm on my feet as soon as my mum says his name, cos I already know how quickly those ten minutes go. I race down the stairs, three at a time, and I almost slam straight into my mum. She gives me a funny look as she hands me the phone.

'I've never seen you move so fast!' she says, and then she disappears into the living room. I press the receiver to my ear.

'Dadir?!' I say, and I hear that familiar noise in the background. The shouting and banging and screaming. I'm suddenly transported back to Ryecroft. Back to being in that tiny cell.

'Yo, Ty,' Dadir replies, and he says my name quietly. Probably to make sure that no one overhears. I feel this mix of emotions, cos it's so good to be talking to Dadir. I've proper missed him too. But he's still locked up, and at least I'm out, trying to get on with the rest of my life. I feel this pang of guilt, cos I didn't write to him like I said I would. Even tho it's not even been a week since I got out, when you're inside, those letters mean everything.

'What've you been up t—?'

'It's good to hear y—'

We both start at the same time.

Dadir laughs, and then he goes: 'How's life on the out?'

I don't wanna tell him how tough it's been, cos no matter how hard I've found it, I know that for Dadir, it's a million times worse.

'Yeah,' I say. 'I can't complain. It's been all right. And remember that Malik who came in to run those workshops?'

'Yeah, yeah, yeah,' Dadir goes. 'The poet guy?'

'That's him. Well, he did some spoken-word thing last night and I went to it. It was proper sick, y'know. I only saw him perform a few of his poems cos of my curfew, innit. I had to get back. But it was like nothing I've ever seen before. You'd like it.'

'That sounds good,' Dadir goes. 'Did you read your stuff out?'

'Nah,' I say. 'They had an open mic night, but there's no way I can do that ...'

'Why not?' Dadir replies. 'You read a poem out that time in front of us, and it was something else, Ty. Like, seriously. Next time you go, you should defo read.'

'Maybe,' I say, then change the subject. 'What's going on with you anyway? How's Ryecroft? What happened with your appeal?'

323

Dadir goes quiet and I feel the weight of his silence down the phone. 'Ryecroft's the same old,' he goes. 'Got moved to the older wing last week, literally the day I turned eighteen. It's like they couldn't wait to move me there! It ain't nothing like Jay tho. I don't really know anyone, and people are just moving proper mad.' He pauses. 'My appeal got dropped as well. The Criminal Cases Review Commission decided not to take it on. After all the stuff that came out as well. This is it, innit, Ty? This is just gonna be my life from now on. It's, like, you can't have any hope, cos as soon as you do, it gets taken away …'

Dadir trails off and I can't speak. I feel even worse that I forgot about Dadir's eighteenth birthday coming up – everything's just been so mad since leaving Ryecroft – and now his appeal's been chucked out too? I feel angry and broken, and I know that whatever I say to him, it won't be enough. How can it, when his freedom's been taken away? When he'll spend the next nineteen years inside.

'Dadir …' I start. 'I'm so sorry. How is this shit even allowed?'

Dadir goes quiet again. 'I should've known,' he says. 'My barrister said there was a really slim chance it would get overturned, cos even when people are told they have grounds to appeal, they still get knocked back, and even when an appeal is 'successful,' it don't really change anything cos you still serve time in prison and end up with a serious conviction. I guess, even tho I knew that, a small part of me still thought that maybe my case might be different. That I might be the one to get my sentence overturned and be released. But I guess not.'

'That's fucked up!' I shout. 'There's gotta be something we can do – that your solicitor can do?'

'Nah,' Dadir goes. 'It's the law, innit … Anyway,' he says after a minute. 'It is what it is.'

It's mad, hearing him say something like that over something so huge, but I get it too. It ain't like me or Dadir can do anything to change it, no matter how much we both want to. I swallow hard. Dadir always seemed to get by in Ryecroft, but maybe that was cos he thought he had a tiny bit of hope. Like, he could maybe see a glimmer of it, just out of reach above him. But, now, instead of getting his freedom back, it's like he's being sucked further and further into the system, and there's no other way out.

'Dadir,' I go. 'Listen, yeah. You're gonna get through this, do you hear me? And one day, you'll be out. *You will!* You've just got to hold on …'

'I know,' Dadir replies, but his voice is barely above a whisper. 'Ty,' he continues. 'Listen, my ten minutes is almost up—' And then the phone goes dead.

I stand there for a minute and I don't move. I'm just trying to make sense of it all. Trying to take it all in. Maybe a tiny part of me thought that Dadir would end up getting his sentence overturned too. Cos it's so fucking obvious how wrong and unjust it is. I hang up the phone and I make my way upstairs. And all I can think about is how Dadir will spend most of his life inside. And how when he gets out, he'll have to deal with this shit.

I close my bedroom door and I pick up a pen and some paper. I think about how Dadir had everything taken away from him. His home, his life, his future, his freedom. How he'd even had his love of music taken away from him too. And I think about being strip-searched the other day in my kitchen. How I felt so powerless. Like nothing belonged to me.

But there's one thing they won't ever be able to take from me, and that's my voice. *My words.* They belong to me and no one else. So I press my pen down on the page, and I begin to write.

26

When I go over to Elisha's the next day, she's already putting some protest placards in the back of Remi's car. I catch sight of one that says PROVEN INNOCENT FOUND GUILTY and another one that says SMASH JOINT ENTERPRISE! Leesh smiles when she sees me and I go over and give her a hug.

'They look good!' I say, gesturing to the signs.

'I stayed up most of the night making them,' Leesh says. 'Even roped Remi into it. I might've made too many tho. What if no one turns up?' I can see how worried she is. 'If it's just you and me, and a handful of people – won't be much of a protest, then, will it?'

'It don't matter,' I say, and I nudge her gently with my elbow.

'The only thing that matters is that we – you – tried to do something. That's what matters!'

'Ty's right!' Remi says as he comes down the garden path. 'I'm proud of ya,' he adds, wrapping his arms around Leesh. 'My little sister, organizing protests! You're gonna change the world one day, mark my words!'

Elisha pushes Remi away, but she's smiling. 'Yeah, all right,' she says. 'I ain't used to you being this nice. I appreciate it tho.'

Remi laughs, then puts a couple more placards in the boot. 'You both ready?' he asks.

'Yeah!' Leesh replies, and I nod. Remi looks like he's about to give us the car lecture all over again, even tho we only just had it the other night, but Elisha shakes her head.

'I swear, Remi,' she says as she yanks the door open. 'Don't even start with that. We're already gonna be late. We don't need to be listening to you for another five hours—'

'*Gent-l-y!*' Remi says. 'Gent-l-y!'

But Leesh is already inside. Remi looks at me and I climb into the back of the car, then close the door so carefully, like my life depends on it. Remi slides into the driver's seat.

'That's how you do it!' he says with a nod, and Elisha rolls her eyes.

Remi starts the engine and I stare out the window. We're meeting in the middle of town first, by Piccadilly Gardens, where the bus station is. And then we're gonna walk to the super court.

It's gonna feel weird going back there. Especially as I ain't even been into town or anywhere near the courts since I got sent down. After speaking to Dadir yesterday, tho, I'm even more determined to do this. Dadir can't speak out about what's happening to him and so many other kids, but I can. Remi's car slows down. There's so much traffic that he pulls over onto a side street.

'This is probably as close as I'm gonna get!' he says. 'D'you know where you're going? You turn down that street and you'll come out near the art gallery. I'm just gonna find somewhere to park – then I'll come and join ya, all right?'

Leesh nods. 'All right,' she says. 'Thanks, yeah, for driving us!'

Remi smiles, then shifts around in his seat so that he's facing me. 'Look, yeah,' he says, and I notice the seriousness in his voice. 'It'll probably be all right, but just in case anything happens and the police show up, just make sure you get out of there. *Okay?* You don't need to be getting kettled in.'

I suddenly feel worried and I see a look of fear flash across Elisha's face too. Remi must clock it as well, cos he goes: 'Like I said, it'll probably be fine, Leesh. But just in case, all right? That goes for you as well, Ty.'

Elisha nods. 'Okay!' she says. Then she leans over and gives Remi a hug. I can tell that he's caught off guard, but he hugs her back.

A car starts beeping from somewhere behind us.

'I'd better move!' Remi says. 'Before I get a ticket. Go and kill it out there, tho, you two. I'll come and find you both!'

'See you over there,' I say as I climb out of the car.

Me and Leesh pull all the placards and banners and stuff out, and then Remi drives off. Both our arms are full and I give Leesh a nudge as we make our way down the street.

'Yo, you sure you made enough?' I tease.

'Shut up, Ty!' she says, but as we turn the corner and make our way towards the gardens, Elisha looks nervous again. 'What if no one turns up tho?' she says, for what must be the hundredth time. 'Maybe I didn't tell enough people ... We probably should've given ourselves longer to organize it. It was all so last minute, Ty ... What if it's just a waste of time?'

We turn onto the street that runs alongside the bus station, and Leesh is so distracted, scrolling through her phone to see if anyone's put that they're here, that she doesn't even notice.

I stop.

'Leesh!' I say with a smile, and I point to the bit of Piccadilly Gardens that you can see behind the buses. It's full of people with placards and banners too. There must be about three hundred, maybe more. Elisha's mouth hangs open in shock and I can't help but grin.

'See,' I say, and I nudge her again. '*You* did this!'

We make our way through the crowd and I start to feel proper nervous. I've never been around this many people in my life, and everyone's so close together too. My heart starts beating fast, but I try to concentrate on the ground and I tell myself that nothing bad's gonna happen. Not just that, tho, but that I'm doing this for Dadir and those boys in Manchester, and all those other people who are inside for joint enterprise. It seems to help, knowing that it ain't about me; that it's about something bigger. We make our way to the middle and put the placards and banners down and Elisha scans the crowd.

'*Woah!*' she says, and she pulls her phone out to take a picture. There's all sorts of people here. Old and young, different ages and races. There's even some people who've brought their kids with them too. Elisha points to a mixed-race woman with brown hair, who looks like she's in her forties, wearing a T-shirt that says SJE.

'That's the woman I told you about who I've been speaking to on Instagram,' Elisha says. 'The one from that charity called Smash Joint Enterprise. Come on!'

We head over to her. There's a few other people wearing T-shirts with SJE on them too. The woman smiles when we approach.

'Marianne?' Leesh goes. 'I'm Elisha, and this is Tyrell. We organized the protest.'

Marianne pulls Elisha in for a hug, even tho this is the first time they've ever met. 'Hi,' she says, and she gives me a wave. 'I've heard a lot about you, Tyrell. It's so good to meet you in person.

It's such a good turnout as well – you should both be proud!'

Elisha nods. 'I didn't expect there to be this many people!' she says. 'I guess it shows just how important it is tho.' She pauses. 'We've never done anything like this before – what are we supposed to do? Do we just start walking when it gets to eleven?'

'Well,' Marianne says, 'sometimes people say something about why they're marching, to start it off. You could say a few words – or I could, if you don't fancy it?'

'No, that's all right,' Leesh says. 'I wanna say something. Thanks tho. Are people gonna be able to hear me? Cos the crowd is pretty big.'

Marianne reaches down and rummages inside a canvas bag that's by her feet. Then she pulls out a blue-and-white megaphone and hands it to Leesh.

'That's why I don't go to any protest without one of these!' she says.

Leesh stares down at the megaphone in Marianne's hands; then she glances at me. Elisha doesn't even have to say anything, I already know what she's thinking. That's what happens when you've been best mates with someone for most of your life. I know she's wondering if she can do it. If she'll be able to say the right thing. And the thing is, there's no one who would be more perfect to do it than Leesh. I step forward and I gently pull on her arm.

'It's all right,' I say. 'Take it, Leesh. You got this, yeah?'

Leesh nods. Then she sucks in a sharp breath and takes the megaphone from Marianne, and we make our way to the front of the crowd. It seems like we were only talking to Marianne for a second, but since then, even more people have joined us in the gardens. All I can see is banners and placards and a few T-shirts as well. Elisha turns to face the crowd, and I stand next to her but a bit to the side.

'Can everyone hear me?' she says, but she must be holding the megaphone too close, cos her voice comes out proper loud. Leesh looks embarrassed, but I give her the thumbs-up. A few people closest to us nod, and there's a few cheers from the crowd as well.

'We're all here for the same reason,' she says. 'For the boys who are on trial for murder, even though they didn't kill anyone. All cos of this deeply racist, messed-up law. How many more innocent people are gonna go to prison for joint enterprise? Where's the justice in that?' The crowd cheer and clap, and I can tell that Leesh is starting to feel more comfortable speaking in front of everyone, cos she adds: 'Those boys shouldn't even be on trial for murder. This is the fourth case to happen right here, in our city, and we're here to say enough is enough! This law needs to change. The system needs to change. So, we're going to march to the super court. For the Manchester Eight and anyone else who's been affected by this law. Are you ready?'

The crowd erupts and it's deafening. Leesh reaches down and pics up a placard with her free hand and she holds it in the air.

'No justice, no peace!' she shouts, and the crowd echoes it back. 'Not guilty by association!' she yells, and the phrase echoes around Piccadilly Gardens. Leesh lowers the megaphone and looks at me, and I couldn't be prouder. I can't even describe how amazing she was up there.

'You were incredible!' I say, and I pick up my placard and hold it up.

'Thanks!' Leesh says, and I see her cheeks colouring. 'No justice, no peace!' she chants again, and we start to walk in the direction of the court.

Me and Leesh are right at the front leading all these people and it's crazy, cos I've never felt anything like it before. I feel free for the first time in my life. Like I actually have some sorta voice. Marianne manages to get to the front to join us and she tells Leesh how amazing she was. Everyone's cheering and shouting the SJE slogan, and at I hesitate at first, but then I join in, yelling out: 'Not guilty by association!' And it feels good. We carry on down the road, and when I sneak a look behind me, there's a sea of people and banners. It feels incredible to be part of something.

Leesh takes a phone call as she searches through the crowd. Then the next minute, Remi and Isiah are here. Remi stands next to Leesh, holding a placard, and Isiah falls into step with me. He

334

puts a hand on my shoulder and gives it a squeeze.

'You all right?' he asks.

'Yeah!' I reply, and I actually am. 'I dunno why I've never been to one of these protests before!'

Isiah smiles and he yells out the slogan. Then he says to me, 'I'm sure it won't be your last!' and he drapes his arm around my shoulder.

We turn onto this street that's mostly glass offices and old buildings, and you can tell that it's the posh part of town. It's different seeing it from this angle, cos the last time I was in court, I came up through the holding cell. I've never really seen it from the outside. Some of the buildings are actually kind of beautiful, which is weird, considering what goes on in there. They're definitely kinda intimidating, tho, cos everything just seems so grand and big. Like you have no business even being in there. We pass the magistrates' and the crown court. Then Leesh slows down and we come to a halt outside the super court.

I look up, trying to take it all in. It's 'super' all right. There's all these stone steps leading up to three huge archways. The building's made up of these solid stone pillars and all this glass. I suddenly get a flashback to being on trial. This is what my mum and Isiah would've seen every day. I freeze and Isiah nudges me.

'You okay?'

'It's weird,' I say. 'Being back here. I mean, I know it's not like I'm going inside or nothing, but it's, like ... my whole life changed here.'

I feel Isiah looking at me. 'I know, but you don't have to worry about any of that now. You ain't ever gonna be stepping foot in there again.'

I nod, but I can't get over how huge this super court is. Everything else – even the other buildings not too far from it – just seems tiny in comparison.

'Can you believe they spent nearly three mil on that?' Isiah says. 'So they can deal with "gang" cases. More like joint enterprise cases.'

'Yeah, I know!' I say. 'It's mad.'

Leesh comes back over to us. 'Shall we just stand here?' she goes. 'Away from the steps? So they can't say we're obstructing the court or nothing?'

I don't really know what to say, cos it ain't like I've done anything like this before. I don't really know what you can and can't do, but I nod. 'Sounds good!' I say.

The rest of the crowd gathers around outside the super court, and Elisha holds the megaphone to her mouth again and shouts, 'Not guilty by association!' Everyone cheers and people shout it back. Then Marianne goes to the front and starts talking about what the charity she works for does. I turn in the crowd and I notice some guy who must be a journalist, cos he's got one of those proper cameras and he's taking a few pictures. I nudge Isiah, and he follows my gaze.

'I mean, it's definitely a big turnout!' he says. 'I'm not surprised there's press here!'

I look back at Marianne just as she's shouting: 'No justice, no peace! No justice, no peace!' I shout it back, and so do Isiah and Remi and Leesh. Then the next minute, I see some guy coming down the steps of the super court. He's wearing a suit and he turns to Marianne and Leesh and goes: 'Right, you've made your point. Can you all just go and do this somewhere else?'

I stare at him. We've made '*our point*'? Like it's some dumb argument we're trying to win in one of those lame English debate classes at school. This is people's lives. *Dadir's life.* It's more than 'making a point'. It's something that needs to change.

Elisha turns to him. 'We've got a right to protest!' she says. 'I've looked it up – we're not doing anything wrong. Maybe you ought to listen to what we're saying.'

The guy doesn't seem to even care. I don't know what his job is – if he's a barrister or a judge, or something else completely – but he says, 'This is a working court. So if you and your friends don't turn around right now, then I'm calling the police.'

'For what?' Elisha says. 'Speaking out?'

'For disruption to community life!' he spits, and then he storms off back up the steps.

337

Elisha sticks a finger up at him. But I'm mad now. Disruption to community life? How is that fair? I don't even know what it means. I see a look of worry flash across Elisha's face, probably cos this guy mentioned the police, but why should we have to leave? It's not like we're hurting anyone, or even blocking the way. I dunno what happens next, but it's like everything from the past few years, the past few weeks, comes surging up to the surface – Dadir; this case; getting searched in my kitchen – and I can't just block it out. I can't stay silent. *I won't stay silent.* And the guy sitting in this super court, trying to ignore us, needs to hear it too. Before I know what I'm doing, I go over to Elisha.

'Can I have this?' I say, and I gesture to the megaphone.

Leesh looks surprised, but she gives it to me. And I feel my hands trembling as I lift it to my mouth. It makes a weird high-pitched sound and I clam up. A few people cover their ears at that and I realize I don't even know what I'm meant to say. There's a sea of faces in front of me and I'm suddenly rooted to the spot. I feel that nauseous sensation rising inside me again and I'm worried that I'm about to have one of those panic attacks.

I hear my heart pounding in my ears and I find myself looking at the crowd again. This time, I see Malik standing there near the front, and I can tell by the look on his face that he's willing me to go on. I suck in a deep breath and even tho a small part of me wishes that I could run, I don't. I wanna do this for Dadir. Maybe I can't give a speech like Leesh and Marianne did. But there's another way I can get my words out – there's another way that I can be heard – and seeing Malik reminds me of that. I think of Dadir in his cell at Ryecroft. How broken he sounded on the phone. Then I hold the megaphone back up to my mouth and the crowd seems to disappear.

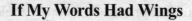

If My Words Had Wings

If my words had wings
They'd soar, taking flight into the night
Escaping iron cages
With broken dreams trapped inside
They'd flutter through the darkest moments
Whispering hope to those who've given up
They'd remind the boy kicked out of school
That his destiny is more than a self-fulfilling prophecy
That there's more for his life than prison or death
They'd glide through steel bars, with the stories of
those untold
And go to places where futures are decided
They'd make sure that words from drill, hip-hop and
grime aren't used as weaponry
But are viewed the same way as poetry:
Art
They'd give a voice to the silenced, making sure they
are heard
Inspiring protests and bravery
Cos my freedom may have been taken from me
But my language knows no bounds
And my words and my voice can never be chained
So let my words fly, let them take to the sky.

*

I get so lost in my own words that I barely notice that people are filming me ... or the police officers in riot gear making their way through the crowd. Now that I've started, tho, it's like I can't stop. I see a few police officers with shields pushing some people in the crowd away, and I hear one of them say:

'That's enough now. *Stop!*'

But I don't. I say another line and another. Cos all I can think about is Dadir. How he'll never get to use his voice and be heard. I say another line and another, and it feels like I'm getting louder. Like I'm finally allowing everything to come out. I'm not even listening to what's going on around me. I get to the end of my poem and repeat the last two lines over and over again: '*And my words and my voice can never be chained. So let my words fly, let them take to the sky.*'

Then the next minute, I'm on the floor, with my arms twisted up behind my back. I feel a sharp shooting pain in my wrists and I yell out. And I hear Isiah and Remi and Elisha shouting my name from somewhere to the side. I try to turn my head, which is at a weird angle cos it's been pressed to the pavement, and I realize that I'm on my own, being restrained on the pavement outside this massive super court. There's shouting and yelling, but there's a wall of plastic shields, separating me from everyone else. One of the officers reads out the number that must be on my tag to a voice on the other end of their radio. I hear another

341

police officer go, 'Tyrell, is it? We're arresting you for disruption to community life.' And I feel like I've been punched in the gut.

'No!' I say as they hoist me up. 'I didn't do nothing wrong . . . All I did was read a poem!' And I try to stop them from dragging me away, but they ain't listening. My legs are trembling and I can feel my heart pounding in my chest. 'I didn't do nothing wrong!' I repeat, and I hear the officer say something about using 'reasonable force' if I keep resisting arrest. And even tho I know I might get into even more trouble, I can't calm myself down.

'I didn't do nothing!' I say again. 'You can't recall me over this . . .'

But they take me off to the side.

In the crowd, I hear Isiah shout, 'Ty! Ty! Yo, where you taking my brother? Let him go . . .' And even tho he's trying to reach me, he can't get beyond the wall of riot police. 'Ty!' I hear Isiah screaming after me 'Ty!'

But all I can think is that I can't go back there. I can't go back to Ryecroft.

27

I sit in the low plastic chair at the back of the police van. It's dark and hot in here and there's the same shouting and arguing from the other prisoners in the little cubicle things, like there was the last time. It's almost like going back to being fifteen again, and I dunno if I'm less or more scared now, cos I know what to expect. I just feel numb. My mum's gonna be wondering where I am as well, but I won't get my first phone call till I get to prison. I kinda hope that it is Ryecroft, cos at least it's somewhere that I know, tho I really don't wanna bump into Spider again. I'll be here for twenty-eight days, on a fixed-term recall, which is the standard number of days you have to do if you breach your licence conditions for the first time. I know that I've already done eighteen months, but being back here somehow feels worse. The van finally stops and I'm glad, cos I really need some air.

One of the officers opens the van doors, and even tho it's dark, when I walk down the steps and towards the back entrance, I can see that it's Ryecroft. I feel myself shaking as I stare up at the prison building and walk back in. As soon as I get into the bit where they process you and search you and that, I see Longman. I can't look him in the eye, cos the last thing I'd wanted to do was prove him right. I feel all this shame and embarrassment creeping up inside me again.

'Forrester,' Longman goes. 'Didn't take you long, did it? I knew you'd be back, but I didn't think it would be this soon! Come on, you know the drill by now,' he says; then he takes me to a holding cell. He looks like me being back has made his day.

I sit in the holding cell while the other guys around me ask each other what they're in for and try and size each other up. I don't say anything when someone asks me tho. I can't believe I ended up back here again. Once we've been searched and all that stuff, Longman tells me that I'll be on Quail this time. I know that I'm gonna be put on the induction wing in Kingfisher tonight, even tho I don't need to be 'inducted' into a place I've already been in. When we go to the phones to make our one phone call, a screw I don't recognize says, 'Two minutes,' but I already know.

I almost think about calling Elisha instead of Mum, cos I don't wanna have to have this conversation with her again. I know that if I do that, my mum won't forgive me tho. Plus she's probably worried sick already. I dial my house number and part of me is praying that she don't pick up. It barely even rings.

'Mum, it's me,' I say.

'Tyrell?' my mum replies and I can hear the panic in her voice. 'Isiah told me what happened – are you okay?'

I swallow hard. 'It was over nothing, Mum, I swear!' I say, and I feel my voice crack. 'I dunno how I'm gonna get through twenty-eight days in here again!' I add, and I mean it. I half expect her to go off on one. To tell me that she knew I'd end up back in Ryecroft again, or how I'd disappointed her. But she doesn't.

'I know!' Mum says. 'Getting recalled over a protest is just ridiculous … It's okay, though,' she adds firmly. 'You've done it before, Ty, for much longer. You can do it again. I love you, okay!'

The phone beeps to tell me that time's nearly up on our call. 'Mum,' I say. 'It's gonna cut out. I love you too—'

Then the phone goes dead. I hang up, then turn to look at this new officer, and I follow him up to my cell.

It doesn't take long for word to get around that I'm back at Ryecroft. Spider, Jason and Kofi are all on the older wing with

Dadir, and I wonder if Dadir's heard that I'm back too? I've been in for a week now, and I just need to get through the other three. You'd think it would be easier this time around, but that ain't the case. If anything, it seems harder, cos I've seen just how easy it is to end up back here and I'm worried that when my twenty-eight days are over, I could end up in the back of a sweatbox again. I know that I can't give up hope tho. I can't stop trying. I'm still getting those panicked feelings too, but I'm trying to do the things that were on the information sheet that Doctor Kaminski gave me, and I'm writing as much as I can too, which definitely seems to help.

And maybe I didn't know how I was gonna get through Ryecroft before, but I do now. I move over on the tiny plastic table I'm sitting at in my cell, and I pick up my pen and turn over a page in the notebook Malik sent me a few days ago. It's a proper one that's got my initials printed in the corner, not like that exercise book I was using. Leesh told him that I'd been recalled, and he sent me the book and a letter with it as well, telling me that I had a place to keep all my new poems now. I finish one of my sentences, and then the key turns in my door. Davidson opens it wider.

'Forrester,' he goes. 'You ready?'

'Yeah,' I say, and I put the pen down.

I follow Davidson out my cell and along the landing, and he stops at a few more cells and collects a few more inmates.

There's only six of us, but he leads us through a set of doors, then another one, until we're in this bit where we need to get searched. I hold my arms out; then some of the screws pat me down and they check inside my mouth. Then they let me into the visiting room.

It's always weird when you first go in there, cos it's so quiet and empty, apart from a few of the inmates and some screws. I sit down at one of the tables and I put my thumb up towards Morgan, who's sitting on the other side of the room. I suck in a deep breath, and you can almost feel how restless and excited everyone is. Then the next minute, this other door opens and people come flooding in. They head over to the different tables, making their way to the inmates they're here to see. People's parents and grandparents and stuff like that. I see Morgan's girlfriend come in.

Then the next minute, Malik's here. He walks over and gives me a hug, and I'm so pleased to see him.

'You all right, Ty?' he asks.

'Yeah,' I say, and we both sit down. 'I'm doing all right.' It feels awkward for a minute, but then I say: 'Thanks again, for the notebook. It's almost full.'

'What?' Malik goes. 'Already? You really aren't messing about!'

'Yeah,' I reply. 'Not much else to do in here.'

Malik gives me a smile, but it doesn't quite reach his eyes.

'I'm so sorry you got recalled, Ty,' Malik says. 'It's a load of bullshit that it happened.'

I shrug. 'I guess it's just one of them things,' I say.

I feel the mood shift slightly, and I know we ain't got long for this visit. I don't really wanna waste it just sitting here quietly and worrying about the future, but I can't help but wonder if I'll just be stuck in this cycle of Ryecroft – if Clinton was right all along. I've probably got even less of a chance now that I've got two prison sentences on my record as well.

Malik must be able to see that I'm a bit upset, cos he goes, 'Listen, Ty, the reason I wanted to see you, apart from checking that you're okay, is cos we're doing another spoken-word night in three weeks'. You'll be out by then, right?'

'Yeah,' I say. 'I should be.'

'Well, I wanted to come and ask you if you'd read something? I meant what I said that time, about people needing to hear your words.'

I'm taken aback, but it feels good that he genuinely wants me involved. And even if the thought of doing it is still terrifying, a part of me wants to.

'I dunno,' I say. 'What if I freeze and that?'

'Listen, Ty,' says Malik. 'You read your poem out in front of the courthouse. Do you know how powerful you were that day?'

'Thanks,' I say, and I can feel myself getting hot cos I can't handle how good it makes me feel.

'You just need to hold your head high and project your voice,' says Malik. 'And if you like, we can run through your poems as many times as you want beforehand.'

I pause, remembering how much I loved the spoken-word night and how I can use my voice to make some sorta difference in the world.

'What are people gonna think when they see me tho?' I say. 'Cos it's obvious from some of my poems that I've been inside.'

Malik gives me a smile. 'They'll think the same thing that I do, and they'll see exactly what I see, Ty.'

'A criminal?' I ask.

'No,' Malik says, and he shakes his head. 'A poet. And a pretty damn good one at that.'

28

THREE WEEKS' LATER

I wait by the side of the stage with Malik and a couple of his friends, and I stare down at the poem in my notebook. I must've practised it a million times already, and I know every single word by heart. It doesn't stop me from feeling scared or nervous tho. I look out across the crowd and I see my mum, Isiah, Kias and Elisha sitting in the front row. Elisha catches my eye and she gives me a thumbs-up. The host is on stage, introducing all the acts. My palms are sweaty and I can feel the adrenaline pumping through my body.

'Hey,' Malik says, and he nudges me. 'Do you remember what I told you?'

'I think so,' I reply. 'Chest up, stand tall, project my voice . . . ?'

'Yeah,' he says. 'You'll be great!'

'Thanks,' I say.

The host says my name and I hear a round of applause. I freeze, and for a minute, I feel like even tho I've done this once before, I can't do it now. But Malik gives me a nod.

'You've got this, Ty!' he says.

I take a deep breath and I walk up onto the stage. I hear the applause from the audience get louder and I see my mum, Kias, Isiah and Elisha are clapping the hardest. I give them a wave and Kias waves back. My mum looks so proud and I can see she's crying.

I'm ready to share my words. I'm ready to speak. I look down at my notebook and see my initials in the corner. I open it at the right page. Then I reach forward and grab the mic.

Acknowledgements

This book wouldn't exist without the help and support of so many people. Firstly, I would like to thank my incredible agent, Chloe Seager, for not only being my biggest champion, but for always allowing me to tell the stories that truly matter to me. To my editor, Amina Youssef, thank you so much for your keen editorial eye and always being able to get the best writing out of me. To Carla Hutchinson, thank you for understanding this book and Ty so deeply, for your insightful edits and the comments that made me laugh, scream and cry (in a good way!). Thank you to my copyeditor, Veronica Lyons, and proofreader, Anna Bowles, for your precision and ability to keep track of any changing numbers I might have missed! Thank you to Rachel Denwood and the wonderful team at Simon & Schuster for all that you do. To Ben Ee and the S&S design team, thank you for such a stunning cover.

To Becks, I'm eternally grateful for the Zoom meetings, voice notes and responses to my many, many questions. Thank you for always getting back to me (even on a weekend), and for all of your help and feedback on the very first draft. Georgia, thank you so much for your help with the research. To Becky Clarke, I feel so honoured to have a friend like you. I wouldn't have been able to get through writing this book without you. Thank you so much for your support and encouragement, for your invaluable feedback, and for everything you've done to help me to write *Wings*.

To Sam Davey, Brett Milner and Emmanuel, thank you all so much for your time, honesty and help with this book. Thank you to the Care Leavers' Association for holding a space where these much-needed and important conversations could happen. To Leon Nathan-Lynch, thank you for your help. Thank you to my dad for your continued support and love. To Lakeisha Lynch-Stevens, thank you so much for everything and for always being there; I'm so lucky to have you in my life. To Natasha Bowen, Alex Sheppard, Samantha Hayden and Roisin Quinn, thank you for the laughter and support, and for getting me through many breakdowns. To Aisha Jarbale, I wouldn't have been able to write large chunks of this without you; thank you so much.

To Andy Forbes, thank you for all of your support and encouragement. To Ruth McShane, for your kindness. I'm grateful to all of the wonderful poets that I've mentioned in this book, thank you for your words. Thank you to all of the amazing young people I meet, who constantly inspire me. And, last but not least, thank you to my readers. I couldn't do what I do without you all, and I'm truly grateful.

Author's Note

Dear Reader,

When I first sat down to write *If My Words Had Wings*, it was important for me to tell the story of a young person whose experiences we rarely get to see represented in books. If some of the events in the novel feel all too real, then, sadly, that's because the things that happen to Ty, Clinton, Dadir and many of the other characters that we meet along the way happen to so many young people.

While editing this book, I was devastated to hear of the passing of Benjamin Zephaniah. His poetry has been so influential to entire generations of young people, who, like myself and Ty, have found great comfort and strength in his words. If you're discovering Benjamin Zephaniah's poetry for the first time, I urge you to read everything, it will change your life.

Although the themes that are explored in this book are deeply upsetting, it was important for me not to shy away from the reality of these experiences. I hope that anyone who sees themselves in any of the characters is able to find some strength from Ty's story.

I hope that you remember how important you are, how much you matter, and how powerful your voice is, no matter how small it might feel right now.

Danielle xx

If any of the issues in this book have affected you, you might find some of the following organizations helpful.

Suicide Prevention
PAPYRUS HOPELineUK – confidential help and advice
Call: 0800 068 41 41
Text: 07786 209 697
Website: www.papyrus-uk.org

CALM (Campaign Against Living Miserably) – helpline and support
Call: 0800 58 58 58
Website: www.thecalmzone.net

Samaritans – 24-hour helpline and advice
Call: 116 123
Email: jo@samaritans.org
Website: www.samaritans.org

Survivors
Survivors of Bereavement by Suicide – support for young people over the age of 18
Call: 0300 111 5065
Email: email.support@uksobs.org
Website: www.uksobs.org

Mental Health Support
The Association for Child and Adolescent Mental Health –

information, help and support for adults and young people
Call: 0207 403 7458
Website: www.acamh.org

Shout – a confidential and anonymous 24/7 text support service for anyone struggling to cope. It is free to text Shout from all major mobile networks in the UK. To speak to a trained volunteer, text SHOUT to 85258
Website: giveusashout.org/

YoungMinds – mental health support for young people, parents and carers. Includes information about mental health problems and medication
Website: www.youngminds.org.uk/

Alumina – free online self-harm support for 10–17-year-olds
Website: selfharm.co.uk/#help

Anxiety UK – advice, support and information for people who experience anxiety
Text: 07537 416 905
Website: www.anxietyuk.org.uk/

Stop and Search
StopWatch – research, action and advice for anyone impacted by stop and search. Includes information on knowing your rights
Call: 0208 226 5737
Website: www.stop-watch.org/

Justice System Support

Appeal – a charity and law practice that fights miscarriages of justice
Call: 0207 278 6949
Email: mail@appeal.org.uk
Website: appeal.org.uk/

JENGbA – an organisation that campaigns for those wrongfully convicted of Joint Enterprise, they can also help to signpost you in the right direction if in need of support or advice
Call: 0203 582 6444
Email: jointenterpriseinfo@gmail.com
Website: jengba.co.uk/

Maslaha – an organization that looks at long-standing social issues affecting Muslim communities and challenges inequality within the justice system
Email: info@maslaha.org
Website: www.maslaha.org/

Youth Organizations/Support for Young People

The 4Front Project (London) – a community-led youth organization that helps to empower those harmed by the criminal and legal system
Call: 0203 489 5654
Email: info@4frontproject.org
Website: www.4frontproject.org/

Kids of Colour (Greater Manchester) – a project for young people of colour aged twenty-five and under, which creates spaces for young people to feel supported, validated and celebrated, while also working to challenge the racism that affects young people and their communities. Kids of Colour also donate free books to teenagers across Greater Manchester
Contact: kidsofcolour.com/contact
Website: kidsofcolour.com/

Young People in Care/Care Leavers
The Care Leavers' Association – a national charity aimed at improving the lives of care leavers of all ages
Call: 0161 826 0214
Email: info@careleavers.com
Website: www.careleavers.com/

Become – information and support for young people in care and young care leavers
Call: 0800 023 2033
Website: becomecharity.org.uk/

Danielle Jawando is an author, screenwriter and Lecturer in Creative Writing at Manchester Metropolitan University. Her debut YA novel, *And the Stars Were Burning Brightly*, won best senior novel in the Great Reads Award and was shortlisted for the Waterstones Children's Book Prize, the YA Book Prize, the Jhalak Children's & YA Prize, the Branford Boase Award and was longlisted for the CILIP Carnegie Medal, the UKLA Book Awards and the Amazing Book Awards. Her second YA novel, *When Our Worlds Collided*, won the YA Book Prize, the Jhalak Children's and YA Prize and the Diverse Book Award, and was longlisted for the Yoto Carnegie Medal for Writing. Her previous publications include the non-fiction children's book *Maya Angelou (Little Guides to Great Lives)*, the short stories *Paradise 703* (long-listed for the Finishing Line Press Award) and *The Deerstalker* (selected as one of six finalists for the We Need Diverse Books short story competition), as well as several short plays performed in Manchester and London. Danielle has also worked on Coronation Street as a storyline writer.

HAVE YOU READ?

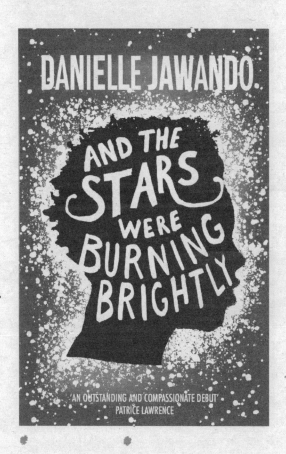

DANIELLE JAWANDO.

AND THE STARS WERE BURNING BRIGHTLY

'AN OUTSTANDING AND COMPASSIONATE DEBUT'
PATRICE LAWRENCE

HAVE YOU READ?

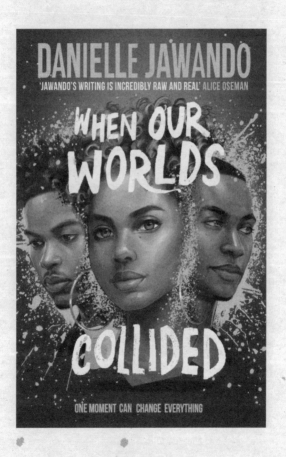